Secrets of the Blood

Books by Felix Jackson

SECRETS OF THE BLOOD

MAESTRO

SO HELP ME GOD

Secrets of the Blood

Felix Jackson

Atheneum   New York   1980

Library of Congress Cataloging in Publication Data

Jackson, Felix.
   Secrets of the blood.

      1. Germany—History—1933–1945—Fiction.
J. Title.
PZ4.J133Se   [PS3560.A2153]   813'.54   80–14389
ISBN 0–689–11076–6

Copyright © 1980 by Felix Jackson
Published simultaneously in Canada by McClelland and Stewart Ltd.
Manufactured by American Book–Stratford Press, Saddle Brook, New Jersey
Designed by Harry Ford
First Edition

For I L K A , *with love and gratitude*

Author's Note

This narrative is a work of fiction based on reality.
The events took place as described.
The characters are authentic.
Only their names have been changed.

The commissioned ranks of the S.S. and their American army equivalents:

Untersturmfuehrer	2d Lieutenant
Obersturmfuehrer	Lieutenant
Hauptsturmfuehrer	Captain
Sturmbannfuehrer	Major
Obersturmbannfuehrer	Lieutenant Colonel
Standartenfuehrer	Colonel
Oberfuehrer	Brigadier General
Brigadefuehrer	Major General
Gruppenfuehrer	Lieutenant General
Obergruppenfuehrer	General

Secrets of the Blood

When we talk about yesterday,
we talk about today and tomorrow.

April 22nd, 1933. St. Moritz, Switzerland.

This is my last day in St. Moritz: tomorrow morning I leave for home. I wonder if Berlin has changed since Hitler came to power. It's been almost four months since I left Germany, but it seems like four years.

Of course, I've had letters from Klaus and Magda, my secretary, but they've been short and not very informative. Karin has written (in the last two months not as frequently as at first), but mostly about parties and celebrations and her American girlfriend, Margie, who seems to be close to the new regime.

This has been my first vacation since Klaus von Isenberg, Siegmund Schwartz, and I established our law firm eight years ago. I needed these four months of complete rest. When I went for my medical checkup shortly before Christmas, Dr. Aaron said to me, "How old are you—thirty-three? You look ten years older."

He wouldn't say that now, if he could see me. I am suntanned. I have lost six pounds. The skiing and mountain air have rejuvenated me. I feel great.

The only thing that has disturbed me has been the arrival of those documents. I'm glad they came only a few days ago. If I'd received them earlier, when I was still weak and tense, they could have spoiled my vacation.

April 23rd. On the train to Berlin.

I hadn't touched a newspaper in months—until today. Whenever anybody turned on the radio news in St. Moritz, I walked off, buried my head in the sand—deliberately. I didn't want to get upset. I wanted to enjoy my vacation.

I am a registered member of the Democratic Party and never liked the Nazis. I could never have believed it possible that Hitler would become Reichskanzler, but when it happened, while I was in Switzerland, and when I read about the inauguration ceremony, with all the old Kaiser trimmings and our dearly beloved President Hindenburg tottering about, I knew I wouldn't have the stomach to read and hear all the bombastic speeches and to digest the glorification of the "Fuehrer." There would be time enough to face the situation when I was back in Berlin, I thought.

Today, however, I picked up some German newspapers on the train. Exactly one month ago, on March 23rd, the Reichstag passed the Enabling Act, giving the Hitler government dictatorial powers. I found this item on the front page:

DECREE

All non-Aryan attorneys are ordered herewith to apply for an indefinite leave of absence. The order is effective as of today. Deadline for these applications is the 15th of May 1933. In exceptional cases concerning non-Aryan attorneys who served in the German armed forces during the last war, written requests for an extension of said deadline will be considered by the Ministry of Justice.

As I read the decree, I thought of Siegmund Schwartz, our partner. He is a Jew, older than Klaus and me, in his early fifties. A sharp mind. A brilliant lawyer. What's going to happen to him?

Then I thought of myself. I look like the common concept of a German: blue eyes; six feet one; a rather undistinguished, slightly elongated face; light hair. Even my name is common: Hans (Johannes) Bauer. My father's ancestors settled in Bremen more than three hundred years ago, to build ships and send them out onto the North Sea. They traded with England and the Scandinavian countries and, later on, when the Pacific Ocean opened up, they sailed and steamed as far east as Singapore, Burma, and Japan. They were proud of their heritage. When I grew up, the name of Herman Bauer and Sons was one of the most respected names in our free city.

My mother's family came from Annaberg in Saxonia near the Czechoslovakian border. Her father injected Slavonian blood in the genealogical tree.

I was fourteen when the big war broke out. I knew about the glory of victory and the honor of dying for Germany. I saw the shining image of the Kaiser, the flags and banners, the flashy pictures of attacking hussars and dragoons. I didn't know about the agony of dying, of basket cases, or of drowning in swamps and mud.

Nor did I know about commercial credits, overextension, and sudden collapse. It wasn't until much later that I would understand why my father had turned the gun on himself and pulled the trigger.

I was the only child. After my father's death, I lived with my mother, but she couldn't stand the sight of me: I looked too much like the man she had loved . . . the man who had deserted her in ultimate betrayal. She took sick. I was raised by well-to-do guardians in an impersonal fashion: first by a governess, then by a tutor. It was all very cold and rigid. I learned early to suppress my craving for warmth and love—in fact, I myself adopted the well-mannered chill with which I had been forced to grow up. Even now, I hate becoming demonstrative, showing my emotions.

I never saw my mother again before she died. I wanted to be a musician or a writer, but my guardians insisted on a "more substantial" profession, so I went to the university in Freiburg, a lovely old city in the southwestern part of Germany, to study law. Within a short time, the avalanching German inflation annihilated the fortune of one of my wealthiest guardians, and I lost whatever there had been left of my own large inheritance.

Some of the most famous and most perceptive teachers of law and economics were members of Freiburg's faculty at that time, and they succeeded in awakening and deepening my interest in my not-chosen profession. What I had always thought dry and boring suddenly became alive and exciting.

It was a time of great unrest in Germany. Right-wing former commanders of the regular army organized their own private volunteer corps and fought lawless border battles, spreading terror among the population. Communists usurped state governments in sudden savage insurrections, and when the federal government called on the right-wing military organizations to help check the Communist danger, it only strengthened the brutal power of those corps leaders who hated the Weimar Republic. The National Socialist Party rose rapidly, using the latent German anti-Semitism to gain followers and supporters.

The military defeat of the German army was forgotten. No one wanted to remember that the army's high command had issued an ultimatum to the Kaiser's government to ask for an immediate armistice. In fact, it was the same generals who had insisted on that armistice who created and spread the "stab in the back" legend: the victorious German army, they claimed, had been betrayed by Communists, Socialists, and Jews.

The Freiburg university was a microcosm of all the infighting, hatred, and violence tearing Germany apart, its student body split into innumerable factions. There was still a strong liberal group at that time, but even there Jews were merely tolerated.

By upbringing and by nature, I was a German liberal—our city and our family business were both cosmopolitan-oriented—but we were and had always been German patriots. In 1871, after the founding of the German empire, the slogan of the Herman Bauer shipbuilding works had been changed from "Onward with Bremen" to "German ships in German waters."

And now I was a German ship out of German water. When my secretary informed me of the new law requiring documentary proof that no Jewish blood had been in my family for (at least) the last four generations, I asked her to send me my personal files. I received them a few days ago in St. Moritz and glanced at them cursorily. But then I saw to my surprise that one of my grandmothers had been of Jewish descent. I was unprepared for that.

Under the new Nazi laws, I no longer qualify as an Aryan.

I thought about all that on the train.

We arrived in Basel, the border between Switzerland and Germany. I heard the clicking of heels, snapping voices, "Heil Hitler!" Before this, I'd heard the salute only in newsreels picturing Nazi rallies, but I knew that it had replaced "Good morning," "Good evening," "Good night."

The sliding door opened. The customs official, a *Sturmabteilung* man in his brown uniform, came in. Click. Snap. Heil Hitler! The right wrist flicked up the right hand.

"Anything to declare?"

"Nothing," I said.

A middle-aged woman shook her head and continued her knitting.

"Your passports, please."

I handed him mine. The woman sighed and put her knitting

aside. Two more passengers shared our compartment: a bespectacled young man who was reading Alfred Rosenberg's *The
Myth of the Twentieth Century*, and an elderly man in a black
suit who had been sitting motionless, in quiet isolation. He was
the last one to submit his passport. The official looked at it and
handed it to the S.A. man.

"Your name is Herbert Cohn," the S.A. man said.

The man nodded tensely.

"I didn't hear your answer."

'Yes," the man said. "Herbert Cohn."

"You were in Zurich for three weeks."

"Three weeks and two days."

"What was the purpose of your visit, Mr. Cohn?"

"Business," the man said. "I was there on business."

"Meaning what, Mr. Cohn?"

"In the interest of several of my clients." Herbert Cohn was
getting more and more excited and beginning to sweat pro-
fusely. It was embarrassing to watch him.

The S.A. man said to the customs official, "Let him open his
suitcase."

"Which one is your suitcase, sir?" the official asked. The
S.A. man looked at the official, then said in a harsh voice, "Get
it down, Cohn! Open it!"

Herbert Cohn reached up. His bag was heavy, difficult to
handle, and I got up to help him. The S.A. man stared at me. I
stared back. He said nothing.

"Thank you. Thank you very much," Cohn said to me.

We put the suitcase on the seat. His hands trembled. He had
trouble inserting the key.

"Take your bag and come with me, Mr. Cohn," the S.A. man
said.

"No, no—I'm getting it—I have it."

The man's body shook. He managed to insert the key. The

lid swung open. The customs official proceeded to examine the bag.

"What is the name of your firm, Mr. Cohn, and what is your position?" the S.A. man asked.

"The National Bank. I am—I am a vice-president."

The S.A. man chuckled. "Vice-president Cohn," he said. "You mentioned your clients, Vice-president Cohn. Are they Germans or Jews?"

For a moment Herbert Cohn didn't answer. Finally he said, "German Jews."

"There is no such thing, Vice-president Cohn," the S.A. man said. Herbert Cohn was breathing heavily.

"Two of them are Jewish. One is—not."

"And you had the money of your Jewish friends transferred to Zurich, Vice-president Cohn?"

"No—God help me—no."

"Leave your God alone, Vice-president Cohn," the S.A. man said. He turned to the official.

"What did you find?"

"Nothing."

"Nothing?"

"You may close your luggage, sir," the official said.

"What about your money, Vice-president Cohn?" the S.A. man asked. "You smuggled that out, didn't you?"

"Everything I own is invested at the National Bank," Cohn replied.

There was a pause. The official asked the S.A. man impatiently, "Can we proceed to the next compartment?"

The S.A. man nodded. He said, "Your answers have not been satisfactory, Mr. Cohn. I must ask you to leave the train with me."

Herbert Cohn's body began to sway. His voice broke. "Please, sir—"

"You go first, Cohn," the S.A. man said.

Without looking at us, Herbert Cohn went through the open sliding door, hitting the seats and the door with his suitcase.

"Heil Hitler!" the S.A. man said to us.

The bespectacled young man murmured "Heil Hitler!" without raising his eyes from his book. The middle-aged woman took up her knitting again.

We three remaining passengers sat quietly, our eyes averted from each other. Where was the S.A. man taking him? What had Herbert Cohn done? Had he really smuggled German money across the border? Was he guilty? Or was it possible he had been treated like that just because he was a Jew?

The train moved on.

The campus of the Freiburg university. A day in June. The day Rathenau was shot. Rathenau had been a rich industrialist, a famous father's famous son, a statesman, and an intellectual. A Jew—the first and only Jewish foreign secretary the German republic had ever had.

When Rathenau was assassinated by members of one of the most notorious volunteer corps, the university's right-wing fraternities were jubilant, their only quarrel being over which one of them should be credited with the kill. The liberal groups rose up in arms. Duels, officially forbidden, were fought in secret. Fist fights broke out. The big question was, would the faculty take a stand? Occasional remarks, colorings of certain lectures, had revealed the political gap between teachers to be as wide as our own, but most of them were too prudent or too cautious to declare themselves openly for one party or the other.

The most popular lectures were given by an internationally recognized authority on law and economics, who was also a titled member of one of the oldest aristocratic families in Germany. Every one of his lectures filled the auditorium to capacity. He had the magic gift of capturing the imagination of his students with his very first words and then holding them spellbound with his eloquence and forcefulness until he had finished. It was plain from the way he related historical events and sociological developments to the evolution of law and economics that he had a profound knowledge of history. But he had never commented on contemporary politics.

On this day in June, however, the conviction had grown among us that the Baron—that was his title and nickname both—would address himself to Rathenau's assassination. The rumor grew during the early morning hours and electrified the campus. While none of us expected the Baron to approve of an act of murder, the question uppermost in everybody's mind was whether he would denounce the crime outright or qualify his condemnation out of political expediency. Fights broke out between us, bets were made. By the afternoon, the tension had become almost unbearable. The Baron's lecture was supposed to start at three o'clock in the afternoon, and the auditorium was jammed by two thirty. Students were sitting in the aisles. The standing room behind the seats was packed. At ten minutes to three the doors had to be locked.

The students in German universities applaud by stamping and express their disapproval by scraping their feet. Precisely at three o'clock the side door opened, and the Baron entered, greeted by a deafening storm of stamping feet. He was a small man, in his middle fifties, immaculately dressed in a gray suit. He walked slowly to the lectern without acknowledging the ovation, stepped up to the desk and put his papers and several books before him, then stretched his arms and seized the outer edges of his lectern with his hands, as was his habit. Then he looked up and nodded at us. There was a trace of a smile on his strong and sensitive face with the gray goatee. He knew what we were expecting of him. He waited until the stamping of feet diminished and, finally, stopped.

11 «

Into that stillness fell his first soft-spoken words: "The Jewish philosopher Jesus Christ—"

That was as far as he got before pandemonium broke out, a cacophony almost equally divided between stamping and scraping. The Baron had lowered his head, but then, in a sudden dramatic move, he raised it and looked at us, and we could almost *feel* the passion in his large, dark eyes. Gradually the scraping began to fade and the stamping to grow until in a powerful crescendo it had wiped out the opposition. Nothing could be heard but the thundering of hundreds of feet.

At that moment, factions ceased to exist. The student body had been welded together by one man's humanity.

The Baron proceeded to read from Rathenau's books: observations on philosophy, statesmanship, and the meaning of patriotism. After every quotation, the Baron raised his voice: "This was the man of whom his murderers screeched: 'Beat to death the Jewish sow! Kill, kill Rathenau!' "

The train was moving faster now. In the evening's twilight I could see the swamps and lakes, the monotonous sandy plains and marshes, and the thickset forests of old, crippled pines.

Rataplan. Rataplan. Herbert Cohn. Herbert Cohn.

Two days ago I had been skiing in the crisp, powdery snow from St. Moritz down to Celerina, with Fritz von Theiss and his French girlfriend. His brown and gray and silver-blue chows had been racing with us. Sometimes their hind legs had hurled the snow in our faces. We had had to stop twice to wipe our dark glasses.

Rataplan. Rataplan. Herbert Cohn.

Same day. Arrival in Berlin.

The train entered the Anhalter station on schedule at 7:45 P.M. The three of us gathered our luggage and lined up in the corridor. The woman was last. She took her time putting away her knitting.

Through the window I could see that something unusual was going on. Railway officials and police officers were running along the platforms and across the tracks.

As I stepped off the car, I saw a cordon of S.A. men in their brown uniforms facing a train that stood on the next track. Apparently it had just arrived. The train's interior was barred from view by black uniforms. S.S. men, members of Hitler's elite guard, occupied the aisles, their backs to the windows. Some high government officials must be on the train, I thought, maybe the Fuehrer himself.

Some passengers from our train stopped to watch, but two brownshirts advanced toward them, shouting, "Move on, move on—fast!"

A roar went up and echoed in the high dome of the station. The S.A. men raised their arms in the Nazi salute. The roar changed into the rhythmical cry, *"Sieg Heil! Sieg Heil!"*

We were kept on the platform until the roar had subsided and whoever it was had left the station. Then the stream of passengers poured into the crowded streets.

I took a cab. I live in the western part of Berlin, in one of the side streets of the Kurfuerstendamm: a fashionable location. The apartments are spacious, built in the early nineteen hundreds.

Arriving, I unlocked the entrance door and carried my bags inside. The manager came out to help me: a slight man in his forties, married to a buxom Amazon who wears her ash-blond hair in braids. He and his wife have always been most accommodating, if not subservient.

He beamed as he saw me and raised his right hand. "Heil Hitler." I saw that he wore a swastika armlet.

"You'll find much changed, Dr. Bauer," he said. "These are great times for Germany. Great times."

We were in the elevator.

"How is Mrs. Heiliger?" I asked.

"The same," he said. "Heinz is in the Hitler Youth. You should see his uniform. He's our pride and joy."

We had arrived on the third floor. I inserted my key, but the door opened before me, and I saw Hanna's smiling face. Hanna, my maid and cook, a black-haired, rather stout woman of thirty-five, always cheerful, with a handsome face, has been with me for five years, ever since I moved to this apartment.

"It's so good to see you again, Dr. Bauer," she said. "Welcome home."

She took one of the bags from Mr. Heiliger and I noticed she avoided looking at him.

"That's it, Dr. Bauer," he said. His expression was sullen and he didn't cross the threshold.

"Thank you very much," I said and handed him a tip. Inside I took my other bag and followed Hanna to my bedroom. In the corridor I asked, "How've you been, Hanna?"

"The house is clean," she said. "I hope you will be satisfied. I had Stefan here for the windows and the heavy work."

"Everything looks just fine," I said.

The door to my bedroom was open. She went ahead and put the bag down.

"Do you want me to unpack, Dr. Bauer?"

"Not now. Thank you."

"Miss Rieger phoned a few minutes ago. She'd like you to call her as soon as you can."

"I'll do that, Hanna."

» 14

"Did you have dinner, sir? There's some cold roast beef in the icebox and some potato salad."

"Thank you. I had dinner on the train. It's late, Hanna. You should be in bed."

"I'm not tired," she said. "There wasn't much work with you away."

I looked at her. "Is anything wrong?"

She hesitated. "No."

"What about Mr. Heiliger?"

There was a pause.

"I don't mean to snoop, Hanna."

"Oh, no, Dr. Bauer. You don't."

"Did he misbehave?"

"With that wife of his—he wouldn't dare. It's about Paul. My fiancé. I shouldn't bother you with this on your first evening back."

"I'm interested, Hanna."

"Well—Mr. Heiliger found out that Paul is half-Jewish and he said if he ever saw us together again, he'd denounce us to the Gestapo. He called it 'racial disgrace.' " Suddenly she burst into tears. "I'm sorry, Dr. Bauer."

"Don't, Hanna. I'll have a talk with Mr. Heiliger. He's always been quite decent."

"You've been away for four months," she sobbed. "You don't know what's happened." She blew her nose—"Excuse me"—and continued haltingly: "I told Paul that we'd have to be very careful and he got mad at me and called me a coward, and now he doesn't want to see me anymore and he got fired from his job."

"I'm very sorry, Hanna."

"I know you are, Dr. Bauer. You've always been so understanding."

"We'll talk about this some more," I said. "Now I'd better call Miss Rieger."

15 «

"Yes, sir. Good night."

Hanna left and I picked up the receiver and dialed. Karin's voice sounded breathless.

"Oh, darling, I'm so glad you're back."

"So am I," I said. "Shall I come over to your place or do you want to come here?"

"I'll be there in twenty minutes," she said.

The apartment has five rooms, all large and with high ceilings, in addition to Hanna's room, the kitchen and butler's pantry, and a spacious hall. The guest room is used only when Karin stays overnight. She never sleeps there, but Hanna opens the bed every evening and makes it the next morning, knowing it hasn't been used. It's her way of upholding the moral code.

My study is next to the living room. Walking in, I saw a stack of letters on the desk and looked through them: some personal, some advertising; nothing important. There was the morning paper too, the same one I had read on the train. I looked again at the decree.

"All non-Aryan attorneys—"

I thought of Herbert Cohn, vice-president of the National Bank. Then I heard the key in my entrance door and Karin's voice calling: "Hans, where are you?"

"Here, in the study."

She threw the door open and rushed into my arms. We kissed; our bodies touched and clung together, and I forgot everything else. We went into the bedroom.

Afterwards we talked for a long time, lying next to each other in the soft, mellow mood of satisfied desire. I told her about the skiing in St. Moritz and mutual friends of ours I had met: Victor Brandt, the actor, and his wife, Eva; many others. I talked about the lazy afternoons on deck chairs in the sun-drenched snow. She spoke of the many days and nights without me. She had been restless. One night, at a party, she had met a man, an attaché of the British embassy, attractive, smooth; she'd had too much to drink; it almost happened—almost—then she re-membered . . . us. Since then the attaché had called her al-most every day, sent her roses, red roses—

"I had only one letter from you last month," I said.

"Yes, I know, darling."

She had seen him again and told him she was in love with someone else and he had been nice about it and very charming —really, Margie thought so too.

"How is Margie?" I asked.

"All right." There was a slight hesitation in her voice.

"Are you still that close?"

"Yes. Only—"

"Only what?"

"I can never be alone with her anymore," Karin said. "Mar-gie's fallen in love with an *Obergruppenfuehrer* or something, high up in the S.S. He comes every evening and brings his friends, all in black uniforms—you don't know what happens to Margie when she sees a uniform. Carl Adriani is his name, strik-ing looks, a dramatic kind of man. I've never seen him smile."

I thought again of the decree. I rose and took my robe out of the suitcase.

"Is anything wrong, Hans?"

"No."

"Suddenly you're so quiet."

I said nothing.

"I'm getting up too," Karin said.

Her own robe was in my closet, and she put it on now over her naked body. Karin is a slight girl with firm breasts and small shoulders, the subtle oval of her face framed by dark-blond hair. Her eyes are large and brown, her lips very red, even without lipstick.

"You've missed all the excitement," she said. "All the cele-brations of Hitler's coming to power. People are crazy about that man. One party after the other. And the parades! One thing you can say about them, they know how to stage their rallies. We must go to one together."

"Yes."

We went into the study, Karin's favorite room. I sat on the couch. She lit a cigarette and lay down, her head in my lap.

"I missed you terribly," she said. "I missed sex with you. Another month without you and I don't know what I would have done."

"I missed you too."

"Did you sleep with another woman—oh, of course, you did. Don't tell me."

"I didn't."

She chuckled. "Don't you believe me?" I asked.

"No."

"I believe you, Karin."

After a moment she said, "Maybe you shouldn't."

"Is that a confession?"

She shook her head. It didn't look convincing.

"I'm almost twenty-seven," she said. She reached over and put out her cigarette. "And we've been together for three and a half years."

"Three years and eight months."

She looked up at me. "Don't you think it's time we settled down?"

"What do you mean? Marriage?"

"Yes. It does sound frightening, doesn't it?"

"Karin—you're the one who never wanted to—"

She cut in fast. "Yes, I know. I had that one disaster—when I was so young. It's always scared me." She raised her arms and pulled my head down to hers. "We won't be a disaster, darling. We'll be happy together. You're so much better in bed than—"

She stopped. I looked at her. For a moment she was confused . . . but she had said it and she couldn't take it back.

"Well, you know what I mean," she said. "I love you, darling. I want to be your wife. I want your babies."

She let go of my head. I had hoped for this moment ever since I'd met her, but now, when I bent down to kiss her, I stopped.

She sat up. "What is it, Hans?"

"I—I don't know."

I rose and went to my desk and stood with my back to her. I didn't want to face her. I said, "Darling—just a very short time ago, I would have been the happiest man in the world."

Behind me, the silence stretched longer and longer. I thought it would never end. Finally, she asked in a flat voice, "Have you met another woman?"

"No, Karin. No. That isn't it."

"Then what is it? Why don't you want to marry me?"

I turned and handed her the morning paper with the decree. As she was reading it, she began to frown. She finished and, still holding on to the paper, she asked, "What's this got to do with you? You aren't Jewish."

"No. But my grandmother's father was a Jew."

"You're joking."

"No. It's true."

"I don't mean that. The fact that a hundred years ago someone in your family was Jewish doesn't make you a Jew."

"According to the new law it does."

She sat down. "I don't believe it."

"Don't you read the newspapers, Karin?"

"Of course I do, but—I've talked to so many people. They all say this anti-Jewish business is only temporary. Hitler promised it to his Nazis and now he has to do something about it. But it won't last."

"What makes you think that? Have you ever read *Mein Kampf?*"

"No, darling. Please—let's not talk politics."

19 «

"We're not, Karin. We're talking about our lives. I have to know what I'm facing."

She turned her head away from me. I went to her.

"Can't you understand that, darling? It wouldn't be fair to you."

She said in a hard voice, "What the hell does that mean—fair?"

"You want me to spell it out for you?"

She didn't answer.

"It's really very simple, Karin—I might not be able to support you."

"I have my own money," she said glumly.

"As long as you don't remarry," I said. "That's stipulated in your divorce contract. Don't forget, I've been handling your affairs for the last three years."

She lowered her head. I sat down next to her and put my arm around her.

"Maybe everything will be all right, darling."

She nodded and turned her face to me and kissed me. "It's all so confusing," she said. "You left me alone for four months—"

"Karin, you know why—"

She cut in impatiently, "Yes, I know. It's part of that divorce agreement. I can't leave the country without my former husband's consent. Nobody's ever heard of such an idiotic clause!"

"You agreed to it, Karin—in exchange for almost double the alimony the judge would have awarded you."

"You shouldn't have let me do it."

"I hardly knew you then. I didn't handle your case and I didn't write the agreement."

There was a pause.

"I was so happy you were back," she said. "Finally, I'd made up my mind to marry you. I couldn't wait to tell you."

"I'm sorry."

"Yes." She took a deep breath. "I'll go and get dressed."
"Aren't you staying?"
"No."
She rose and touched my hand: a palliative gesture.
"I'll see you tomorrow."
For a moment we stood silently and looked at each other. It was almost like a farewell, I thought. She must have felt that too.

April 23rd. Berlin.

No. It is one o'clock in the morning.

April 24th.

After Karin left, I called Dr. Aaron at his home, to let him know I was back and in excellent health.

A woman's voice answered the telephone. "Dr. Kruger's residence."

"Dr. Kruger?"

"Yes."

"I'm sorry. I must have dialed the wrong number," I said and hung up.

I checked the phone number in my book, but it was correct. I must have made a mistake in dialing. Once more.

"Dr. Kruger's residence."

"Well . . . I'm sorry to bother you again. I thought this was Dr. Aaron's number."

"It used to be," the woman said.

"Has he moved?"

There was a moment of hesitation. Then, "Yes."

"Could you tell me where I could reach him?"

"Are you one of his patients?" the voice asked. "I'm Mrs. Kruger. My husband took over Dr. Aaron's practice and his apartment."

"When was that?"

"About two months ago. Many of Dr. Aaron's former patients are now consulting my husband. If you'd like an appointment—"

"Do you have Dr. Aaron's new address?"

"All I know is that he moved to Brussels," Mrs. Kruger said. "My husband's still out on calls. If you could give me your name and phone number—"

"My name is Herbert Cohn," I said.

She gasped. "Dr. Kruger is very busy this month." Click. Mrs. Kruger had hung up.

According to the dictionary, a diary is a "daily record of matters affecting the writer personally." In that sense, this account might pass for a diary, although I didn't set out to write one. It's been a long-standing habit of mine to write down any kind of problem that on the face of it seems difficult, if not impossible to solve. It's helped me immeasurably in some of our legal cases —in rerecording the facts, I've sharpened my memory. Nuances I'd failed to register originally have assumed an unexpected significance and on many occasions opened up new prospects that ultimately have led to a solution.

The same applies to my personal problems. In several instances, important as well as trivial, the very fact that I've recorded what has troubled me has clarified my thoughts enough to enable me to come to a decision.

I hope that this will help me now too. In the few hours since I've returned to Berlin, I've seen and heard many things that have made me apprehensive. I am confused. In St. Moritz I was relaxed, free of pressures—even the discovery that I had a fourth-generation Jewish ancestor hadn't affected me too much. I am a German. Not a Jew. Nobody can make a Jew out of me.

I want to talk about Karin.

She is a pastor's daughter. Her mother grew up in East Prussia on a small farm near the village that used to be the pastor's parish and they married when they were both very young. Shortly thereafter, he was transferred to a larger parish, not far from Breslau. Karin was an only child. Her upbringing was strict and spartan, in the best Protestant Prussian tradition, and as she grew up, her freedom became even more restricted. She was forbidden to go out on dates until she was eighteen, and even then the boys had to be introduced to her parents, and approved, before they were permitted to call for Karin in the evening.

When she was twenty, her parents took her to a fair in Breslau. On the first day, they were looking at a display of optical instruments when they met a man who offered to guide them— but it soon developed that he was interested only in Karin. His name was Joseph Sebaldt. He was fifteen years her senior and not very good-looking: short, with narrow shoulders, glasses, and reddish hair combed straight back to cover his bald spots. His mouth was too large and his nose slightly lopsided, but his teeth were very white when he laughed. And he laughed frequently and loudly. He seemed entirely self-assured and worldly-wise.

He proposed to Karin a few days later, having first informed her parents of his intentions. At first she was scared—she was not in love with him and honest enough to tell him so—but when she was alone with him and he kissed her and touched her as she had never been kissed and touched before, her virginal body succumbed to him easily and she accepted his proposal eagerly and gladly. Only after she had agreed to marry him did he reveal the extent of his holdings and his fortune. As president of the largest optical firm in Germany and owner of most of its patents, he was a very rich man.

The wedding took place in Berlin, where Joseph Sebaldt had made his home. It was a church wedding done in style. Karin's father officiated by special permission, which his new son-in-law had obtained for him.

The couple honeymooned in Paris and London and returned to Berlin four weeks later, to the Sebaldt mansion in the fashionable suburb of Dahlem. To Karin the sudden change from spartan simplicity to the luxurious carnival of international society was overwhelming. It took two full years before she was able to comprehend what had happened to her and to arrive at a true evaluation of her lot.

It was then that she realized she was miserable in her marriage, in spite of the designer clothes, the summer vacations at the villa in Antibes, and her social position as Joseph Sebaldt's wife. After the ardent courtship, the honeymoon, and the excitement of being mistress in a mansion with fourteen servants, she discovered that her husband, her first sexual experience, was actually quite inadequate in bed. She also realized that they had little in common. They were rarely alone—the house was always filled with guests—but when they found themselves, suddenly, by themselves, it seemed they had nothing to say. She became frustrated and lonely; began to feel uneasy at her husband's touch, and the uneasiness soon changed to disgust.

Finally, after two years, she had her first affair. It gave her complete physical satisfaction, nothing else—not that she had wanted more from it, but the affair didn't last. Others followed. In the society in which Karin moved, adultery was considered normal. The women of her acquaintance were only too eager to introduce new candidates to her in exchange for similar services.

When I first met Karin four years ago she had decided to get a divorce. When she approached her husband about it, however, he refused: he had known about her affairs and was perfectly willing to tolerate them as long as she remained his wife. It was then that she began to hate him. She faked affairs, paraded her "lovers" openly and stayed away nights to provoke him into action, until finally Joseph Sebaldt's family, associates, and friends prevailed on him to give her the divorce. Faced with the inevitable, he proved to be amazingly forgiving and generous. With her record of adultery, she was not entitled to any alimony, but, claiming he was still in love with her, he insisted on large alimony payments anyway. And when she agreed to conditions that would keep her still dependent on him to an extent, he doubled the amount voluntarily.

Karin and I fell in love with each other just before the divorce. One year later, I asked her to marry me. She stalled for a while and, finally, refused. She was scared of marriage and confessed that she didn't dare risk losing the alimony payments which gave her financial security. I suppose, basically, she mistrusted her own feelings, as well as mine. While our relationship ostensibly remained the same, it soon began to suffer from her lack of confidence, which affected me too.

About five months ago I started to have dizzy spells and severe headaches. At Dr. Aaron's advice, I decided to rest several months to recover from what he termed an extreme case of physical and mental exhaustion.

At first Karin had written frequent, affectionate letters, then, shortly after the Hitler regime came to power, her letters changed in tone and concentrated more and more on descriptions of parties and Third Reich celebrations. I still felt very much attached to her and wrote to her often . . . but during the last months, her letters virtually stopped.

Karin had changed. I could see it quite clearly now, in spite of her passion in bed, in spite of her surprising proposal of marriage. Maybe I shouldn't have left her alone for four months.

The 26th of April.

I haven't had the time to write until today. And even if I had, I don't think it'd have been possible for me to put on paper everything I've experienced these last days, so soon after it occurred.

What I've seen and lived through transcends reality as I have known it. In terms of human behavior—or rather what I always understood human behavior to be—it is incomprehensible. I can only try to describe the events and facts in as much detail as I remember. Maybe there'll come a time when I'll be able to analyze my own reactions. Right now, I still feel numb.

It was raining on the morning of the twenty-fourth. I couldn't get a taxi and took the bus to my office. The bus was crowded, people were standing in the aisle.

But two young S.A. men were seated. In front of them stood an elderly, well-dressed couple. He was trying to hold on to a strap, but he was short and his extended right arm could only just reach it. She clung to him tightly, both hands linked to his left arm.

The two brownshirts were staring at the couple. One of them formed a hooked nose with his forefinger. The elderly man turned his head.

"Jews shouldn't be allowed in the same bus with Germans," the S.A. man said. "They stink up the air."

He continued to stare at the couple. A man next to him unfolded a newspaper and hastily started to read. The other S.A. man chuckled. Just then the bus came to a sudden stop, the man lost his grip on the strap, and his wife fell against the S.A. man.

"Get back on your hooves, you Jewish sow!" the first one shouted, and pushed the woman hard. She uttered a cry and slapped both her hands on her mouth to stifle the sound. The man stared at the two S.A. men, hatred in his eyes. His body shook in hopeless frustration.

A blond girl across from the two brownshirts said, "Leave them alone. They're old."

The one who had hit the woman leaned forward. "What are you—a Jew lover?"

"It's none of your business what I am," the girl said. Her face was red with indignation and embarrassment. Everybody looked at her. Nobody spoke. The other S.A. man whispered something to the first one. Both of them grinned.

The bus started again. The influx of new passengers had moved the elderly couple away from the brownshirts.

On the next stop, the blond girl got up and went to the exit door. The two S.A. men rose too. Shoving people aside, they got off the bus behind the girl.

I sat down next to the man with the newspaper. Both of us turned our heads and saw through the window that the brownshirts had taken the girl between them. The bus moved on. Our eyes met.

"The new Germany," I said.

He lowered his head and looked across the aisle. I saw the sign: "Listen to your neighbor's talk."

Our offices are downtown, near the Friedrichstrasse, on the fourth floor of an old building that has a flat, smoky facade and a jagged roof, with three Gorgon heads jutting out at a dangerous angle. Inside a wide marble staircase swings upward to the top floor, the sixth. The creaky lattice elevator is out of order most of the time.

Our suite is comfortable and spacious. There are three of us: Klaus von Isenberg, whose full name is Eberhardt Anton Klaus Ritter von Isenberg; Siegmund Schwartz; and myself. Between us we have two young assistants, Manfred Schuller and Guenter Sternberg; three secretaries, Magda, Hedi, and Lieselotte; and a filing clerk, Gustaf Angermann.

Magda has worked for me for nine years: a handsome girl in her early thirties, who nevertheless hasn't been able to find a husband. She's six feet tall—that seems to have a discouraging effect on men who are shorter, and she rejects the idea of selecting a husband according to size.

I glanced at the "out of order" sign on the elevator and took the stairs. It was shortly after ten when I entered our offices.

I saw two of the girls, not Magda, talking to a man in S.A. uniform. As I came in, the girls went back to their typewriters and said, "Good morning, Dr. Bauer. Glad you're back."

The S.A. man said, "Heil Hitler!" and asked, "How do I look, Dr. Bauer?" I recognized our filing clerk, Gustaf Angermann.

"Brown," I said, and walked past him.

Hedi chuckled. I shook hands with Magda and she followed me into my office.

» 28

"Sit down, Magda." I went to my desk and looked at the enormous stack of mail.

"It's good to have you here again, Dr. Bauer."

"Thank you." I opened my briefcase, took out some of the letters I'd received at home, and sat down.

"Dr. von Isenberg would like to see you as soon as possible," Magda said.

"Is he in his office?"

"Yes, sir."

"Well, first let's talk for a few minutes," I said. "How're you and how is everything around here?"

She hesitated, then she leaned forward and whispered, "It's been terrible, Dr. Bauer."

"What's the matter? Why are you whispering?"

"The other day Gustaf threatened to put microphones in every office. He's been a party member and a member of the S.A. for years. Nobody knew about it. Then one day after the Nazis came to power, he marched in here in his uniform. He says he's a *Sturmfuehrer*, whatever that is."

"We should have fired him long ago. Dr. Schwartz was the one who insisted on keeping him. He felt sorry for him."

She whispered. "Do you know what happened to Dr. Schwartz?"

"No, I don't." I found myself whispering too.

"He's Jewish. You know. You remember how he used to talk about Hitler and that whole gang—well, last Thursday, Dr. Schwartz was in his office and Gustaf came in with two other brownshirts and they took him away."

"Where?"

"I don't know."

"Couldn't Dr. von Isenberg interfere?"

"He's in court on Thursdays."

The door opened and Klaus came in fast with outstretched

hands. "Hans, for Christ's sake, I didn't know you were here—"

Magda rose and left the office.

"I just got in," I said.

"Am I glad to see you!" Klaus said.

He sat down on the couch. Klaus is of medium height, lean and sturdily built. His dark hair is cut short, and his face, with his long, straight nose, gray eyes and sensual mouth, shows his descent from one of the best-known aristocratic families. He looks exactly like his father, who was a commanding general in the world war, and his grandfather, who served as cabinet minister under the Kaiser. When you enter his office for the first time, it is a startling experience to look from the two pictures on the wall to the man behind the desk.

Klaus became the black sheep when he decided to study law. No member of his Prussian family had ever dreamed of joining the vulgar ranks of ordinary professionals. Junkers supervise the administration of their estates; they join the diplomatic service or choose a military career. They do not exhibit themselves in offices and courtrooms. Gradually, however, in the last few years, the family attitude had changed. Our firm's reputation had grown. So had our income. We could demand top fees and afford to be selective in the choice of our clients. Klaus had used a large part of his earnings to save his family's estate from bankruptcy, and while they still considered the source of the money humiliating, they had to acknowledge, reluctantly, that without Klaus they would have lost most of their holdings.

"Magda told me about Siegmund," I said.

His expression hardened. "Yes. I was in court and couldn't be reached. This son-of-a-bitch, Gustaf, counted on that. Have you seen him?"

"Yes. Just now."

"I haven't yet."

"Can't we find out where they took Siegmund?"

» 30

"I did. I learned about it early the next morning. The S.A. has established 'reeducation centers' for enemies of the state. Jews, Communists—anybody they don't like. What really happens there is torture and murder." He bit those last words off. Then, more quietly, "I'm trying to get him out."

"How?"

He half-smiled. "I've got connections. For the first time in my life, my family name is good for something. Those idiots automatically assume I'm on their side."

"Careful, Klaus!"

"Careful—!"

"Magda just told me Gustaf threatened to put microphones in our offices."

Klaus's face reddened; the muscles on his neck contracted. "Is that so?" he said.

He jumped up, walked to the door, and threw it open. "Get Gustaf in here. Immediately!" He left the door open.

"What do you plan to do?" I asked. He didn't answer.

Apparently Gustaf took his time. When he finally sauntered in, he had a defiant smile on his face.

"Heil Hitler!"

"Shut the door!" Klaus snapped.

Gustaf leaned against the door. It closed slowly.

"Mr. Angermann, you haven't been here, in the office, since last Tuesday and you couldn't be reached at home," Klaus said.

"That's right."

"What's your excuse?"

"I don't need an excuse. I was on S.A. duty."

"As long as you're an employee of this office, your duty is here. Nowhere else."

"Times have changed, Dr. von Isenberg," Gustaf said.

"Your hours are from nine to six. That hasn't changed."

"We'll see about that," Gustaf said.

I began to admire Klaus's patience.

"On Thursday morning you came here with two of your hoodlums and arrested Dr. Schwartz. Why?"

"The Jews are our enemies," Gustaf said firmly. He obviously felt on safe ground with that statement.

"Do you know we kept you in your job only because of Dr. Schwartz?" I asked.

"Personal feelings have nothing to do with it," Gustaf said. "The Jews are Germany's enemies."

"You are incompetent and lazy," I said. "Dr. Schwartz felt sorry for you only because you told him you were the sole support of your mother."

"I heard him slander and vilify the Fuehrer and the party. You've heard him too. It would have been your duty—"

Klaus cut in, "Don't you talk to us about our duties, you scum!"

Gustaf paled. "I demand respect for my uniform—"

"On you, it looks like shit!" Klaus said.

Gustaf's face collapsed. "You'll—you'll hear about that!"

"From whom?" Klaus didn't wait for an answer. "Is it true you intend to install microphones in our offices?"

"That was just a joke, Dr. von—"

"I'm glad to hear that, Gustaf. As it happens, I don't have any sense of humor. Get out and don't ever show your face in this office again! You're fired!"

Gustaf stared at him. "I don't accept that."

"All right, then, accept this," Klaus said. He slammed his fist into Gustaf's face and Gustaf crumpled to the floor, his eyes rolling until only the whites were visible. Klaus filled a glass with water from my pitcher and threw the water in his face. Gustaf sputtered and came to, then got up slowly, his head lowered.

Klaus said, "You understand that you're fired?"

Gustaf nodded.

"And you accept it?"

He nodded again.

"I didn't hear your answer."

The phrase sounded familiar. It was what the S.A. man had said to Herbert Cohn on the train.

"Yes," Gustaf said.

He managed to open the door and leave. I said nothing. The sudden outbreak of violence had unnerved me.

"I know, I've just applied the Nazi technique," Klaus said. "But that's the only thing these hoodlums understand."

"It might not have been very smart," I said.

"Maybe not."

He was breathing heavily as he took a cigarette out of his case and lit it. The buzzer on my desk sounded and Magda's voice said, "I have an urgent call for Dr. von Isenberg."

I handed Klaus the receiver.

"Yes?" He waited a moment. "Yes, heil—good morning, Franz. What's the news?" Pause. "Where is he?" Pause. "Of course, he'll leave the country. He'll have to. Provided, of course, he can get a passport and a visa. Could you have one issued for him, and for his wife too? Her name is Helen, Helen Schwartz."

He listened again and said, "I appreciate that very much, Franz. Please, send them to the office, care of me. Yes, I guarantee that. Personally."

There was a pause. "All right. I'll ask his wife to meet him. At three o'clock. Good. And Franz—thank you again. No, I won't mention it to a soul. So long, Franz."

He hung up.

"God damn it! I can't say it!"

"Can't say what?"

"Heil Hitler."

I said, "That was the call about Siegmund."

"Yes. He's going to be released at three this afternoon. I must phone Helen."

"How did you do it, Klaus?"

"Never mind," he said. "They'll have to be out of the country in four days. Until then he's supposed to be in my custody. I'd better go and make some calls."

He was about to leave, but I stopped him. "Klaus—"

"Yes."

"I need a few minutes with you."

"Now?"

"After you've called Helen."

"All right."

He picked up the receiver. "Magda, please, get me Mrs. Schwartz."

I was growing more and more apprehensive. As Klaus talked to Helen Schwartz, I thought: Siegmund and Helen are being forced to leave Germany because they are Jews. Jews. If Klaus hadn't interfered, Siegmund might be dead by now.

Klaus put down the phone. "She was crying so hard, I could barely understand her." He looked at me.

"You saw yesterday morning's paper with the new decree?" I said.

"Of course. It makes it impossible for us to keep Schwartz in the firm."

"Well, Klaus . . . I'm sorry to say . . . you might lose me too."

He stared at me. "What do you mean?"

"My grandmother made a slight mistake," I said. "She had a Jewish father."

He said nothing, and I knew he was counting the generations. Then he sat down heavily.

"I thought I was prepared for everything—"

"I was surprised myself. The first I knew about it was when I went through my papers."

He covered his face with both hands and thought. After a moment, he dropped his hands and looked at me.

"You're not a Jew," he said. "Any driveling half-wit can see that, even if he wore a uniform. You're not a Jew."

"Of course not."

"Just because one of your great-grandfathers—that's ridiculous!"

"That's what I thought."

He rose. "Give me your papers."

"What do you have in mind?"

"I'm going to try to straighten it out. That can't be tough in your case. With your family background."

He took my envelope and put it in his briefcase.

"I certainly appreciate that, Klaus. I don't want to leave the firm. I certainly don't want to leave the country. I'm a German."

"So am I," he said. "But those lunatics want us to revert to cannibalism. If they succeed, it'll be a caveman's Germany, Hans. Not the country we both know and love."

He went out fast, slamming the door.

In the afternoon, I received a call from Karin. She had a headache and was going to lie down for a couple of hours. She'd phone me in the evening, at home. She said she had two tickets for the first performance of Richard Strauss's new opera, *Arabella*, and she knew how much I loved Strauss's music. Could I go with her? A week from Friday? I certainly could.

She sounded tired. Listless.

By the time I got through my mail, it was almost seven o'clock: I'd lost track of the time. Most of the correspondence had to do with legal problems connected to show business. Over the years I've tended to concentrate more and more in that area, until by now I've become an expert. Most of my clients now are producers, managers, publishers, and actors.

It was dark when I left the office. The rain had stopped. I'd been sitting at my desk all day and the air was cool, so I decided to walk for a while.

The Friedrichstrasse is one of the main arteries of downtown Berlin. The stores were closed now, but I've always enjoyed window shopping. Except for this evening. Wherever I looked, I saw the remnants of the first of April, the "Day of Boycott," on which all Jewish-owned stores had been guarded by S.A. men to keep customers from entering. Whoever had defied those pickets had been photographed. Few if any had dared challenge the brownshirts. As I looked around now, I could see some of the shop windows were broken, and on the fragments of glass, painted in red, the words JEW or THIS IS A JEWISH STORE. Other windows were covered with crude swastikas or had signs THIS IS A GERMAN STORE or ARYAN OWNER AND ARYAN PERSONNEL. Hardly a store was unmarked.

S.A. men rode by in large trucks, singing the Horst Wessel song, which by now had become the second German anthem. It had been written three years ago by an S.A. youth who had later been killed by Communists. "When Jewish blood squirts from our knives—" Nobody in the crowded street turned his head. People were already used to it.

Two police cars came to a sudden halt just a few steps ahead of me, and it was then I saw the brownshirts. They had linked their arms, forming a semicircle that started at a bar across the street and extended to the middle of the pavement, causing a traffic jam. In front of the bar, something burned with a rapidly growing flame, exuding a strong odor. About eight or ten policemen jumped out of their cars and ran toward the brownshirts. As they reached the line, one of the S.A. men turned and shouted, "Get lost!"

Two of the cops tried to break through the S.A. chain, the others stopped. The two policemen pulled out their clubs, but before they could use them, they were kicked and beaten by the brownshirts. One of them fell and was dragged back by his comrade.

By now a crowd of people had collected where I was. A man next to me stood as if frozen, staring at the fire. His face was white.

"What is that terrible odor?" I asked.

The man said nothing. Someone behind me said, "You weren't in the war, were you?"

I shook my head and turned. The man was well-dressed, in his fifties. His cheeks showed two red scars from his student days.

"You'd know that stink if you'd been in the trenches," he said. "That's one thing you don't forget."

"Why don't they scream?" a woman next to him asked. She was sweating. Her eyes glistened with excitement.

"They did," the man said. "It's all over."

My legs gave way. I groped for the arm of the man next to me as he stood, still motionless, staring across the street. When I touched him, he grabbed my hand, linked it in his arm, and put his hand over mine.

The policemen had remained behind the brownshirts. None of them had moved.

"They're Bolsheviks," the man behind me said. "The S.A. men dragged them out of the bar, poured gasoline over them, and set them on fire."

"Those goddamned swine!" a young man in the crowd said. I didn't know if he meant the Nazis or the Bolsheviks.

Someone I didn't see shouted, "All Bolsheviks and Jews should burn like this!"

After that, no one spoke. The policemen climbed in their cars, fast and furtively, and drove off. My arm was still linked to the man next to me. Now he turned and I turned with him.

We walked together in silence and didn't look back. After a while he removed his hand and released my arm, gently. My legs carried me ahead. He remained behind.

The smell of human flesh, burning, was still in my nostrils. I wanted to vomit, but I couldn't open my mouth. I took out my handkerchief to wipe my face, and when I put it back in my pocket, it was soaking wet. I hadn't realized I was crying.

I found a cab and went home.

Mr. Heiliger stood in the door of his ground floor apartment, smoking a cigar and reading the evening paper.

"Heil Hitler, Dr. Bauer."

I looked at him and said nothing. I was still numb. There was something—then I remembered.

"I want to talk to you," I said.

He folded his paper. "Oh, but certainly, Dr. Bauer. Any time." He held his cigar behind his back and stepped away from the door to let me enter. "We've just finished dinner. The apartment is a mess, I'm sorry to say. Does the cigar smoke bother you?"

"No."

"Christine!" he shouted. "She's in the kitchen. Christine! Dr. Bauer is here! Maybe a cup of coffee, Dr. Bauer?"

"No. Thank you."

Christine came in, hot from working, towering over her husband. She wiped her large hands on her apron.

"Dr. Bauer," she said, and as an afterthought, "Heil Hitler! It's so nice to see you. You were gone for so long—Philip told me you were back. . . ." She stood for a moment. "Well, it's good to have you home again. Excuse me now, the dishes—" She retreated.

Mr. Heiliger looked at the glowing end of his cigar. "I'm

always available to my tenants, that's my job. So! Won't you sit down, Dr. Bauer? Take that chair. It's the best one in the house."

"I want to talk to you about Hanna," I said.

We both were seated now and I saw his expression change, his eyes narrow.

"Hanna—?"

"Yes. You know, she has a problem and—"

"I don't think so," he cut in.

"Well, I'm told that you threatened her and—"

"I'm only doing my duty."

"Mr. Heiliger, I prefer to finish my own sentences," I said sharply.

"Yes, of course, Dr. Bauer."

"Hanna's fiancé is a half-Jew," I said. "In the present climate that represents a problem, a very difficult one. But it's her own personal problem. I don't propose we add to it by threatening her."

Mr. Heiliger looked at his cigar again and then at me. "Dr. Bauer, you've been away for some time. This is a new Germany. The Jews are our enemies. Anybody who mixes with a Jew is a traitor."

"Calling Hanna a traitor is ridiculous!"

Red-faced, Heiliger stood up. "The purity of our race must be preserved," he said. "Any German woman who has sexual intercourse with a Jew commits racial disgrace. That is a crime, Dr. Bauer—and it is my duty as a German to inform the authorities."

"You seem to take your duties very seriously, Mr. Heiliger."

"Absolutely."

"Spying and informing on your fellow man used to be contemptible and immoral."

There was a pause. Then Heiliger said, "With all due respect

39 «

to you, Dr. Bauer—you're one of our finest tenants, never a day late with your rent, always nice—but you've got a lot to learn if you want to stay out of trouble."

The door opened and Heinz came in, the couple's son. He was fourteen and he'd always been fat, but he'd gained even more weight since I'd seen him, and he looked almost grotesque in his Hitler Youth uniform.

"Heil Hitler," he said.

"Heil Hitler," replied his father.

"Heil Hitler, Dr. Bauer. You haven't seen me in my uniform, have you?"

"No."

The boy looked at his father and shrugged. He went into the kitchen to see his mother.

"He's growing up in the right spirit," Heiliger said. "That's why the Fuehrer wants them when they're young."

"He's done all right by you, too," I said.

Hanna opened the door for me.

"Good evening, Dr. Bauer. Miss Rieger is in the study."

Karin was elaborately dressed in a pale green, low-cut evening gown, reading a magazine.

"You're so late," she said, rising slowly and putting her arms around me.

"I'd no idea you were waiting for me."

We kissed.

"You left your office more than an hour ago. Where've you been?"

"I walked part of the way and stopped for a moment at Mr. Heiliger's." I didn't want to talk about what I had seen.

"Victor's party is tonight," Karin said. "I almost forgot. I want you to be my escort."

A few months ago I'd seen Victor Brandt and his wife, Eva, in

St. Moritz. He is famous for his performances in Noel Coward's plays: Victor is one of the few German actors who possesses the cosmopolitan flair for those parts. He's a friend as well as a client.

"I couldn't go to a party tonight," I said.

"Why not?"

"I'm much too tired."

"Oh, come on—"

"Really, Karin—"

"Darling, please don't spoil my evening."

"I'm sorry."

"Is it because they didn't invite you? But Victor didn't know you were back. He and Eva were simply delighted when I told them—"

"Karin—"

"Our first party together after all those months."

I took a deep breath. She said very softly, "Darling, I understand . . . you're worried. I thought about it last night. I could talk to Carl—"

"Carl?"

"Carl Adriani, Margie's boyfriend. He's in the top echelon of the S.S. I'm sure he—"

"Karin," I said. "Please, don't. Don't ever mention it to him."

"He's not a monster. He's quite human. Really."

"Please forget it. Promise me. Promise me now."

"All right, I promise," she said wearily. There was a pause. "I was so looking forward to that party."

"Why don't you go?"

"With you," she said.

Hanna knocked on the door and came in. "Excuse me for disturbing you, Dr. Bauer. I just wanted to know about dinner."

Karin looked at me. "Dr. Bauer and I are having dinner out," she said.

"Yes, Miss Rieger, thank you."

I felt exhausted, drained of the energy to put up a fight. The line of least resistance, I thought. Please, let me take the line of least resistance.

I didn't realize I had said it aloud.

"What are you talking about?" Karin asked.

"I'll take a shower and get dressed," I said.

"Black tie," she noted.

I looked in the mirror. I needed another shave, I saw, just a light scrape to remove the evening shadows from my face. The magnifying mirror showed the short hairs on my upper lip and lower chin. Some of the hairs were gray. My temples were turning gray, too, gradually. To the naked eye, they still appeared dark blond. The wrinkles under my eyes seemed deeper today, I thought. Maybe there were more of them. My face was still tanned. I turned my head. My nose was straight, no question about that. Even in profile, I could discover no sign of a curve. It wasn't a Jewish nose.

My lower lip was full. It stuck out, just a little. Maybe that was an indication. My cheekbones were high: quite pronounced. The cheeks drew in and formed a long, pointed chin.

Karin had said "black tie," but I didn't know what shape my tuxedo was in after having traveled from St. Moritz to Berlin. Maybe the pants were wrinkled. I looked at them. No . . . straight and firm, two perfect legs . . . still warm. Hanna. She must have pressed them after seeing Karin in her evening dress.

I rubbed my face with 4711, my favorite cologne, put on fresh underwear, a pair of black silk socks . . .

"Darling—"

"Yes, Karin."

"How much longer?"

"Just a few minutes."

I took out a shirt. Starched and stiff like a cuirass, the damn thing stood up by itself. I had read somewhere that the Americans wore soft shirts with their tuxedos. I must ask Margie about that.

"Karin—"

"Yes."

"Is Margie going to be at the Brandts'?"

"No."

"Why not? Wasn't she invited? I thought she was close friends with Eva."

After a moment Karin said, "She couldn't make it tonight."

I finished dressing and looked in the mirror. There I stood. Going to a party. Business as usual.

But then I smelled the odor again—it was still in my nostrils —and I saw the flames. I took the bottle of 4711 and poured some more of it on my hands and face.

"Heavens!" Karin said. "You smell like a whore!"

"How would you know?"

We were in the elevator going down.

"Hans—"

"Yes?"

"Let's have fun tonight."

"Of course."

We crossed the ground floor hall. Heiliger's apartment door opened and Heinz came out in his uniform. He raised his right arm and hand.

"Heil Hitler!"

He waddled to the entrance door and opened it for us, trying to click his heels, without much success. His legs were too fat.

I have to stop writing. I am too tired.

It is now the 27th of April.

Victor and Eva Brandt's party.

Karin drove her car, a small white Buick coupe, which was part of her divorce settlement. The car is seven years old now, but in perfect condition. She has taken excellent care of it.

It was past nine o'clock. We were an hour late, but it wouldn't make any difference. I knew Eva's and Victor's parties. Some of the guests were actors and came after their performances or after filming; dinner would be a buffet affair with tables set up in every room of the large house.

The Brandts live in Grunewald, a lovely suburb, half an hour's drive away. When we got there, we saw the cars lined up in front of the long white wrought-iron fence. The driveway is wide and leads to a roundel, and there were some parking spaces left there. As I helped Karin out of the car, I saw several black Mercedes limousines with swastika standards.

Times have changed, I thought. Some years ago, Victor Brandt was rumored to have been a card-carrying member of the Communist Party. When it had hit the newspapers, he had come to me for advice. There had been just enough truth to it to make it impossible to deny outright. Victor had joined the party when barely twenty, then broken with them eight months later and sent back his card. I enlisted the help of some newspapermen who owed me favors, and a subtle but articulate campaign, spread over many weeks, restored Victor's fashionable Noel Coward image.

Eva is in her late thirties, and before marrying Victor was a high fashion model. That was sixteen years ago, but she has retained her figure and the shape of her long legs. Her face has gained a new mature beauty. It gives her an almost regal appearance.

She stood now in the hall, kissed Karin, shook hands with

me. Her white evening dress emphasized the red color of her hair. When I saw her in Switzerland, she was sun-tanned. Now she looked pale, nervous.

More people entered while we stood in the hall. Some of the men wore black or brown uniforms. Exchanges of "Heil Hitler" were made, informal, said with a slight upward bending of the wrist.

The rooms on the ground floor were connected by sliding doors which had been opened for the party, and a steady flow of guests passed from one room to another. Victor was at the bar in the living room with Grete Fall, the young film star, who is also one of my clients. Victor is tall and very slender, and the cut of his tuxedo emphasized his narrow waistline and wide shoulders. As usual, the dark hair was parted in the middle—a trademark, as are the brows over his deepset eyes, which form pointed arches, almost triangles, giving his face a sardonic look. When he is forced to think—not one of his favorite occupations—he tugs at his right ear.

Seeing us, he smiled happily and bent down to kiss Karin's hand. His attitude was nonchalant but not without elegance and formality, and his handsome face retained its smile as he grabbed my shoulders and shook me.

"Hans, what a glorious surprise!"

Grete Fall turned and kissed me on the cheek. She wore a large diamond-studded swastika on a gold chain.

"It's good to see you back," she said. "I missed you."

She shook hands with Karin. Karin turned and made a wry face at me. She has never liked that girl. Grete is three years younger than Karin—and a star.

A small man in a tan S.S. uniform approached Victor. "Heil Hitler, Mr. Brandt."

"Heil Hitler," Victor said. "I'm glad to see you, Alfred. Where is your wife?"

"Talking to *Gruppenfuehrer* Grautke."

45 «

"Well, then, Alfred, meet two of our closest friends, Karin Rieger and Dr. Johannes Bauer," Victor said. "This is Dr. Alfred Koenig."

The man's pleasant expression changed. He clicked his heels and shook hands with Karin.

"I didn't recognize you in your uniform," I said.

"I've been a party member for six years," he said stiffly.

"Congratulations."

"Thank you, Dr. Bauer. Victor. Here is my wife."

I took Karin's arm and we moved away from the group. I heard Victor say, "Heil Hitler."

A man's voice called, "Karin!"

She stopped. I saw she was blushing.

"Jimmy."

They shook hands rather awkwardly.

"Darling, this is James Charters—Dr. Bauer."

"I'm awfully glad to meet you, Dr. Bauer. I've heard so much about you from Karin."

He spoke German with a strong British accent.

"James is an attaché at the British embassy," Karin said, blushing even more.

"Nice to meet you, Mr. Charters."

"I didn't expect to see you here," Karin said. "Why didn't you tell me?"

"You know I always try to be where you are," Charters said. He made it sound like a joke. Then he turned to me. "You don't mind, Dr. Bauer . . ."

"Not in the least."

"But—but you never told me you knew Victor," Karin insisted.

"I made it my business to meet him," Charters said. He bowed to her a little too formally. "I hope you'll do me the honor of having a drink with me."

"Maybe," Karin said.

He smiled. "The night is long."

We crossed into the dining room in silence. Finally, Karin said, "That's the man I told you about."

"The 'almost' one."

"Yes."

"I gathered that much."

I pointed to the buffet, attended by several servants. "Are you hungry?"

She shook her head.

"He's good-looking," I said.

Nothing from her.

"Young and virile."

She let go of my arm. "Let's have a drink."

"All right."

Victor wasn't there anymore. Other people stood and sat around the bar. James Charters was talking to Grete Fall.

"You like her, don't you?" Karin said to me.

"Yes, I do."

"Did you see the big swastika? People say that Goebbels gave it to her."

Charters turned and saw Karin. "Your usual drink?" he asked.

She looked at me. "Whiskey," she said.

"And soda."

"Yes."

"What about you, Dr. Bauer?"

"Nothing for me, thank you."

I kissed Karin on the cheek. "I'd like to mingle for a while," I said.

Many of the guests were filling their plates in the dining room now and carrying them to their assigned tables. Victor's study was almost empty. A young couple sat on the couch, holding hands. An elderly gentleman stood talking to a man in S.A. uniform. I heard the S.A. man say, "You have to destroy first in order to build."

The elderly gentleman smiled. "That used to be a Communist slogan."

"The Fuehrer has taught us to learn from our enemies," said the S.A. man.

Eva came in. "If you'd like to go to the buffet, dinner is being served."

The elderly gentleman left, followed by the S.A. man, who bowed to Eva before he walked out. The young people were talking to each other very softly. The girl had tears in her eyes I saw. After a moment, both rose in one motion, their hands linked together.

"I hope everything works out, Anna," Eva said to the girl. The girl stared at her wide-eyed and nodded. They left.

"Those two got married six months ago," Eva said. "Now she's going to have a baby and he's been fired."

"Jewish?"

"She is. His company was very generous. They gave him a choice. He could keep his job if he divorced her."

"He said no?"

"They're very much in love and he's a decent boy."

"And if he weren't, he'd still have his job," I said. "The morals of the Third Reich."

"For heaven's sake, Hans, not so loud!"

She turned around fast to see if anybody had been listening. We were alone. She whispered, "I'm trying to protect Victor's career. It's all he's got."

I half-smiled at her. "All he's got? What about you?"

She shook her head.

"You two are about the only happily married couple I've ever known," I said.

"Don't say that. Not now."

"What do you mean?"

She pointed with her head in the young couple's direction. I looked at her. She nodded.

"I'm half Jewish. Not even that—one-third or something. It sounds idiotic, but too many people know about it and Victor's trying to fix it with the authorities. That's why he's invited all these big shots and been playing up to them."

Before I could say anything, I saw Dr. Koenig come in with his wife. She was carrying two plates, filled with food.

"I hope we're not intruding," he said. "Our table is supposed to be in this room." I noticed that there were indeed two tables set up in the study, each one for four.

"Yes, that's right, Dr. Koenig," Eva said. "Right there."

The Koenigs went to their table. He sat down; she put his plate before him, took his folded napkin, shook it, and handed it to him. He nodded, without looking at her. She took her own plate and sat down.

"Victor invited Carl Adriani," Eva said to me, very softly. "Through Margie, of course. He knows about me."

"But Margie isn't here."

"Adriani refused to come," she said with an effort.

Alfred Koenig picked up the place card across from him. He glanced at me.

"Margie called me back just a few minutes ago," Eva continued. "She said she'd try everything to bring him here tonight. It would be so important—"

"Why Carl Adriani?"

"He's in charge of what they call 'protection of the blood.' "

Dr. Koenig was leaning toward us in an obvious attempt to listen. Eva turned her back to the table.

"If he had accepted Victor's invitation, it would have been the official seal of approval."

"Well, let's hope for the best," I said aloud. "The first five years in a marriage are the most difficult ones."

We went back into the dining room. Victor was standing at the buffet next to Ludwig Butler, the novelist. Butler was speaking to him, but Victor didn't seem to be listening. Instead his eyes were searching the room, his hand tugging at his right ear. Then he saw Eva and motioned her to join him. I looked in vain for Karin, picked up a plate and took my place in the line. Seeing me, Butler waved and pointed to the study. I nodded. I wasn't hungry. My plate was only half full when I left the buffet.

Grete linked her arm in mine as I moved away.

"What's the matter, darling? Did you lose your appetite?"

We were both walking toward Butler, who stood in the door to the study, holding his plate.

"Little Jimmy has quite a crush on Karin, doesn't he?" said Grete.

"Where's Karin?" Butler asked.

"I left her at the bar."

"The place to be. The only place to be. I ran into her once or twice while you were climbing the Alps. She's the sexiest female on two legs—present company excepted."

"Saved by the bell," Grete said. "I seem to be your dinner partner tonight."

"I'll try my best," said Butler. "I'm just admiring your beautiful piece of jewelry."

"Isn't it pretty?"

"Yes. And in exquisite taste."

She glanced at him, but he was bending over the table looking for his place card.

Ludwig Butler is of medium height, lean and athletically built, with a virile face, regular features, and large, dark eyes. In his thirties now, he caused a sensation five years ago with his first book, which dealt with his experiences in the world war. It was the first time war had been treated realistically, in all its ugliness and futility, without heroics. The Nazis have never forgiven him for this "original sin" against the German spirit, but his fame has grown with every new novel he has published. By now his stature as an internationally recognized German writer makes it almost impossible for the new regime to denounce him.

"Here we are," he said.

Grete sat down next to him.

"I'm at the other table," I said.

Alfred Koenig's reaction to Butler's entrance had been very interesting. He had put down his knife and fork and stared at him unbelievingly. His wife had continued to concentrate on her food.

"My name is Johannes Bauer," I said. "We've met, Mrs. Koenig."

She looked up, chewing, and gave me an uneasy smile.

"That's Ludwig Butler, isn't it?" Koenig asked.

"Yes, it is." I sat down.

"How did he get here?"

"He drives his own car."

"That's not what I mean and you know it. I'm glad *I* don't have to share the table with him."

"Well, you have me instead," I said with a smile.

He looked at me. Koenig and I have opposed each other twice in cases where his side did not fare too well. In fact, in the second case, about a year ago, the judge reprimanded him because of "sordid tactics unbecoming to the dignity of the Court."

"Where is your beautiful girl friend?" he asked.

"I don't know."

Mrs. Koenig looked up from her plate. Her pug nose oscillated and her small, pouting mouth half-opened and emitted a grunting sound. Her husband eyed her in disgust.

"We are not in the zoo, Katarina!" he said sharply.

She faced him without any sign of embarrassment.

"You're always so witty, Alfred," she said, turning back to her plate.

He asked, "Is Ludwig Butler a friend of yours?"

He spoke loudly, and Ludwig moved his head and gave me an amused look.

"I think I can say that."

"And a friend of Victor's too?"

"Victor's invited him, hasn't he?"

"He's invited me, too, and I'm not his friend," Alfred said. "I know exactly why I'm here."

"You are eating his food, Dr. Koenig," I said. "Your wife seems to enjoy it."

"What happened to the Jew in your office?" Koenig asked.

I had a difficult time restraining myself, but thinking of the Brandts' precarious situation made me hold my temper.

"If you're referring to Dr. Siegmund Schwartz, he is leaving the firm," I said.

"I've never associated with Jews," he said. "Neither professionally nor socially. There's something subhuman about them. Most of them smell."

He had raised his voice, making any other conversation in the room impossible.

Ludwig turned to him. "Sir, I don't know who you are—but if you're making a speech, please be kind enough to rise and rap on your glass."

Dr. Koenig's face reddened. "Save your insolent remarks for your books, Mr. Butler."

Grete put her hand on Ludwig's arm and looked at him, and just then another couple walked in and took their seats at their table. Ludwig got up and the moment of introductions broke the tension. I rose and bowed to Mrs. Koenig.

"I must excuse myself. I'd better try to locate my friend."

I avoided Koenig's gaze when I left, but on my way out I did glance at Ludwig.

"See you later," he said.

I would have hit Dr. Koenig if I'd remained at the table. He's repulsive to me. It's a physical reaction as well as an utter contempt for the man.

Now that I'm writing this down, it occurs to me that I might have been hypersensitive toward his vile remarks about the Jews for personal reasons. In all honesty, however, I don't think that's true. I cannot identify with the Jews. I'm not one of them. Yet these days the Jewish question is uppermost in everybody's mind. People hardly talk about anything else. What we **are** witnessing is the enforcement of one of Hitler's first internal objectives: the elimination of Jews from Germany's life. I've never had any anti-Semitic feelings. I can't condone the persecution of the Jews on principle. Personally, I don't feel involved. I am not a Jew.

Karin was not in the dining room. At some tables the conversation was very noisy. At others it looked as if people were moving their lips without uttering a sound. People were whispering. I am walking among monsters and ghosts, I thought. And the monsters have conquered the earth.

The odor of human flesh, burning, returned and filled my nostrils. My legs weakened. I had to hold on to the back of a chair. A man in a brown uniform turned around and patted my hand. "That can happen to the best of us." He laughed.

I managed to move on. Karin was still at the bar, with Charters on a stool next to her. He had his arm around her shoulders. Their faces were very close.

"A brandy, please," I said to the bartender.

Karin turned when she heard my voice.

"Where have you been?"

"I was having dinner."

"By yourself?"

"No. With some very agreeable, some very sweet people."

"We've been sitting and talking," Charters said. "Karin wasn't hungry."

His hand held on to her shoulder. Tightly.

"That's good," I said. I emptied my brandy glass. The bartender looked at me. I nodded. He filled it again.

"Let go of me," Karin said to Charters. Then she shouted, "Leave me alone!"

He put his fingers to his lips and rose. "Time for you to take over, Dr. Bauer," he said with a smile. "So long, Karin."

He went. As he was leaving, I heard a commotion outside, a roar of motorcycles which ebbed, then stopped. A few harsh words sounding like orders. Then silence.

Suddenly Eva and Victor came rushing to the entrance hall. The conversation in the living room ceased.

"What's going on?" Karin asked.

I took a few steps to see into the hall.

The door was opened by two S.S. men who stood at attention as Margie entered, followed by a tall S.S. officer who removed his cap and handed it to his aide. The man's bearing spelled authority. His black hair was cut short, his face was narrow, with a wide mouth and dark eyes, veiled by very long eyelashes —almost like a woman's. He moved gracefully and easily, without self-consciousness, but sure of the impression he was making.

Margie's dark-haired beauty was a perfect physical match to him. She wore a silver fox over a low-cut dress, her face beaming with a show of triumph and delight. She said, "May I introduce *Obergruppenfuehrer* Carl Adriani—my dear friends, Eva and Victor Brandt."

Adriani's expression didn't change. He didn't smile. He shook hands, first with Eva, then with Victor.

"It was nice of you to invite me to your party," he said. "I have seen you on stage, of course, Mr. Brandt, and I have always admired your skill—if that is the correct word for it."

"Thank you very much, *Obergruppenfuehrer—*"

"My name is Adriani."

"Mr. Adriani," Victor continued. "I am delighted that you came."

Margie was hugging and kissing Eva, who started to cry. Adriani turned, walked into the living room, trailed by Victor, and flipped his wrist in a wordless Nazi salute, acknowledging the other guests.

When he saw Karin, he went up to her and they shook hands.

"This is Dr. Bauer," she said.

"Oh, yes." He shook hands with me. "I hope you'll be very happy together," he said, surprisingly.

I looked at Karin and saw she was blushing. She'd done a lot of blushing this evening, I thought.

Dr. Koenig came storming in, almost losing his balance as he came to attention and raised his arm.

"Heil Hitler, *Obergruppenfuehrer* Adriani."

"Heil Hitler," Adriani said and looked at him. "Have we met?"

"I had the honor to meet the *Obergruppenfuehrer* at one of the Fuehrer's receptions," Dr. Koenig said in a loud voice. "If the *Obergruppenfuehrer* would be kind enough to remember—"

Adriani cut in. "I'm afraid I don't," he said softly. He left abruptly and went up to Eva and Margie, who had entered the room. Eva was smiling, but her hands were nervously playing with a crumpled handkerchief.

"Your friend is a very beautiful woman," Adriani said to Margie. He turned to Victor. "Many men must envy you, Mr. Brandt. And envy is the source of many false rumors and the cause of much aggravation."

I hadn't realized until now that almost all the guests had

risen from their tables and were standing in a wide semicircle, watching the scene as if they were attending a theatrical performance.

"Aren't you hungry, Carl?" Margie asked.

"To be perfectly frank, I am," Adriani said.

He followed Eva and Victor to the buffet. Margie took Karin's arm.

"Come, join us. You too, Hans."

"I've already had my dinner," I said.

Karin looked at me. Her eyes narrowed. I shook my head and she turned around fast. They left.

I felt ashamed. Ashamed for Eva and for Victor. For Margie. For everybody participating in this charade. I didn't want to be with Karin either. I felt no closeness to her. I felt no closeness to anybody. For a while I remained at the bar, then I heard someone call my name.

I turned and saw Ludwig Butler standing in the entrance hall, motioning me to come to him and holding what looked like a bottle in his hand. I went. He pointed at the staircase. I didn't know what he had in mind, but I followed him upstairs, and when we came to Eva's sitting room, he motioned me inside, then closed the door and showed me the bottle triumphantly. I looked at it.

"Napoleon brandy."

"Read the date."

"1833—!"

"One-hundred-year-old Napoleon brandy," Ludwig said. "Let's see if that will restore our sanity."

"Where did you get it?"

"I stole it from under the bar," he said, "and I uncorked it in the kitchen."

He took two small glasses out of his pocket and filled them.

"Courtesy of Victor Brandt. To the Jews, the Communists, and to our beloved Kaiser Wilhelm the Second."

We emptied our glasses and he filled them again.

"I saw one of the gang this afternoon. The honorable Dr. Joseph Goebbels," Ludwig said.

"How was it?"

"Lovely. Lovely. He is a charming man. He licked my shoes—the ones I'm wearing—I shall never take them off. He wants me to become a member of the Reichs Culture Chamber. I asked him if it was true that the president of the chamber had said, 'Whenever I hear the word "culture," I release the safety catch on my gun.' Goebbels didn't like to be reminded of it, but he admitted that the quotation was correct. He said that it referred to the Jewish so-called intelligentsia, certainly not to the pure Aryan culture of the German people. I asked him what the word 'Aryan' meant. He got a little irritated. I played it wide-eyed and straight: the unworldly poet. I said I had learned that the original Aryans had been the Indo-European ancestors of the Indo-Iranians, and I asked him if he considered those tribes to be the ancestors of the German people.

"At that point Goebbels got angry, but for reasons of his own, he tried to hide it. He clubfooted around the desk to tell me that the Fuehrer himself was interested in my active participation in the National Socialistic effort to purify the national culture. I said that I had lecturing obligations in several foreign countries and that I would need a few days to coordinate and reorganize my activities. He didn't like that one bit. I'm supposed to see him again next week to give him my reply. By that time I'll be in Paris, which I didn't tell him."

"When are you leaving?"

"Tomorrow morning at seven," Ludwig said. "I'm not taking any chances."

Both of us had been drinking steadily but I felt no effect. I'm sure he didn't either. He said, "You know, Hans, during this whole conversation with Goebbels, there was only one question in my mind. If I had a gun, would I have the guts to shoot that swine?"

"You'd have been killed and his death wouldn't have changed anything."

"I know." He filled our glasses again. "Other people risk their lives every day."

He took out his wallet and extracted a small piece of paper. It was folded many times and, unfolded, was the size of an average sheet of stationery.

"Have you ever seen one of these?"

The text was crudely printed:

The Rape of Germany

Germany is in the hands of a gang of murderers and lunatics. Brought to power by the machinations of greedy industrialists and the corrupt members of the aristocracy, Hitler and his brutes have now started to murder their opponents.

During the last elections, the Nazis received forty-four percent of the German vote. Hitler's opponents were in the majority. Only due to the Nazi plot of the Reichstag fire and the senility of an eighty-two-year-old man who was duped into signing an emergency decree was it possible for the Hitler gang to outlaw the Communists and remove their eighty-one elected representatives from the Reichstag, thus giving the Nazis a parliamentary majority. Now, with the passage of the Enabling Act, Hitler's dictatorship has been firmly established. The constitution is a thing of the past. Jews and non-Jews are dragged into concentration camps, tortured and murdered.

The German rearmament is beginning. That can mean only one thing: preparation for a war of aggression.

Even at this hour, it is not too late to rally the majority of the German people, to have them join the underground in the battle for freedom. We must fight the Nazis with their own weapons: with terror, assassinations, and arson until these vermin have been exterminated.

THE COMMITTEE FOR FREEDOM AND
THE EXTERMINATION OF THE NAZI GANG.

After a moment I said, "It's very well-written."
"Thank you."
I looked at him, startled. I hadn't expected that.
"Are you—are you active in this?"
"I've written some of their pamphlets, that's all."
"But . . . where do they print them?"
"When they started, they had a shop in the cellar of a mutual friend of ours. The Nazis found out about it. Five people were arrested. One of them broke when he was tortured, and talked. Nineteen more were arrested and disappeared. Seven were women."
"And . . . our friend?"
"He wasn't home at the time of their arrest. But the Nazis have his name."
"Who is he?"
Ludwig shook his head. "It is safer for you not to know."
"How do they distribute these pamphlets?"
"One by one—in doorways, houses, public toilets, automobiles—"
"And they're still printing them?"
"Yes."
We had another drink. He said, "They found a new place. Underneath the Anhalter railway station. It was an excellent location, but they were betrayed." He paused to fill our glasses again. His face was calm, almost expressionless. "There was a rather original aspect to this betrayal," he said. "The informer was a Jew."
"A Jew?"

"Yes. A member of the chosen people. Chosen by God to be exterminated by the Nazis."

"How is it possible that a Jew—"

Ludwig cut in. "The explanation is simple. His wife and his four children were being held hostage by the Nazis. He was promised an exit permit and passports for his family and for himself. After he did what they had asked, he went to the authorities to get his reward. They had never heard of him. They knew nothing about his wife and children. He went berserk and tried to strangle the man in charge. He was arrested and cut his throat. End of story."

Suddenly I realized we'd been standing all the time. I felt weak and sat down.

Ludwig said, "I'm getting out of Germany for very selfish reasons. I want to save my life and I want to continue my writing. My interview with Goebbels was a trap. They want me to feel secure until they're ready for the kill. They don't give a damn about my reputation. Goebbels isn't stupid. He knows where I stand. But even if that weren't true, I couldn't live under Hitler, and I'm too much of a coward to work in the underground. It's too late anyway. There's no center of resistance anymore."

He took the pamphlet, folded it again, and put it back in his wallet.

"You're staying?"

"Yes."

"Well, it's different for you. I'm a writer. I can work anywhere. You're an attorney. You wouldn't even be allowed to practice in a foreign country."

"Yes, it is different," I said.

Ludwig looked at his empty glass. "You know Konrad Willman, don't you?"

"Yes, of course. He and his wife are friends of mine. Is it true he's joined the party?"

He hesitated a moment before replying. "Yes, he has. But you can trust him. He happens to be my ex-brother-in-law, and I want him to let Agnes know where I'm going to be. He's the only one who has her address. She wouldn't give it to me. She hates my guts."

I've known Ludwig Butler for a long time and I knew his wife. She was an exquisite beauty and in love with him, but she couldn't be faithful. It wasn't in her. Finally he had to break with her . . . but I have always sensed he is still in love with her.

"Please, go and see Konrad for me," he said. "Don't use the phone. Just go there. Any day after seven in the evening. I told him you'd contact him."

He wrote his address down on a piece of paper and handed it to me. Suddenly there were voices outside and footsteps. The door opened and Victor was saying, "This is my wife's sitting room. She—"

He stopped when he saw us.

"What the hell are you—"

Behind him Carl Adriani had entered. The paper was safely in my pocket.

"We were having a quiet talk," I said.

"A charming room, Mr. Brandt," Adriani said. His eyes were fastened on Ludwig. "My name is Carl Adriani," he said. "You're Ludwig Butler. I recognize you from your pictures. It's a privilege to meet you in person."

They shook hands.

"Thank you, sir. This is Dr. Bauer—we're old friends."

"I've met Dr. Bauer," Adriani said.

Victor discovered the bottle and reached for it. "Oh, no!" The bottle was almost empty.

"It was very good brandy," Ludwig said.

"Very good—" Victor turned to Adriani. "One-hundred-year-old Napoleon brandy! I've been saving it for years! They drank the whole bottle!"

"I'm afraid so," I said.

"I've read every one of your books, Mr. Butler," Adriani said. "I'm a layman, of course, but I consider you a brilliant writer."

"Thank you very much."

"I hope it won't be too difficult for you to adjust yourself and your work to our new Germany," Adriani added softly.

"What do you mean by 'adjust'?"

"I've told you, I'm just a layman. You're the writer." And Adriani lowered his head in a demure gesture.

Karin and I left the party soon after that. I shook hands with Adriani and with Ludwig, who said, "See you tomorrow at lunch." Both of us knew it would be a long time before we saw each other. I thanked Eva and Victor for the splendid evening. Grete said she would call me at my office. On the way out Dr. Koenig seized my hand and told me he and his wife would love to have Karin and me for dinner next week, and that it had been so delightful to see me again—not in the courtroom. He said all that in a loud voice to make sure that Adriani, who stood nearby, would hear him.

The air was cool outside. Karin drove and said she had had a terrible evening and she would never speak to Jimmy again. She'd thought he was a decent guy and that she could trust him. She was tired of his running after her and trying to touch her and all that. I said that if a girl went to bed with a man, she could expect him to take some "liberties" afterwards: a man can't always know why a woman sleeps with him—a sudden impulse, a physical need, something more. Men are vain, I said, more sentimental than women, and a man doesn't like to think that a woman he went to bed with can forget him so easily. I thought I was expressing myself very delicately.

"I said 'almost,' didn't I?" Karin said.

"Yes, you said 'almost,' but it wasn't the truth."

She was driving fast and passed a car and then had to turn in sharply to avoid a car approaching from the opposite direction.

"No, it wasn't the truth. I went to bed with him," she said finally. She didn't look at me. She kept her eyes on the road and her hands on the wheel.

I didn't know whether to be jealous or not. I didn't even know if I was still in love with her. I had missed her while I was in Switzerland, but now that I was back in Berlin, sitting next to her, I felt nothing.

People were being tortured and burned alive in the streets. Pamphlets were being written and printed. Jews were subhuman and smelled. And I was supposed to be a Jew myself. Not by birth. Not by choice. By decree. I didn't know how it felt to be a Jew. I didn't know if a Jew's thoughts and emotions differed from ours. I did know that the Jews kept their hats on in their synagogues when they were honoring their stern and revengeful God.

I remembered the story of Job. God had taken from him his flock, his cattle, and his sons and daughters. "And Job fell down upon his face before the Lord and he said, 'With nothing I came into the world and with nothing I shall leave it. The Lord gave it and the Lord has taken away; blessed be the name of the Lord.'"

Why was Job blessing the Lord who had made him poor and killed his children? Wasn't Hitler doing the same thing to the Jews? Was Hitler an instrument of the Lord? Or was he the new Lord, who should be blessed by the Jews for what he was doing to them?

I saw that Karin was crying, soundlessly. I wondered why. I couldn't remember the reason for it. She stopped the car in front of my house, and when I leaned over to kiss her good night she clung to me. "Please, darling, don't leave me alone."

She got out of the car with me. I unlocked the heavy entrance

63 «

door and we went in, then I turned on the lights and pressed the button for the elevator. It took a long time to come down.

Karin held my hand and moved closer to me. I could feel her body: she wasn't crying anymore. While we were still in the elevator, the automatic lights went out, and I had to grope around in the darkness to find the keyhole to my door in frustration, before finally turning on the lights again. Inside I found a few telephone messages on the table in the hall. One from Klaus von Isenberg and one from Guenter Sternberg, one of our two assistants. It was past one o'clock in the morning. Too late to return phone calls.

"I'm very happy for Eva and Victor," Karin said. "Margie did a great job. At first Carl was adamant. He wasn't going to set foot in a Jewish house."

"How did she get him there?"

Karin chuckled. "Very simple. She refused to go to bed with him unless he went to the party. Don't you think that's hilarious?"

"That's the right word for it. Yes."

The irony didn't register.

"Now Eva and Victor won't have to get divorced," Karin said.

"Was that discussed too?"

"Why, of course. Victor has to make a living, doesn't he? And he's an actor. He can't do anything else. Eva was the one who suggested it."

"How did Victor feel about it?"

"I don't know, darling. Please, let's talk about something else."

We were in the bedroom. Karin was getting undressed. She asked, "Do you still love me?"

"Yes."

"Jimmy doesn't mean anything to me. Please, believe me. It was just . . . you were away so long. I missed you. I missed your body."

» 64

"So you fucked Jimmy. That's logical. A prick is a prick."

She stared at me. "Don't say that. Don't be so vulgar! I can't stand it—you've never talked to me like that!"

"I'm sorry. Maybe I had too much to drink. Ludwig and I polished off a whole bottle of Napoleon brandy."

I was getting into my pajamas.

"Why are you putting those on?" she asked.

"I'm cold," I said. "Cold and tired."

She stood naked. "Don't you want me anymore?"

"Darling, it's very late and I—"

"Is it because of Jimmy?"

"Oh, to hell with Jimmy!"

She threw her arms around me and thrust her body at mine. She whispered, "I want you, darling, I want you right now—I can feel you. Come to bed—"

I reached up and broke the grip of her hands. "Don't, Karin."

She dropped her arms.

"Can't you understand?" I asked.

"Understand what?"

"Something has happened to me. To everybody—"

She looked at me uncomprehendingly.

"Give me time," I said.

"Of course I will." Her face was blank.

"Let's go to sleep."

"You really want me to stay?"

"Yes."

She lay down and pulled the cover over her body.

"Give me your hand," I said. "Let's be with each other like this. Quietly."

She squeezed my hand. "I love you very much."

"I'm glad."

"You think . . . you think you'll be able to forget—?"

"Forget what?"

"Jimmy," she said.

"Oh, Karin—"

It would be easy for me to forget Jimmy. I didn't even remember what he looked like.

When I wrote that down it was true. And as I read it again now, it is still true. I've retained the picture of someone young and fairly tall, with long arms and a lot of hair, but I can't recall anything else about him. I've been trying to think of his face, the color of his eyes—I draw a blank every time.

The telephone woke us at six o'clock in the morning. I groped for the receiver and heard Magda's voice.

"Dr. Bauer, I'm sorry to be calling you so early, but could you please go to Dr. Schwartz's apartment right away?"

"Why? What happened?"

"I don't know. Mrs. Schwartz called me. She couldn't find your home phone number and seemed to be in hysterics. I called Dr. von Isenberg too."

"All right, thank you, Magda. I'll be there as soon as I can."

I got out of bed. Karin asked, "What's the matter, darling? Where are you going?"

"It's an emergency, Karin."

"What time is it?"

"Six."

Her head fell back on the pillow. I rushed into my clothes. "Go back to sleep, darling. I'll phone you from the office."

"All right."

Downstairs I ran into Mr. Heiliger sweeping the floor.

"Heil Hitler," he said. "Aren't you the early one—"

"Yes."

"Did you read the Fuehrer's—"

I was outside, hailing a taxi.

I must stop. I cannot write any more. I'll have to let one or two days go by before I can face what I witnessed then. I know I was there, in Siegmund Schwartz's apartment. I stood there and sat there and saw people come in and go out. I heard what they said. I saw what they were doing. None of it sank in. I can imagine that an author like Ludwig Butler would have the power to write the story of that early morning in words of fire and compassion. But as for me . . . I'll have to wait until my emotions are stilled. Until my mind is clear again.

April 29th, 1933.

Dr. Schwartz's apartment is only a short distance from where I live, and as I pulled up, a man carrying a black bag was getting out of another taxi. We arrived at the second-floor apartment at the same time and found the door open.

Helen Schwartz stood in the hall, motionless, rooted to the spot. In her late forties, she is still a handsome woman, but on that morning she looked worn out and feeble, her face pale gray, her cheeks flabby and spongy, as if they were about to melt. Her black hair was in disarray. She wore a faded blue robe.

I went up to her. "What happened, Helen?"

She opened her mouth, but no sound came out. The man who had arrived with me said, "Mrs. Schwartz, I'm Dr. Hirsch. I came as soon as I could—I'm sorry your regular physician is out of town. Where's the patient?"

Helen didn't move. The maid came in with a cup of coffee: a pleasant-looking girl, quite young. She put the coffee on the table and I asked, "Where is Dr. Schwartz?"

The maid pointed at a door and started to cry.

Dr. Hirsch turned to me. "Dr. Schwartz is Jewish, isn't he?"

"Yes. Why?"

"I'm not permitted to treat Aryan patients," he said matter-of-factly.

I opened the door to the study. Siegmund Schwartz was lying on the carpet. He was on his back . . . and he was dead. A gun lay next to his right hand. He had not been a handsome man: small, with short legs and a broad face, his nose large and slightly curved, his lips too full. Last November he had been fifty-three. His dark-brown eyes, which had always held a melancholic expression even when he laughed, had been his most eloquently attractive feature. Now they were lifeless and glassy.

Dr. Hirsch took some instruments out of his bag and bent over the body. He shook his head. "There's nothing I can do," he said. "I'll get an ambulance and call the police." He went to the phone on the desk.

I looked at him as he dialed. He couldn't have been more than forty-two or forty-three, but his hair was white, his body angular and thin. His clothes hung on him loosely: he must have lost a lot of weight since buying them. He walked stiffly, from arthritis, I thought.

The door was opened gently, and Klaus von Isenberg came in. He nodded at me and looked at Siegmund Schwartz's body, then swallowed heavily. I saw the tears shooting up into his eyes. He said nothing. The doctor talked softly into the phone.

I saw a piece of paper on the desk and went to look at it. It was a short note, neatly written:

My beloved Helen,

I'm sorry I have to do this to you. I cannot face a future that will bring us nothing but humiliation and insults and poverty. I know your sister in Chile will be happy to have you with her. For me, a change is too late. My home and my work are here. And if my country doesn't want me anymore, it means the end for me. I'm sorry, Helen, but I know that you will understand me, as you have always understood and loved me in the twenty-eight years of our marriage.

All my love,

Sieg.

Dr. Hirsch put the receiver down and said, "Don't touch anything."

"Have you seen this note?"

"No."

"You should read it, Doctor. It's important to the death certificate."

He came around the desk and read the note. It took him a long time. Finally, he raised his head. His eyes were moist.

"My country . . ." he said softly. He went to pick up his bag. "I'll take a look at Mrs. Schwartz," he said. "She needs help."

As he left the study, Klaus came up to the desk and he too read the note.

"God damn it," he said in a hoarse voice. "They could have gone to London. Everything was arranged." He looked again at Dr. Schwartz's letter. "Of course, he wouldn't have been allowed to dispose of his property. Or to take much money out of the country."

"Could he have practiced law in England?"

"No—but he wasn't an old man."

He was fifty-three, I thought. I was twenty years younger.

After a short while, Dr. Hirsch came back.

"Mrs. Schwartz is in a state of shock," he said. "I gave her an injection. She's asleep now—the maid helped me put her to bed. A nice girl." He glanced at Siegmund Schwartz's body. "You were friends of the deceased." It wasn't a question.

"Friends and partners," Klaus said.

I had almost forgotten that Siegmund's body was in the room. We were all together, all three of us: three partners. One was dead. Our silent partner.

Twenty years would make a hell of a difference, I thought. I was only thirty-three. If something should go wrong, I might be able to start from scratch. But where? I didn't want to think about it. I didn't need to. Nothing could possibly go wrong.

The maid stuck her head in and told Dr. Hirsch that the ambulance had arrived. He asked her to tell the driver he was still waiting for the police.

"What time is it?" I asked. I'd been in so much of a hurry, I'd left my watch at home.

"Seven fifteen," the doctor said.

We heard voices outside, then the door opened and four men walked in. One of them was dressed in a business suit, another was a young policeman in his regular uniform. With them was an S.A. man who wore the white armlet that marked him as attached to the police force, and a photographer.

The S.A. man raised his arm. "Heil Hitler."

His face was pockmarked and red and he was built like an ox, with a wrestler's arms and bulky hands with stubby fingers. Dr. Hirsch introduced himself to the man in the business suit, who knelt down to inspect Dr. Schwartz's body. The man was middle-aged and stout. His head was bald.

"My name is Inspector Sontag," he said in a low and pleasant voice. The photographer was busy setting up his camera.

"Hirsch," the S.A. man said. "You're a Jew."

"Yes," the doctor said. "The deceased was Jewish too."

The inspector picked up the gun with his handkerchief. "I suppose nothing has been touched or moved," he said.

"Not since we arrived," Dr. Hirsch answered. "This man and I got here at the same time."

"And who are you?"

"Dr. Bauer," I said. "I'm a lawyer. So is Dr. von Isenberg. Dr. Schwartz was a partner in our firm."

The inspector put the gun back on the floor next to the body's right hand.

"You mean this Jew was your partner?" the S.A. man asked.

Klaus's face reddened. "Dr. Schwartz was an outstanding attorney and as fine a man as I have ever known."

"We don't appreciate Jew lovers in the Third Reich," the S.A. man said. "What was your name again?"

"Eberhardt Klaus Ritter von Isenberg."

The inspector straightened up. He had taken no notice of the S.A. man.

"Are you related to the general?"

"He's my father."

"I served under him at Ypres," the inspector said. "Of course, he wouldn't remember me. I was just a captain. It's a privilege to meet his son."

The young policeman said, "There's a note on the desk, Inspector."

The inspector read the note without touching it. The expression on his corrugated face was grim and sad. The S.A. man stood next to him.

"I suggest we destroy this scribble," the S.A. man said.

"I suggest . . . not, Storm Trooper Brause," the inspector said. "The note is evidence. It confirms that the deceased committed suicide."

"I disagree with you," Brause said.

The inspector looked at him. "I don't give a damn if you disagree with me. You can't disagree with the facts. Did you make out the death certificate, Dr. Hirsch?"

"Not yet, Inspector. I have the form here." He put it on the desk.

"Go ahead, then," the inspector said. He motioned to the photographer.

"Just a moment," said Brause, and walked to the body and kicked the gun out of camera range with his boot. Klaus rushed at him with clenched fists.

The inspector cut in sharply, "Stop it! This is a police matter!"

Klaus stopped. The inspector turned to the S.A. man.

"Put that gun back where it belongs. Use your handkerchief. That's an order."

"I'm not subject to your orders, Inspector. I am attached to your detail to guard the interests of the party."

The inspector shrugged, took out his own handkerchief, picked up the gun, and placed it next to the body's right hand again. The flashlight on the camera went off.

The brownshirt's upper lips curled back, baring his teeth, and he said coldly, "The death certificate and the police records will show heart failure as the cause of death, Inspector. Anything else will get you into serious trouble."

The young policeman looked at his superior. Inspector Sontag kept still. The camera lights flashed again.

"You're supporting anti-German atrocity propaganda," Brause said. "Your colleagues have been much more cooperative on these matters."

Dr. Hirsch finished writing. He got up, leaving the death certificate on the desk. The inspector took it and read it. His hands were shaking and his face was white.

"You've signed that, Dr. Hirsch," he said. "You are a physician and—"

"I am a Jew," Dr. Hirsch said.

» 72

He picked up his satchel and left without looking back. The storm trooper reached across the desk for Dr. Schwartz's suicide note and struck a match. The flame hit my eyes and I smelled once more the sickly odor of burning human flesh. The inspector stood motionless. The young policeman stared at him as if he couldn't believe what he was witnessing.

The paper blackened and writhed and fell into ashes on the carpet.

I sleepwalked through the streets. I had no sense of being alive. In fact, I was not alive. I was lying on the carpet, the gun next to my hand. The inspector was looking down on me. So was Klaus. His face came very close to mine. I saw the tears in his eyes. He was mourning for me.

"You could have left," he said. "You could have gone to America."

"I do not want to leave," I said. "I am not a Jew."

"Then why did you kill yourself?" he asked.

I didn't answer. Klaus rose. Two shiny black boots were towering over me. With my lifeless eyes I saw that he wore the uniform of an S.S. colonel. He raised his right arm and hand, and his voice blared the Hitler salute, his body tore back, farther and farther, until it was a tiny figure, seen through the wrong end of a telescope, and I was alone on the vast cemetery of the carpet.

I tried to open my eyes. Held by magnetic power, the lids wouldn't lift. I pulled with all my strength, gritting my teeth . . . and then I saw the entrance to my house. I felt my blood return to my body, but I did not enter yet. I stood still to be sure the twilight had gone.

The elevator was not on the ground floor. I didn't want to wait and took the stairs, and as I climbed, one of the apartment doors opened. Mr. Heiliger came out, carrying a carton filled with what looked like pictures. The carton was very large.

"Dr. Bauer. Is anything wrong with the elevators?"

"No."

I noticed that he had not said, "Heil Hitler." He motioned with his head toward the closed door.

"The Gutmans are leaving." He added, "They're Jews."

I wanted to pass him to get to the third floor, but he continued to speak. "Some old family pictures," he said. "The Gutmans can't take much luggage. I promised to send them by railway express. Jews are very sentimental about family pictures. They're going to Amsterdam. You know them, don't you?"

"Slightly, yes."

"They're Jews. But they're in their seventies. One must be kind if one can afford it."

"Excuse me, Mr. Heiliger."

He stepped aside. "Oh, of course, Dr. Bauer."

I searched my pockets for the keys. I couldn't find them. I had forgotten my wristwatch *and* my keys. I rang the doorbell. After a moment Hanna opened the door. She looked at my face.

"Is anything wrong, Dr. Bauer?"

"No," I said. And then, "Yes."

She didn't ask what it was. She just stood.

"Dr. Schwartz is dead," I said.

"Oh, no. That nice man. Was he sick?"

"He killed himself," I said. "It's called 'heart failure.'"

She gasped. "Poor Mrs. Schwartz. That poor woman!"

"Yes."

I took the newspaper from the table in the hall.

"Would you like breakfast, Dr. Bauer? Miss Rieger isn't up yet."

"Oh, I—" I stopped. I had forgotten that Karin had spent the night with me. "I'm not hungry," I said. "I'll go in my study and read the paper."

"You must eat something, Dr. Bauer. I'll fix you a tray."

I was glad that Karin was still asleep. I couldn't have talked to her then.

The 30th of April.

I wrote as much as I could last night. My memory functions very well. It always does. I can still quote questions and answers from cross-examinations that took place three or four years ago.

I thought of Mr. Gutman. I want to retell the story of his last visit to his department store. It was told to me by a former associate of his who had heard it from Mr. Gutman himself.

Reinhold Gutman is the founder and owner of a well-known department store in Berlin, a wealthy man who contributed generously to liberal causes to help stem the Nazi avalanche. Accordingly, he was one of the first Jewish businessmen to be dispossessed.

He came to his store on a Monday morning and found the entrance guarded by two brownshirts who refused to let him in. Gutman is seventy-two, a giant of a man, six feet three, with wide shoulders and an imposing head, topped by a shock of unruly white hair. He is also a courageous man.

"I built this store and I own it," he said.

"We're under orders," one of the S.A. men said.

"Under what orders?"

"You're not to enter this store."

"Then follow your orders and kill me," Mr. Gutman said. "That's the only way to keep me out."

One of the brownshirts shrugged and the other one drew his gun. Mr. Gutman ignored the gun and walked through the revolving door. There was no shot. He went down the aisle on the ground floor which led to the executive elevator, greeting his employees as he'd done every morning for almost forty years.

When he arrived at the executive suites on the fifth floor, he saw a man removing the name plates from the doors and replacing them with different ones. He found his own name plate lying in front of the door to his office, and picked it up. In his outer office sat a strange girl in a brown Nazi uniform. She jumped up as she saw him. He paid no attention to her and opened the door marked PRIVATE.

Seated at his desk was one of his floor managers, Martin Sommer. Seven other men were sitting in the room, two of them in Nazi uniform. He knew most of them.

His entrance caught them by surprise. Sommer got up and walked around the desk. Mr. Gutman proceeded in the opposite direction and sat down in his habitual chair. He looked at the men from behind his desk. By now they were standing in an irregular semicircle, uncertain what to do. Behind him on the wall was a large colored picture of Adolf Hitler. He turned around and looked at it for a moment, remembering the picture of his father that used to hang there. Then he turned back to face his employees.

"We didn't expect you today, sir," Sommer said.

Mr. Gutman nodded. "I gathered that much. You may terminate your standing ovation, if you'd be kind enough to explain to me what all this means."

"This is not your office anymore."

"It isn't?"

"No."

"Whose is it then?" He put his name plate on the desk.

"It's my office," Sommer replied. "I am the new chief executive."

One of the men in uniform said, "Why make so much fuss about this old Jew?"

"Who are you?" Mr. Gutman asked.

"Richard Kreutzer."

"Do you work in my store?"

"Yes, but it isn't your—"

"Where, may I ask?"

"Ladies' gloves, first floor."

Mr. Gutman nodded. "Ladies' gloves, first floor," he repeated softly. It sounded like a breeze. He got up.

"Let me tell you something, Mr. Kreutzer and Mr. Sommer, and the rest of you. If you consider the word 'Jew' an insult— it isn't. It's a very proud word. I am proud of being a Jew. My father, my grandfather, all of my ancestors were Jews, and in our family, it would have been a social disgrace to marry a non-Jewish girl. So if you want to apply your racial theories to me, nobody's blood can be purer than mine."

There was a pause. When no one else spoke, Mr. Gutman continued, "As to the nature of this improvised meeting in my office—I am an old man. I've had a good life. I'm happily married. I've learned to accept facts, whether I like them or not, and I have no desire to be tortured or killed. That goes for my wife, too."

He sat down. "If you're telling me—which so far none of you has done—that I am dispossessed, that this store is not my store anymore, I don't quarrel with that. How could I? Mr. Gutman against Mr. Hitler. That sounds ridiculous, doesn't it? I am offering you two alternatives: I want an exit permit for myself and for my wife. And I want it now, before I leave this room."

He paused.

"What—what is the second alternative?" Sommer asked.

"I have a gun in my pocket," Mr. Gutman said. "If you refuse to get me the permit, I shall shoot myself. Here and now."

They left him alone and he sat in his office for two hours, waiting. After two hours, Martin Sommer came in with the two exit permits. Mr. Gutman took them and picked up his name plate from the desk. At the door, he turned and looked at the picture of Adolf Hitler and at Martin Sommer.

"I hope you're not going to make a mess out of this," he said. "I'm very much attached to this store."

The former associate of Mr. Gutman supplemented the story by telling me that Mr. Gutman had known exactly what he would be up against on that Monday morning, that he had discussed his planned behavior with his wife, and that he had had to promise her not to carry a gun on him. The associate said that, knowing the relationship between Mr. Gutman and his wife, it would have been unthinkable for him to have shot himself, thus leaving her alone and helpless.

"And, of course," the associate added with a chuckle, "none of those fellows in the room knew anything about Mr. Gutman's personal life. They didn't know, for instance, that Mr. Gutman was the most feared poker player at the Berlin Merchants Club."

Now, back to myself.

While I sat in my study, glancing at the newspaper, turning the pages without actually reading, I thought of my encounter with Mr. Heiliger. He'd been surprised to see me, and not agreeably surprised. He'd looked as if my sudden appearance on the staircase had come as a shock to him. He had talked too fast. Too much. Why? I hadn't asked any questions. He had said something about "being kind"—kind to Jews? That from Mr.

Heiliger, who was constantly quoting the Nazi doctrine, "the Jews are our enemies!"?

Hanna came in and put my breakfast tray on the desk.

"I spoke to Mr. Heiliger about you and your fiancé," I said. "I couldn't get anywhere with him."

"I didn't think you would, Dr. Bauer . . . but thank you for talking to him." She was clearing the tray and added, "I haven't heard from Paul."

"Have you tried to reach him?"

"I called his number several times, but never got an answer."

"He could have been out."

"Yes."

She held the empty tray in one hand and walked to the door, then turned and looked at me.

"It must feel terrible to be a Jew," she said.

I called Magda at the office and told her I wasn't coming in and to cancel or postpone my appointments. She said Dr. von Isenberg wanted to talk to me. After a moment I heard Klaus's voice.

"I just got off the phone with Alfred Koenig. I understand he's a friend of yours."

"Is that what he said?"

"Yes. You saw him last night at Victor Brandt's party, didn't you?"

"He's no friend of mine," I said. "He's the worst shyster I've ever encountered and he behaved like an idiot last night."

"Well, that settles that," Klaus said.

"Settles what?"

He seemed to hesitate. Then, "He'd heard we were looking for a new partner—and he suggested himself."

"That's a nice touch."

"Yes, isn't it?"

"What did you say to him?"

"Nothing. I wanted to check it out with you first."

"Tell him to go to hell."

"Talk to you later," Klaus said.

Karin looked sleepy when she came in. She kissed me, took my coffee cup and drank the rest of my coffee.

"What was the emergency?" She poured herself a fresh cup and sat down.

"Dr. Schwartz, our partner. He died."

"Oh, I'm so sorry," she said. "Was it sudden—I mean—what did he die of?"

"He killed himself."

She was drinking, stopped and put the cup down.

"Why?"

"I'd rather not talk about it, Karin," I said.

"I understand. I don't think I've ever met him. Was he—was he Jewish?"

"Yes."

She frowned and finished the coffee. "Hans, I must tell you something. But it's confidential. So please, don't talk to anybody else about it."

"What is it?"

"Really, Hans. Don't ever mention to anybody that I told you about it."

"I won't."

"Margie phoned me. Carl spoke to her about you."

"Yes—"

"He likes you."

"But—?"

"Well, he is—I don't know how to say it—he's 'concerned' about some of your friends."

"For instance—"

"Ludwig Butler."

"What's wrong with him?"

She rose. "That's where the confidential part comes in. Carl is suspicious of him. He thinks he's unreliable and dangerous."

"Goebbels invited Butler to join the Reichs Culture Chamber."

She shrugged. "All I know is what Margie told me." She sat down on top of the desk next to me. "Darling, Adriani is a very powerful man."

"I know."

"You must be careful with him. With all of them."

"What else did Margie tell you?"

She hesitated. "Maybe this will sound silly to you, but it isn't . . . Adriani was watching you last night. You never gave the Nazi salute. Not once."

"You mean—'Heil Hitler'?"

"Yes. I'm warning you, Hans, they notice everything. Even when they don't talk about it right away."

"Do you say 'Heil Hitler'?"

"Of course. At first I felt a little ridiculous, but now—I'm used to it. It isn't really important, is it? If that's what they want."

I didn't answer. Karin said, "The only one who can afford to ignore it is Margie. She's an American citizen."

"How does she feel about this whole Nazi business? America is a democracy."

"She doesn't care about politics. She loves Carl."

She put her bare feet on my lap and brought her face close to mine. "Darling, please—promise me one thing."

"What?"

"Stop seeing Ludwig Butler. At least in public."

A few hours from now, Ludwig Butler's train would cross the border between Germany and France. I said, "I promise."

She drew back surprised. She hadn't expected it to be so easy. She smiled happily and kissed me. "I'm so glad, darling. Thank you."

I moved my chair back and got up. Karin remained on top of the desk and moved her feet up too. I said, "Adriani seems to assume that you and I will get married."

She lowered her head. "Yes. That's my fault. I told Margie about it. And she told him." She was speaking very softly. "I was so sure of you, darling. I know, I shouldn't have been. Nobody has the right to take anybody for granted. But—that's what I did. It never—I mean—I never thought that you—"

She didn't finish the sentence. It stayed suspended in midair. Finally she asked, "Aren't you going to the office today?"

I shook my head. She moved her legs down, slid from the desk, came to me, and put her hands on my shoulders.

"Do you want me to leave?"

"No."

"Tell me, please. I'll understand if you'd like to be alone."

"I don't, Karin. I just don't know what to do with myself. I want to close the windows and doors and live behind sound-proof walls. I want to forget that there are Nazis and Jews and torture and death. But I know that I can't."

"It won't be that bad tomorrow," Karin said.

I felt a choking pain in my throat. I tried to speak. I wanted to tell Karin that I was dead tired, that I needed sleep, that I needed it now. Maybe she understood anyway. She made no movement as I walked out.

I went into my bedroom and dropped down on the bed.

I slept.

Hours later when I awoke, my pillow was drenched.

Maybe I had cried in my sleep.

May 1st, 1933.

Yesterday afternoon, when I woke up, I realized I had thrown myself on my bed fully dressed. I hadn't even removed my shoes. I realized, too, that I was sweating and had a stinging headache, so I took a bath, which made me feel better. The clock said ten to four. I put on my robe and went to the study. As I passed Hanna's room, she opened the door.

"Miss Rieger had to leave," she said. "She left a note for you on the desk."

It read,

Darling, I couldn't wait. Hope you feel better. Please call me later. I'll be home. Love, K.

I was disappointed, and relieved. She'd been right. It was better for me to be alone—and then, suddenly, it occurred to me that it wasn't so much that I wanted to be alone as that I didn't want to be with her.

I'd been away for four months. I had come back to my hometown—I was born in Bremen, but I had lived in Berlin ever since I had returned from the university, so Berlin seemed my hometown to me. But Berlin had changed. The street signs and the buildings were the same, but the people were strangers and the strangers had transformed the town. The city I had known was a thing of the past . . . and for some inexplicable reason, Karin had become part of that past.

For a while I sat on the couch and read. When it got darker, I moved to the chair behind my desk and switched on the lamp. I noticed that the desk and some of the chairs were arranged much like the furniture in Siegmund Schwartz's study. My eyes were drawn to the carpet. I couldn't concentrate on reading. I turned my head and saw the small piece of paper next to my calendar: Ludwig Butler's address in Paris.

Konrad Willman's phone number had changed, but Konrad himself answered the telephone.

"This is Hans, Hans Bauer," I said.

"Hello, Hans."

"I'm calling you because Ludwig—"

He cut in fast. "Yes, I know. Why don't you come over to-night? Any time after seven."

"I'll do that. And Konrad—"

"Do you have a car?"

"No, I don't but—"

"My driver will pick you up at a quarter to eight. Same address?"

"Yes. That really isn't—"

"So long," Konrad said and hung up.

I put the receiver back slowly. What was the matter with him? Why had he been so short—so rude? I knew he was about to direct the new Gerhart Hauptmann play: maybe rehearsals had started and he was nervous, tense. Quarter to eight, he had said. Almost four more hours to wait. I kept staring at my car-pet. Somewhere in the shadows, Siegmund Schwartz was lying dead. I had to get out of my apartment.

I remembered a new American film playing at one of the large movie houses that was supposed to be good. I would have plenty of time to see the picture and be back by a quarter to eight.

The film's title was *It Happened One Night*. I came in while the short subject was still playing, something featuring a Bavar-ian song-and-dance group. The girls were tall and buxom and the men were broad-shouldered, and most of them had legs like a dachshund. I closed my eyes and tried to enjoy the music, which was based on the melodies of Schubert.

Then came the newsreel. It started with a mass meeting at the

Sports Palace in Berlin, about to be addressed by Hitler. It showed the audience crowding in—men and women, S.A. and S.S. uniforms, some civilian clothes—then a shot of everybody in their seats as the parade began in the center aisle: the Nazi standards and flags, the oldest ones first, the "sacred" ones that had seen the abortive Munich beer hall putsch. Thousands rose, their arms stretched in the Nazi salute, the brass band playing the Horst Wessel song—then came the Fuehrer himself in his slick S.A. uniform, and the deafening ovation, "*Sieg Heil! Sieg Heil!*" which Hitler acknowledged by whipping up his right hand at the wrist. He was followed by Goering, drenched in medals; Goebbels, white-faced and solemn; the other members of the cabinet.

Then Hitler mounted the platform and stood at the lectern. Cameras flashed and clicked. "*Sieg Heil! Sieg Heil! Sieg Heil!*"

Hitler began to speak in his hard, rural Austrian accent.

Close-up: his face.

Suddenly, a roar of laughter swept the theater. For years there'd been a whispered joke about Hitler's resemblance to Charlie Chaplin, and suddenly there it was on the screen. Chaplin's face exaggerated into the grotesque: the small mustache, the hair down to his forehead, the crude voice—it was irresistibly comic. Everybody around me was laughing. I don't remember whether I did or not.

Just as suddenly the lights went on and the picture on the screen died out, the sound whining to an end. S.A. men stood in both outer aisles, surrounding the audience.

Several rows behind me, a man got up and, motioning to the brownshirts, pointed at his neighbor, who rose in panic. No, he hadn't laughed! He threw himself at the informer, but two S.A. men were already at him and dragged him out. The woman next to him screamed. They took her too; fights broke out all over the theater. People in the last rows tried to run out. Some managed to escape, most were caught. The resistance in the audience grew—citizen against storm trooper—until a pack of brownshirts pulled a man out in the aisle, clubbed him till he collapsed, then jumped and trampled on his body. The man lay motionless, smeared with blood. A girl staggered into the aisle and threw herself over his body. One of the S.A. men tore at her blond hair. She screamed in pain. He dragged her off the body and threw her down.

No one moved.

The brownshirts picked up the bodies and carried them out.

Now many people rose, but one of the Nazis shouted, "Nobody leaves the theater!"

The lights stayed on as people went back to their seats. The brownshirts resumed their positions in the outer aisles. Watching the audience.

Once more, Hitler's face appeared on the screen. The comic image had changed into a monstrous visage, shrieking terror, smelling of burning flesh. The deadly quiet lasted through the end of the Fuehrer's speech, then the lights dimmed and went out. The newsreel finished. The movie began.

Slowly, my tension ebbed. Another world was unfolding on the screen. A fairy tale. I was wishing it true . . . and it became true. There were still people in the world with simple problems . . . poor and rich . . . people who loved and fought and won, smiling and laughing, speaking lines that moved me and made me smile and laugh. When, finally, the words "The End" appeared, I yearned for more. I wanted it to continue forever.

The lights went on and a sigh came from the lips of hundreds. Applause began and grew, and held for minutes . . . to prolong the fairy tale. Next to me an elderly couple rose reluctantly. I saw the tears in their eyes. They smiled at each other.

The audience filed out in silence.

Outside the street was crowded. I heard the noise of drums, the voices of children, the Horst Wessel song. A formation of the Hitler Youth was marching by, ten- and twelve-year-olds with innocent, glowing faces. One, ahead of the group, proudly carried the swastika flag.

"When the blood of the Jews squirts from our knives—"

I was jerked back into reality, into today. And parading before me was the reality of the future.

I arrived back in front of my house shortly before a quarter to eight and found a man already waiting for me.

"Dr. Bauer—?"

He was very tall and thin, with a haggard face: in the light of the lamp post, it looked cadaverous. He wore a dark leather jacket which reached below his knees, and he led me to a gray Rolls-Royce, parked around the corner.

The window between the driver and the back of the car was closed. We drove for quite some time through heavy traffic until we entered the suburbs, when the car picked up speed. After a while we came to a crossing and slowed down again to turn into a side road that seemed to be unpaved and full of holes.

After about twenty minutes, I saw glaring lights ahead of me. Closer up, the outlines of a massive structure took form, a walled enclosure, with high towers at the corners from which the lights originated. They appeared to be searchlights covering the inside of the compound, moving slowly in a full circle of three hundred and sixty degrees. I rolled down my left window to get a better look. The searchlight next to us hit the Rolls-Royce and stayed on it for a few seconds until it moved on. Apparently we were on the approach road to the main gate of one of the S.A.'s concentration camps. It conformed to the descriptions I had been given. Suddenly I heard the melody of a Viennese waltz, bursting forth in full blaring strength from loudspeakers mounted underneath the searchlights. The driver stepped on the accelerator and the main gate raced toward us, flooded in white, flanked by brownshirts who were armed with rifles.

Sudden fear struck me. I leaned forward and knocked on the window. Just then the Rolls-Royce made a sharp turn to the right and I had to hold on to my seat with both hands. The car sped over another unpaved road away from the compound, and after a few minutes we were back on the main highway. The driver hadn't turned around once. His whole attention had been focused on the road. I let the window down that separated us and told him sharply to stop the car.

He turned onto the right shoulder of the road and brought the Rolls-Royce to a halt. He moved his head to face me.

"Yes, sir?"

"What the hell are you doing?" I asked angrily.

"I thought you might like to see it, sir," he said. "Everybody who comes to this neighborhood asks where it is and wants to take a look at it."

"It's a concentration camp, isn't it?"

"A reeducation center, sir."

"Why didn't you ask me ahead of time?"

"I should have done that, sir. I'm sorry," the driver said.

His voice was low, his face in the dark. I couldn't see it. I was still shaking.

"I didn't mean to upset you, sir. I'm very sorry," he said.

I was trying to calm down. "All right. Go ahead. How far is it?"

"About five minutes, sir." He turned back to the wheel and I closed the window again.

I thought about the stories I had heard about those camps from Ludwig Butler and Klaus. Ludwig had said that the inmates were tortured with instruments revived from the Middle Ages until the victims broke or died. So-called enemies of the state were executed and cremated or buried. Without even the pretense of legal proceedings. He had told me—and I must confess that I hadn't believed it—that gay music was blared to the outside whenever people were tortured, to drown the pleadings and screams of the victims.

Now I had heard the hideous sound for myself. I had seen the sinister structure, the glaring searchlights, the armed S.A. guards. Now I knew that the inconceivable was true.

The car stopped at a large wooden fence, the gate swung open, and we drove in. The house was a two-story ranch-style building, surrounded by fruit trees and flower beds. A huge lilac bush stood next to the entrance. I had been at the Willmans' house before. This house looked unfamiliar to me.

Konrad Willman came out to greet me, a heavy-set man in his early forties with the sensitive face of an intellectual and bushy eyebrows set over large blue eyes. His hair is dark brown. He loves to dress like a man of the soil: overalls and boots. That's what he was wearing now.

He took the pipe out of his mouth and we shook hands.

"I'm glad to see you, Hans."

"How are you, Konrad?"

"Rotten. I'm rehearsing."

The cadaverous driver had remained at the door of the Rolls-Royce. Konrad looked at him. "Have your dinner, Satan, and stand by," he said. "You might have to drive Dr. Bauer back to Berlin."

"Yes, sir."

As Konrad and I walked on the pebbled footpath to the house, I still felt the impact of that weird drive.

"What did you call him—Satan?"

"Yes, it fits, doesn't it? At least, it fits his appearance. He's really a nice fellow, been with us for ten years."

I didn't comment.

"He didn't upset you, did he?" Konrad asked unexpectedly.

I shook my head.

We entered a long, wood-paneled living room dominated by

a large fieldstone fireplace. The ceiling was formed of massive beams running the whole length of the room, with V-shaped crossbeams giving the ceiling the appearance of a roof. The room was carpeted, the furniture heavy and grouped in orderly, symmetrical fashion. A concert grand stood in one corner and a great number of filled bookshelves covered one entire wall.

Two women sat at the fireplace. The younger one rose and came to greet me. I had known Barbara long before she had married Konrad Willman, then a young and upcoming stage director. Under her name, Barbara Teilhaber, she had been a well-known young actress, close to fame, but she gave up her career when she fell in love with Konrad. She wanted to be a wife and raise a family. She got pregnant almost immediately, but the baby was stillborn, turning her almost overnight into a moody, melancholy introvert, shying away from her husband's touch.

It took her two years to regain her vibrant and warm personality. Three months later she was with child again. Continuously under doctors' care, she spent most of her pregnancy in bed. This time the baby was born prematurely, alive but too frail to survive. It died ten days later.

Barbara was in a state of shock. She lost her power of speech and became partially paralyzed. The doctors recommended an institution, but Konrad refused to give his permission. He discontinued working for a year and instead devoted all his time to his wife's needs. With love and patience, he nursed her back to health.

She is now in her early thirties. The painful experiences have left scars on her face. There are sharp lines at the corner of her mouth. Her forehead is permanently wrinkled. But her dark eyes are still the same, and the rich color of her blond hair has not changed.

We shook hands and I kissed her on the cheek. She led me to the woman in the armchair.

"Mother, this is Dr. Bauer, a friend of ours."

Mrs. Teilhaber was a woman in her sixties, tall, with wide shoulders and a straight-lipped mouth set in a rosy face. She looked at me without a smile.

"Have you had your dinner?"

"I'm not hungry, thank you."

She nodded. "We have had our dinner."

Around her neck was a gold chain that held a diamond swastika much like Grete Fall's, but considerably larger. Over the fireplace hung an oil painting of Adolf Hitler.

"We're enjoying Mother's hospitality," Barbara said. "This is her house. She was in Munich for several months and wanted the house occupied."

Mrs. Teilhaber drew in her chin. "Nonsense. You know you're staying with me to save money. Konrad hasn't been doing so well."

Nobody spoke.

"Serves him right," she said. Mrs. Teilhaber looked sharply, first at her daughter, then at her son-in-law. "All your life, you've been working with black frocks and Jews. Now you see."

"See what?" Konrad asked. His pipe had gone out and he lit a match.

"Stop it, you two," Barbara said. "Mother, you know that Konrad joined the party. There is nothing wrong with him, or he wouldn't have been accepted and he wouldn't be directing Hauptmann's new play."

"Hauptmann is a Communist. He wrote *The Weavers*," Mrs. Teilhaber said.

Konrad shrugged. Barbara said, "Wouldn't you like a cup of coffee, Hans?"

"I'd love a cup of coffee. I won't stay long. I only want to give you—"

Konrad cut in, "We'll talk about that later."

Mrs. Teilhaber's head flew up. "Secrets?"

"It's not a secret, Mother. It's private," Konrad said. "There's a difference." He drew on his pipe. "A personal problem."

"And you're the one who's going to solve it," she said dryly to her son-in-law.

For a while nobody spoke. Obviously, Konrad didn't want to discuss Ludwig Butler in front of his mother-in-law. I thought I could still hear, faintly, the gay rhythm of a Viennese waltz.

Into the silence walked Barbara with sandwiches and a cup of coffee. "Here we are."

"Thank you so much."

She put the coffee down. "Black?"

"Yes, thank you."

After a while Mrs. Teilhaber asked, "Is there a window open? I can still hear the music from the center."

"It's very loud, Mrs. Teilhaber," I said. 'We drove by there and—"

"Drove by there—!?" Konrad said. He reached for a pipe cleaner.

"Yes. Your driver thought I'd be interested in seeing it."

I noticed a quick exchange of looks between husband and wife.

"It's a reeducation center," Mrs. Teilhaber said. None of us commented. She glared at us defiantly. "That's what it is. No matter what anybody else tells you, Dr. Bauer, that's what it is."

"Of course, Mrs. Teilhaber," I said.

Somebody had to say something. Konrad put his pipe on the table. He looked fatigued. His skin had an unhealthy color.

"Mother's upset about all the atrocity stories," he said.

His mother-in-law nodded. "The international Jewish conspiracy."

"But nobody believes these stories," Konrad said. "I was in Prague recently. In the restaurant where I had dinner, a man, obviously an emigrant from Germany, told his Czech companions how he had been tortured and beaten by S.A. men. I tell you, he was laughed out of the place."

"There'll always be isolated acts of violence in every revolution," Mrs. Teilhaber said. "The Fuehrer himself has ordered everyone guilty of them executed."

"Where the hell did you read that?" Konrad asked.

"I don't have to read it, I *know*," Mrs. Teilhaber said. "And don't use curse words in my presence." She pointed at the picture of Hitler. "Look for yourself. His face radiates greatness. There is not an iota of meanness in it. Firmness and resolution. No cruelty."

The three of us stared at the picture. Mrs. Teilhaber rose. "That music makes me nervous," she said. "I'm going to bed and turn on my radio, then I won't hear it anymore. It was pleasant meeting you, Dr. Bauer. You didn't talk very much, but then—maybe you're just as shy with strangers as I am."

"I am, indeed," I said.

"Good night. Good night, children." Walking stiffly erect, she disappeared.

There was a pause; both husband and wife seemed to be listening. Upstairs, a door closed. Konrad turned to me.

"Didn't Ludwig tell you not to phone us?"

I thought back and remembered. "Yes, he did. I'm afraid I forgot."

"Our telephone at home is tapped," Barbara said. "And as soon as we moved here, to Mother's, her phone was tapped too. Fortunately, she doesn't know it."

"But why would they do that?" I asked.

"Probably because of Ludwig," Konrad said. "He's my ex-brother-in-law, after all, and a close friend. He stayed with us for several months."

"I'm very sorry that I called."

"I don't think it did any harm," Konrad said. "I tried my best to cut you off whenever you approached dangerous territory."

Barbara looked at Konrad, then at me, then abruptly got up and took a few steps toward the door through which Mrs. Teilhaber had disappeared. She had left the door open.

Konrad whispered, "What is it?"

"I heard a noise," Barbara whispered back. Aloud, she said, "To be perfectly frank, Hans, I don't understand your problem."

She continued to listen. Konrad picked it up. "Women never understand this kind of situation."

Barbara whispered, "She's standing on the staircase, trying to overhear."

"Basically, all women are bitches and all men are dogs," Konrad said, picking up his pipe again. "Sex drives them together. For a short while, they're hung up and become a couple. Then they separate again and are what they were before copulation: bitch and dog."

"Your dialogue is terrible," I whispered.

"It's from an old play," Konrad whispered back. "The only passage I remember."

"You're being unfair to both sexes," Barbara said in a loud voice. "Unfair and vulgar. I'm glad Mother can't hear you."

"Chances are she would agree with me," Konrad said. "She disapproves of me, but she likes me. Most women do. I'm that kind of man and—"

"You can stop your panegyric on yourself," Barbara said in her normal voice. "She's back in her room."

She went to the couch and sat down. Neither she nor Konrad spoke; they just sat there, looking at each other. I didn't want to be the first one again to talk. Finally, Konrad said, "My mother-in-law doesn't trust me. She doesn't even trust her own daughter. She's not sure if we're real Nazis, or just affect it."

I wasn't sure either, but I hadn't asked the question.

"Ludwig wants you to know that he's safe," I said. "Here's his address in Paris." I handed him the paper.

"That's good news. Agnes will be delighted," Konrad said. "I'm going to write to her tomorrow morning."

My mission had ended. I got up.

"My mother hates Butler," Barbara said. "She hates everybody who is against the Nazis. She was supposed to stay in Munich another two months, and then all of a sudden she came home this afternoon."

"If we'd known she was going to be here, we'd have warned you," Konrad added.

I was getting more and more confused. Konrad was a member of the party, Barbara had confirmed that. . . . Still, there was something peculiar about his attitude. Maybe I should ask them bluntly—no, it was safer to leave.

The answer to the question came from an unexpected source. As I was preparing to go, there was a soft knock on the entrance door. Barbara and Konrad looked at each other and froze. The knock came again: still not very loud. Konrad went to the door and opened it.

A woman came in very slowly, without speaking, and walked past Konrad with stumbling steps. She had to hold on to the wall when she entered the living room. Konrad followed her, frowning, a puzzled expression on his face.

Barbara just stared at the woman.

Her head was a skull, pale yellow. Her torn dress hung loosely on her bones; her legs emerged as sticks, folding at every move. Her hands were heavily bandaged, grotesque in size, at the end of bare arms on which almost no flesh was left. Her hair was white. The cave of her mouth opened. Two or three teeth showed. The rest was dark and red. It thrust out syllables.

Barbara was still staring at the apparition—then she screamed.

In a split second Konrad was by her and slapped his hand on her mouth.

We listened. There was no noise from upstairs.

The woman was leaning against the wall. Barbara began to shake. Konrad let go of her. She whispered, "It's Berta—"

"No!"

The woman bent her head twice. Her mouth closed and widened. It might have been an attempt at smiling. Barbara stepped forward and knelt at the woman's feet.

"Berta—"

The skeleton bent her head again.

I had never seen eyes like that: naked, without lashes or brows . . . night-dark globules, reflecting infinite despair and pain. My tears were choking me. I stumbled and had to hold on to Konrad.

He said to me softly. "She's been held by the Nazis for two months. No one knew where she was." His lips were trembling. "Look at her! She's twenty-five years old—! Look at her! Those swine, those goddamned swine!"

Barbara was still kneeling. She turned to us and I saw her face and neck tense in a major effort to control herself.

"Berta—"

She picked up the girl and held her in her arms. She took her to the couch and laid her down gently.

"A doctor—call a doctor—"

"Which one?" Konrad asked.

"Who is closest to us?"

"Fabricius. He won't do. He's a Nazi."

"Hansen is Mother's doctor so he's out."

A thought came to me. I forced myself to be rational and calm. I asked, "Is she Jewish?"

Barbara looked at me. "Yes."

"I might have a doctor for you. Where's your phone?"

"Use the one in the study," Konrad said. "But keep in mind that it's tapped."

I dialed Siegmund Schwartz's home and spoke to the maid, who gave me Dr. Hirsch's telephone number. I'd heard a soft click after putting the receiver to my ear. I heard it again when Dr. Hirsch answered.

"I met you earlier today on a case, Dr. Hirsch," I said. "It was supposed to be heart failure. The patient is now fast asleep."

A pause. The doctor said, "I'm glad that he got some rest."

"Yes. I'm interested in his condition, Doctor. Could you call me as soon as possible and tell me how he is?" I added, "It's extremely urgent."

It took a long time before he answered. "What is your phone number there? And your address?"

I gave him both.

"I'll get back to you in about an hour," he said.

"Thank you very much, Doctor."

I went back to the living room. The girl lay motionless—asleep or not, I didn't know. Her eyes were open.

"The doctor should be here within an hour," I said. "I tried to disguise the call as well as I could. But I had to give him your address."

Konrad nodded.

"Dr. Hirsch," I said. "He's a Jew. He wouldn't be allowed to treat Aryan patients."

"Berta is Jewish," Barbara said. "Her boyfriend isn't, but they suspected him of being a Communist. He managed to escape, so—they got to her. They must have tried to learn his whereabouts from her."

The girl's body was hit by a convulsion. When it stopped her mouth opened and articulated the word ". . . yes . . ."

"Don't talk," Barbara said.

"Questions . . ." the mouth brought out. "And . . . after . . ." Her head came up and fell back. ". . . after every . . . question . . . they slapped . . . my face . . ."

"She can't stay in this room," Konrad said.

". . . Jewish sow . . ."

"Your mother might come down any moment."

"Yes."

The girl was almost inaudible. "Days . . . and . . . nights . . ."

"Please don't talk, Berta," Barbara said. "Let's take her to the basement. We have a cot there. Mother never goes to the basement. She fell on the steps once and broke a leg."

Konrad lifted the body from the couch and Barbara and I followed him. We went through the pantry and kitchen to a locked door. Konrad reached in his pocket and handed the keys to his wife. She unlocked the door. Steep steps of stone led to the cellar.

The place was roomy and relatively uncluttered, only the furnace, hot water heater, and pipes. At the far end stood a cot. The air was warm. A ventilator swinging from the ceiling kept it from getting too moist.

Konrad placed Berta on the cot. "Shouldn't we undress her?"

Barbara shook her head. "There is so little left of her," she said. "Wait until the doctor arrives."

The girl tried to lift her bandaged hands. "My nails . . ." she gasped. ". . . one by one . . ."

Liquid began to flow from her eyes. You couldn't call it tears. It was a trickle of water that ran for a moment and stopped as if cut off by a faucet.

"Where is . . . he . . . where . . . tell us and . . . we stop . . . day and night . . . you . . . Jewish sow . . ."

"Maybe your mother should see this," Konrad said.

"No. I know my mother. Hitler's spellbound her ever since she met him in person. She'll betray her and you and me."

» 98

Berta spoke again and we listened. To me, her words were nothing but a hollow rushing sound. I didn't understand their meaning. Maybe I didn't want to understand it.

Berta began to move her head back and forth. Very slowly.

"I . . . stood . . . stood . . . stood . . ."

The movement of her head accelerated. It became faster and faster. It frightened me. Any moment her head will fall off, I thought. What was it that held this bundle of bones together?

Suddenly the head lay still. "They . . . let me go . . ." she said. "I . . . I don't . . . know . . . if I . . . if . . . I . . . betrayed him."

"I'd better go upstairs and watch for the doctor," I said. "He shouldn't ring the doorbell."

I climbed the steps and the skull danced ahead of me and smelled of burning flesh.

I don't remember how long I had to wait until I heard the car. I opened the door. Dr. Hirsch's face was unshaven, his eyes dead from fatigue. He nodded at me.

"Yes, I remember you. Dr. Bauer, isn't it?"

"Yes."

"The patient is Jewish?"

"Yes, of course."

He followed me with his black bag to the basement. The introduction was brief. He stared at the girl's body for a long time before he knelt down to listen to her heart. Then he began to undress her with gentle hands. I couldn't watch it; neither could Konrad. We went to the other end of the basement. Barbara stayed with the doctor.

"How is it possible for anyone who sees and hears and feels to do that to another human being," I said.

It was not a question, but Konrad answered it.

"You only have to be able to commit the first act of violence. After that, it's the guilt that drives you farther and farther. You try to still the screams and the pleading and the voice of your own conscience."

"You're being too charitable," I said. "Those men are driven by sadism and hatred, not by anything as noble as guilt."

Konrad shook his head. "There is nothing noble about guilt. It is the most reprehensible feature God planted in our souls. Guilt follows sin. Whether the sin is real or imagined is irrelevant. Guilt itself is a sin—a most deceptive one. It lulls you into believing it is a virtue—that it will absolve you eventually from whatever you have done—but in fact it will corrupt your soul and your mind. It perpetuates your sin and makes you its slave."

Dr. Hirsch straightened up. "If we're to have any chance at all to save her life, she must go to a hospital immediately," he said.

We dared not call an ambulance: the noise would certainly wake Mrs. Teilhaber. We carried Berta upstairs on the cot.

"I'll take her to the hospital myself," the doctor said. "It's on my way home."

"One of us should go with you," Konrad protested.

"No. It's a Jewish hospital," said Dr. Hirsch firmly.

We had set the cot down in the living room. The girl was conscious. The doctor didn't want to give her a sedative before he'd had the chance to examine her thoroughly. He wasn't sure her body was strong enough to tolerate medication. He sat at the table, jotting down notes.

"Please, don't . . . don't . . ." the girl said. Her voice became louder. "I . . . can . . . can't . . . stand it . . . any longer . . . !"

She tried to lift her head. A scream came out of her. It was not a human sound. Dr. Hirsch rose quickly and went to the cot, bent down to Berta, talked to her very softly.

Barbara rushed to the door and opened it, then turned to us, her face white. "Mother—"

There was no time to hide the cot. We simply stood there,

frozen. Only Dr. Hirsch continued as before, still speaking to the girl. He didn't look up.

Mrs. Teilhaber was dressed in a gold-colored robe. "What's all this noise?" she asked.

At the sound of her voice, Dr. Hirsch straightened up and turned. Mrs. Teilhaber stared at the girl on the cot.

"The girl is sick, Mother," Barbara said.

"She looks dead."

"Dr. Hirsch is taking her to the hospital. He will try to save her life."

Mrs. Teilhaber turned to the doctor. "Are you a Jew?"

"Yes."

Her mouth tightened. "What happened to the girl?"

Konrad and I said nothing. It was safer to let her daughter do the talking.

"She's been tortured," Barbara said.

Mrs. Teilhaber went to the cot and looked closely at the girl's face. "How did she get here?"

"I don't know," said Konrad. "I can't imagine she was able to walk. It's fifteen miles from the camp to here. She must have crawled."

"What camp?" Mrs. Teilhaber asked.

"You call it a reeducation center," Barbara said.

"Is that where she came from?"

"Yes, I'm sure of that," Konrad said.

Barbara added, "Berta is a friend of ours. She knew we were staying at your house."

"She's an old woman," Mrs. Teilhaber said.

"This old woman is twenty-five," Barbara said. "That's what they did to her."

"Who?"

"The Nazis. She is Jewish."

Mrs. Teilhaber gave out a short, harsh laugh. "And you believe what a Jewess tells you?"

I looked at Dr. Hirsch. He had just closed his bag. His face was rigidly controlled, but his hand on the grip tightened.

"We'll have to take the cot out," I said to Konrad. Together we lifted it.

"Get those two out of this house as fast as possible!" Mrs. Teilhaber said. "Now!"

Suddenly, Barbara's self-command broke. She screamed at her mother, threw herself at her, and hammered at her face with both fists. Quickly we put down the cot, and Konrad grabbed his wife and pulled her back.

"Barbara, don't! Stop it!"

She stood leaning against him, breathing heavily.

"We'll be leaving tomorrow," Konrad said to Mrs. Teilhaber. She took out her handkerchief and wiped her battered face.

"I'll never speak to you again," she said to her daughter, her voice trembling. She drew herself up. "So that's how you used my house while I was away," she said. "Infesting it with Jews and Communists. That's what I get for my hospitality! My own daughter—"

"Go to bed, Mother," Barbara said quietly.

Dr. Hirsch had taken Konrad's place at the cot. The two of us proceeded through the hall and took the cot outside to his old-fashioned landau. He opened the rear door. I picked up the girl, wrapped in her blankets, and laid her carefully on the wide back seat. She was so light. It felt like carrying a small, wounded bird.

"She weighs nothing, Doctor," I said. "She weighs nothing."

I put a pillow under her head. Her night-bird eyes were on me. There was an urgent question in those eyes. I turned away and closed the car door.

"I hope she's going to pull through," the doctor said.

"Will you let us know?"

"Yes."

"I'm very grateful to you, Dr. Hirsch," I said. "All of us are."

"I don't want gratitude," he said harshly. "Where do I send my bill?"

He was inside the car. I gave him my business card.

"I won't see you again," he said. "A friend of mine in Mexico City has sent me an affidavit."

"I'm glad for you, Doctor."

"Yes." He started his car. "I was born in Berlin," he said.

I didn't stay long after Dr. Hirsch left. Mrs. Teilhaber had gone to bed. Barbara sat on the couch with Konrad. I saw she had been crying.

"I should apologize for my mother," she said. "But I really don't know what to say."

"Has she always been such a fanatic?" I asked.

"No. Not always. Except—she never liked Jews. She was brought up to dislike them. You knew my father, didn't you, Hans?"

"I met him years ago," I said. "He came backstage to see you. I happened to be in your dressing room."

"I remember. I was playing in *The Green Hat*. Two years later he died of a heart attack. He had high blood pressure all his adult life. He never paid any attention to it."

"He was an imposing-looking man," I said.

"Yes. I loved him very much, in spite of his prejudices and his ruthlessness in business. At home he was kind and warm. Mother never got over his death."

"I didn't know him," Konrad said. "He died before I met you."

"Yes. Father supported Hitler when the Nazi Party was still struggling. Many industrialists did at the time. Mother went to one of Hitler's receptions—he was already very powerful then —and came back raving about him. She was fascinated by his eyes. She thought he was a genius, the savior of the German people. The savior—"

Her voice failed. Konrad rose.

"You're tired, Barbara. This whole damn thing was too much for you, too much for anybody. Take a sleeping pill and go to bed."

She got up slowly. Konrad put his arm around her. She leaned over and kissed me on the cheek, then she asked her husband, "Are you going to take Hans home?"

"I'd like to—if you don't mind."

"I wish you would," Barbara said. "You'll be able to talk."

The night was cold, the sky clouded. No stars. The Rolls-Royce was parked at the entrance. The cadaverous driver lifted his cap and opened the car door for me. Konrad said, "I'm going to drive Dr. Bauer home, Satan."

"Yes, sir."

He closed the rear door and opened the front door for his employer. Konrad was about to get in and stopped. "Satan, why did you drive Dr. Bauer to the camp?"

"I thought he might be interested in seeing it, sir. Most people are," the man said.

"Are you in the habit of taking my guests there?"

"Only if they request it, sir."

I had not requested it, but I didn't want to get the man into trouble. I was silent. Konrad shook his head.

"Please, don't do that anymore," he said to the driver. The man said nothing. Konrad looked at him.

"I won't, sir," he said reluctantly. Then he added, "But so many people are incredulous, sir. They only believe what they see." His face showed the trace of a smile. Konrad got in the car.

Soon we were on the highway back to Berlin.

"He's right, of course," Konrad said. "Most people don't believe what they don't see, especially if they don't want to believe it. The story about Prague I told this evening is true. It happened to Ludwig Butler. He was telling a friend of his of his experiences, of some incidents he had witnessed himself. They looked at him and smiled. They had heard those 'atrocity stories' before and didn't believe them. In Prague, Hans! In a city that close to Berlin! Dr. Goebbels is doing quite a job!"

A car raced toward us with blinding lights. Konrad blinked his lights, but the others remained unchanged. Konrad slowed down. The car roared past us at high speed.

"Son-of-a-bitch!" Konrad said.

After a long silence he said unexpectedly, "I'm not so sure that I should keep Satan."

"You've had him for ten years."

"Yes."

"What's wrong with him?"

"Well, I'll tell you. I've never talked politics with him, but I know he hates the Nazis and I wouldn't be surprised if he were secretly working for the underground."

"What makes you say that?"

"I've been watching him. What he said, just now, about showing the camp to people confirmed my suspicion again. Two or three times a week he asks if he can have the evening off. He takes the car—not this one, he owns a small 1922 Opel—and stays out until four or five in the morning."

"The Prince of Darkness might have a nymph," I said.

Konrad shook his head.

"Out of curiosity, I checked his mileage indicator a few times. One night he had driven more than two hundred and fifty kilometers, another night close to three hundred. Those weren't nights of love, Hans. He must have been on the road six to eight hours each time."

"Did you ask him about it?"

"Yes. He said the indicator was broken."

We were both silent. Then he said, "One morning I came into the living room. He was just leaving. That was in our house, not here. After a few minutes I discovered a pamphlet from the underground on one of the chairs. Of course he said he had never seen it."

"Was it one of Ludwig's?"

He nodded. "That's another thing. I had no idea that Ludwig was involved in this. He told me about it only after he had made up his mind to leave Germany. I raised hell with him. For Christ's sake, I have to watch out for Barbara and myself! He had no right to work on those leaflets while he was staying at our home. It made us part of a conspiracy. People are getting shot for less."

"I agree with you."

"A couple of weeks ago I asked Satan outright if he was in the underground. I told him that if he was, he was jeopardizing not only his life but ours too. He denied that he was involved and then he said, 'Mr. Willman, nothing I ever do will endanger Mrs. Willman and you. I promise you that.' "

"That's almost a confession, isn't it?"

"Yes. But unfortunately I didn't realize it until later."

We were getting closer to Berlin. Konrad said, "To top all that, we have the enemy in our closest family. God knows what she's going to do after tonight. I tell you, she's capable of denouncing us to the Gestapo—'harboring a Jewish traitor,' or something like that."

The traffic was getting heavier. He had to slow down. "I'm scared," he said.

"Is that why you joined the party?"

"No, not really. It's very simple. I want to work. I can't without joining. And I love my work."

He tried to beat a traffic signal and failed. Stopped for a moment, he looked at me. "Are you going to stay in Germany?"

"Yes."

We drove on. Konrad said, "I don't like the Nazis. I hate what they're doing to the Jews. But I don't want to leave."

"You could, though, couldn't you?" I asked. "You'd be welcome in Paris or London—you could continue your career there."

"Yes, I could."

We were both silent for a while.

"I guess you feel the same way I do," I said at last. "It's something indefinable. I don't want to leave either. Germany is my country—my roots are here—and, aside from that . . . I'm a lawyer. Where would I go? What would I do?"

Konrad offered no answer, and we both sank back into thought. When we got close to my house he suddenly said, "Sometimes I wish I were a Jew. At least I wouldn't have any choice. Can you understand that?"

"No," I said. "I wouldn't want to be a Jew."

May 3rd.

It was long after midnight when I returned from the Willmans', and I immediately went into my study and began to write. Early next morning, however, when I checked what I had written, I crossed out everything. It didn't make sense.

Just to remind myself of my confusion, I am going to quote some of it here.

I could have killed Konrad when he said, "Sometimes I wish I were a Jew." What an idiotic blabber! He wishes to be tortured or murdered? Didn't he take a look at Berta?? They beat her into a subhuman embryo. [I'm not sure about the last word, but I think it's "embryo."] Is that what Konrad wants to be?? The great director who hides his intellectualism in overalls and Nazi boots?! God damn

107 «

it, I hated them all last night! Mother *Obergruppenfuehrer* with the rosebud face; Barbara, the wailing *Compassionata* —she really hammed up that part! Dr. Hirsch, who flaunts his Mogen David the way the Nazis parade their swastika. Konrad, the honorary king-sized rabbi of stage and screen; Berta, the poor, smashed-up victim—I hate victims! They tell you their rock-bottom bedtime stories of human decay and humiliation, then they haunt you in your dreams and turn them into the terror of purgatory. Don't they understand? There is one straight line from the crucified Jewish philosopher, Jesus Christ, to the shattered skeleton of the Jewess Berta. All Jews are condemned to be eternal victims —the professional quarry of the people of this world.

That's about one-third of what I wrote that night. The rest is illegible. From now on, I shall force myself to stick to the mere facts without erupting into paragraphs of self-indulgent emotionalism.

And, of course, everything gets out of focus. Konrad did make me mad with his remark, but this fury I wrote myself into had nothing to do with my true feelings. I don't hate the Willmans. They are my friends. I can even understand Mrs. Teilhaber. That's the kind of woman she is: so what? What is Hecuba Teilhaber to me? And Berta—how could I write down this nonsense about hating her?? Hating victims. I don't hate victims. I don't hate Jews. I'm just not one of them.

Breakfast. Hanna.

She used to smile all the time. Even early in the morning when everybody else was still trying to wake up. Now she smiles very rarely. Come to think of it, not many people smile these days.

Hanna came in with my coffee, her face a thundercloud, her voice almost inaudible. She wanted me to know she was in a bad mood. I was sure it involved her half-Jewish fiancé, and I didn't feel like talking about half-Jewish fiancés or anything else Jewish—but just the same, I did ask her if anything was wrong, and she told me she had just received a letter from Paul. He had emigrated to Sweden and he hoped to find a job within a few months. He had been told there was a lot of interest in young architects in Stockholm. He was still very much in love with her, and he wanted Hanna to join him and marry him as soon as he was settled again.

I looked at her. "This isn't bad news, Hanna. It's good news. For one thing—Paul is safe."

"Yes, I know," she said. She was close to tears.

"He loves you and he wants you to be his wife."

She nodded and blew her nose. "Yes—but when—when??"

"In a few months, he says."

"Oh, he is always too optimistic."

She tucked away her handkerchief and sighed.

"I don't know if I want to live in a strange country. I have my parents here. My two brothers."

"Stockholm is not that far, Hanna."

She cleared her throat. "I would have had a fight with them anyway, Dr. Bauer. They don't like Jews. They've always been against Paul. I think I could have stood up to them—here—with him around. But when my parents hear that I'd have to leave Germany to marry Paul—" She shook her head. "I don't know what to do."

"You don't have to do anything now," I said. "In a few months everything might look different to you. You're not a little girl anymore, Hanna. Don't pay too much attention to other people's opinions. Make up your own mind."

"Yes, I know I'll have to, Dr. Bauer."

As far as I'm concerned, all bets on a happy honeymoon for these two are off. That'll teach me again how little I know about people. And I'm an attorney, a good one. I'd always thought that Hanna was a steadfast German peasant, strong-willed—a one man's woman. But when it comes to the test . . .

Glancing at the newspaper. New decrees:

"Non-Aryans are not allowed to serve on juries."

"Jews are not permitted to have female servants under the age of forty-five. . . . Suspicion of sexual intercourse . . . Jews are known to be a lecherous race. . . . Racial disgrace. . . ." That would be another blow to Hanna—if I were a Jew.

The sky was dark: it was raining. I put on my raincoat and took my umbrella. It was much too early to go to the office, but I had a heavy day ahead of me and I wanted to prepare myself for the various meetings.

As I was crossing the downstairs hall, the door to the Heiliger apartment opened slowly and Heinz backed out in his Hitler Youth uniform. There was something furtive and secretive about the way he closed the door behind him. He turned and jumped when he saw me.

"Dr. Bauer—"

"Good morning."

"Good—Heil Hitler," he said.

At that moment a flash of lightning and a deafening crash of thunder split the gray of the morning. Heinz's face went white. He began to tremble. Through the brown topcoat and the martial uniform underneath, I saw a fat kid of fourteen, afraid of thunderstorms. I almost felt sorry for him. Almost.

Outside a taxi splashed by and stopped. The driving was slow. The elevator was out of order again, so I walked upstairs . . . and then I stopped. Through the glass window on top of the door to our office, I saw a light. I unlocked the door. The light went out instantly.

I closed the door carefully behind me—the outer office was

dark—and switched the light on again. The office was empty, but the filing cabinet stood open, some of the drawers had been pulled out . . . and then I sensed it, a moment before I knew what it was. The door to my office was closing very slowly. I tiptoed to it and threw it open. Somebody tore past me—a man, a brownshirt—and I went after him. He yanked at the door-knob, but before he could open the door, I grabbed his arm and pulled with all my strength. He let go and both of us fell down, the brownshirt on top of me, but I was stronger. I hit his head with my right fist. He groaned. I turned his body and nailed him to the floor with my arms and knees.

"I—I haven't done anything, Dr. Bauer," Gustaf Angermann stammered breathlessly.

"What were you doing here?"

"Nothing."

I slapped his face.

"I was looking for something I forgot."

"How did you get the office key?"

"I kept it."

"You never had a key, Gustaf! Who gave it to you?"

"Nobody."

I slapped his face again. Harder.

"Honest, Dr. Bauer. I took it from one of the desks."

I dragged him up by his shoulders and pulled him to his feet. He stood up sluggishly.

"Don't hit me anymore, Dr. Bauer."

I pushed him to the filing cabinet.

"How did you get the key to that?"

"I took that, too."

"I am going to hit you again, Gustaf. You couldn't have taken it. Each secretary has an office key and a key to the filing cabi-net. Both keys are always locked in the middle drawers of their desks. That is a strict office rule."

"They were on top of the desk, Dr. Bauer."

He was leaning against the wall, exhausted. I tried the drawers. Every one was locked.

"I want both keys," I said.

He handed them over.

"What were you doing in my office?"

He didn't answer. I went to the front door and locked it.

"Go in!"

"Where?"

"Into my office."

He shook his head. "No."

I grabbed his shoulders and pushed him ahead of me into my office and turned on the light. Several files were piled up on my desk. One was open.

"Don't try to run," I said. "You saw me lock the front door."

I looked at the open file: *Axner* v. *Bitterfeld*. I remembered the case.

During the transportation strike in Berlin preceding the last elections and Hitler's appointment to the Chancellery, the Communists and the Nazis had formed a united front against the Papen government and taken to the streets. Bloody riots had occurred. In one free-for-all, caused by the basic hatred between the two political factions, who were only cooperating for reasons of expediency, a storm trooper, Josef Axner, had been shot to death by Friedrich Bitterfeld, a Communist. Axner's father had brought suit against Bitterfeld. Our firm had been retained by the defendant's family. Klaus, who had acted as defense attorney, had been able to prove that the incident had been provoked by the Nazis and that Bitterfeld had shot in self-defense. Bitterfeld had been acquitted.

It was easy to understand why Gustaf Angermann had looked for that file. In the present climate, the fact that our firm had successfully represented a Communist who had caused a storm trooper's death would certainly have been distorted. The resulting publicity could have had alarming consequences. It was a conspicuous act of revenge on Angermann's part for his dismissal.

When I looked at Gustaf now, I saw that his expression had changed. There was a mocking smile on his face. He proceeded to sit down leisurely, cross his legs, and light a cigarette, then he asked, "Well, what's next?"

I knew why his attitude had changed. With the physical threat apparently over, he had had time to think. His next question confirmed it.

"Why don't you call the police, Dr. Bauer?"

"Because you know damn well they wouldn't do anything. They're scared of your shit uniform."

The last days' experiences had all taught me the same lesson. Appealing to the police was hopeless. There was no official anywhere who would have proceeded against an S.A. man. I was furious, but I didn't want to give that son-of-a-bitch the satisfaction of seeing it. I said coldly, "You have always been inefficient and clumsy. You fumbled this little piece of treachery, too. I don't give a damn if you get punished. Eventually you'll trip over your own feet and end up where you started—a nobody."

His face and neck turned crimson. He was ready to throw himself at me, but he obviously thought better of it.

"I want to get out of here," he said in a hoarse voice.

"You weren't invited in," I said. "Now that you're here, I want you to wait."

"What for?"

I heard the key turn in the entrance door. I went to the outer office.

"Good morning, Magda."

"Good morning, Dr. Bauer." She looked at me. "Is anything wrong?"

"Please lock the door again."

"Lock the door?"

"Yes."

She locked the door, puzzled, and went to her desk. "You want to dictate, Dr. Bauer?"

"No. Not now. We have a visitor."

Gustaf came out too. "Heil Hitler, Magda," he said with an impudent smile. She gasped.

"Gustaf—"

"Yes—surprise."

The key turned again and Klaus von Isenberg entered. He stopped as he saw Gustaf Angermann.

"What the hell—"

"Klaus, please lock the door," I said.

He looked at me and locked the door slowly. "What's going on?"

"Mr. Angermann tried to steal one of our court files," I said. "Unfortunately for him, I decided to come to the office early."

"How did he get in?"

"You'll see in a few minutes."

"I didn't steal anything," Gustaf said.

I was watching the entrance door. Somebody outside tried to open it. The doorknob turned several times, then came a rap, and finally a second rap, sharper.

Magda rose. "Should I—?"

I nodded. She unlocked the door and opened it. Lieselotte entered—the secretary to our two assistants, Manfred Schuller and Guenter Sternberg.

"I'm sorry, Magda, I forgot my key." Then she saw Gustaf Angermann and paled. "Gustaf—"

"Be careful. They're trying to trap you," he said. "They're going to accuse you of giving me the keys."

The girl was recovering fast. "What keys?"

I showed them to her in the palm of my hand. "These two."

Lieselotte is an attractive girl, a blond with a well-developed figure. The others have always kidded her because she wears nothing but tight-fitting sweaters. It was easy to see what had happened between Gustaf and her.

"I must have forgotten to lock them in the drawer," she said.

I could tell by her expression that she was trying to gain time to think. She unlocked the middle drawer of her desk very slowly. By the time she had it open, she must have realized the futility of further pretending. She sat still with a blank face.

"You're fired," I said.

Gustaf took a few steps toward Lieselotte. "He can't fire you. You didn't do anything."

She shook her head and covered her face with both hands.

"What are you upset about? Don't be so dumb! Who wants to work for these Communists?"

"Don't call me dumb," Lieselotte said.

I saw rising fury in Klaus's face and wanted to avoid another physical clash. "Get out, Gustaf," I said. "Get out as long as you can walk out! Take your girl along!"

Gustaf shrugged. "She knows where to find me."

Lieselotte raised her head and stared at him. He went to the door without looking at her. At the door, he turned and raised his right arm in a defiant attempt to restore his ego.

"Heil Hitler!"

Nobody spoke. Klaus moved and Gustaf left fast. The silence was broken by Klaus's secretary, Hedi, who arrived a second later. She saw only the other two girls and asked, "What was that son-of-a-bitch doing here?" Then she saw Klaus and me and blushed. "I beg your pardon."

"That son-of-a-bitch tried to steal some files," Klaus said. "Dr. Bauer caught him."

I turned to Lieselotte. "I want you to leave right away. Magda will settle your account."

Hedi looked at the girl and shook her head. "He got you in

on it, did he? I've told you again and again that guy is no good."

"So you did," Lieselotte said sullenly. She started emptying her desk.

Back in my office, I described to Klaus my rough encounter with Gustaf. "Even under normal circumstances, it would have been difficult for the police to step in," I said. "It wasn't a case of burglary. Angermann used a regular key. It would have been impossible to prove larceny. I didn't catch him in the act of taking and carrying away the files. They were on my desk."

Klaus took the papers and glanced at them, then tucked them under his arm. "From now on, I'd better keep them in my private safe. I wonder what he would have done with them. Shown them to the Gestapo?"

"That would be my guess."

Klaus went to the door.

"I'm sure we'll hear from Gustaf Angermann again," I said. "He's vindictive and he knows that case record exists."

"Let's not worry about that," Klaus said. "All we can do these days is tackle the problem when it's there. Who the hell worries about tomorrow?"

I looked at him. "I do."

For a moment, our eyes held. His expression was calm. "Yes, I know," he said. "I didn't want to talk about it until I had results. I spoke to Adriani yesterday. You've met him, haven't you? He told me you had."

"Yes. At Victor Brandt's party."

"He's head of the department for 'Protection of the Blood'— an inspired name for it. I don't expect any trouble, Hans. He didn't commit himself, but he doesn't strike me as a fanatic. He'll get back to me in a few days. Maybe he'll talk to you directly."

"Thank you, Klaus."

"The firm might have to pay a substantial amount of cash."

"To whom?"

Klaus shrugged. "Protection of the blood is expensive."

"Whatever we have to pay must come out of my account," I said.

"The primary objective is to have you cleared," Klaus said. "First things first."

In the afternoon I received a phone call from Grete Fall. Her voice is usually low and soft, but when she gets excited, it acquires a harsh twang, stemming from her Bavarian origins— high German doesn't come easily to her even though she needs it professionally. Yesterday she sounded more upset than I've ever heard her. She had to see me urgently. Not at the office. At her apartment. I must promise. I said I'd drop by after office hours.

My intercom buzzed. Klaus asked if I could join him right away. He was talking to Guenter Sternberg when I came in. Sternberg rose and we shook hands.

"Guenter is here to say good-by," Klaus said. "You know he's leaving."

"No, I didn't. I've been back for such a short time. Why?"

"I'm Jewish," Sternberg said.

"God damn it, that again!"

Klaus looked at me.

"I'm sorry. I'm very, very sorry, Guenter."

"So am I," he said. "I've liked my job and you've been very good to me." He added, "Dr. Schwartz, too."

Suddenly I found myself scrutinizing his features. Did his face look Jewish? Maybe his nose—his hair—yes, one could say—

Something in myself rebelled. I turned my head. I didn't want to look at him like that.

"I wrote a letter to John van Dienen in Johannesburg," Klaus said. "You remember him, Hans. We won the Dahlberg mining litigation for him."

"You're going to South Africa?" I asked.

"Yes. My father has a cousin in Germiston. He seems to be well-off and he's offered to send affidavits for all of us. My father didn't even have to ask him."

"How many in your family?" Klaus asked.

"My parents, my sister, and myself. We just got Erna out."

"Out from where?"

"Until yesterday . . . she was in a concentration camp."

Klaus started to pace. "Why?"

Sternberg hesitated. I said, "You don't have to tell us if you don't want to."

"No, that's all right. She was engaged to a man who turned out to be a Nazi, after Hitler came to power," Sternberg said. "He called off the engagement and then—I guess he was afraid for his own skin—he told the authorities Erna had concealed the fact that she was Jewish from him."

"Did they . . . torture her?" I asked.

He shook his head. "They didn't get that far." He smiled. "You see, last year we celebrated Rosh Hashanah as usual. I'm an amateur photographer and I took some group pictures. The guy stood next to Erna before a large Mogen David—and he had his arm around her shoulder."

Klaus stopped pacing. "That's great, Guenter."

"It saved her life," Sternberg said.

After he had left, Klaus and I talked for a while. We would have to look for another assistant. Manfred Schuller, who had been splitting the workload with Guenter, couldn't possibly handle everything by himself. Klaus's secretary called and he said, "Just a moment, Hedi." He turned to me. "Alfred Koenig again. I'd like you to listen to this. Take the phone on the table. I'll do the talking."

He picked up the receiver. "Yes, Dr. Koenig."

"Heil Hitler, Dr. von Isenberg. About the matter we discussed briefly the other day—"

"Which one?" Klaus asked. He winked at me.

"You remember, don't you? You spoke about the possibility of my joining your firm—"

"I don't think I was the one who brought it up," Klaus said.

"Well, it's immaterial who mentioned it first."

Klaus made no comment. There was a pause.

"Are you there?" Koenig's voice asked.

"I'm listening, Dr. Koenig."

I could hear Koenig draw in his breath. He was audibly annoyed.

"It occurred to me that your partner, Dr. Bauer, might influence you against me."

"I haven't discussed it with him," Klaus said. "Why should he do that?"

"On several occasions, we have opposed each other in court."

"That happens every day among attorneys, Dr. Koenig. Those are professional differences. They don't affect personal relationships, unless—"

He stopped deliberately and gave me a caustic smile.

"Unless what?"

"Unless there was more involved than just the usual contention of two legal positions. For instance, if your conduct at a trial, or his, was—detrimental to the dignity of the court, or if the Board of Attorneys happened to have reprimanded—"

Koenig's voice cut in sharply. "The Board of Attorneys is a thing of the past, Dr. von Isenberg. It used to consist of Jews and Communists. The new organization will conform to the principles of the National Socialist Party."

Klaus was silent. I could visualize Dr. Koenig's exasperated face.

"I find your attitude rather intransigent," Koenig said.

119 «

Klaus was getting angry too. "Well, Dr. Koenig, between Dr. Bauer, our late partner, Dr. Siegmund Schwartz, and myself, we've built quite a lucrative and important practice here. I think Dr. Bauer and I have the right to choose our partner—if, indeed, we want one."

Koenig's voice took on added weight. "All right, Dr. von Isenberg, I didn't want to mention it, but I'm afraid I'm forced to now. I am authorized by the minister of justice to tell you that my application has his fullest support."

"Thank you for telling me, Dr. Koenig," Klaus said dryly.

There was a long pause. Klaus waited, looked at me. Shrugged. We hung up.

"That goddamned conniving bastard," I said.

Klaus went behind his desk, sat down, and covered his face with his hands. A moment later, he loked up and I saw his whole face had slackened and his eyes were dull.

"What a mess!" he said. "I'm so tired of all this horse shit! Maybe I should go back to my so-called family and manage the estate. Only I know I don't have the stomach for that either. I'm sure they're all in Nazi uniform by now, including my mother. She even calls Hindenburg a Communist and a creature of the Jews."

It was twenty minutes past six—I was locking my desk, ready to leave the office—when Manfred Schuller came in.

"Excuse me, Dr. Bauer. Dr. von Isenberg wanted you to see these."

Schuller was Guenter Sternberg's age, short and stocky, with a prematurely wrinkled face, a wide forehead, and thinning brown hair. He put two passports on my desk. I opened the first one. It was made out to Siegmund Israel Schwartz. The name Schwartz was underlined. The name on the second passport was Helen Sarah Schwartz. Again, the name Schwartz was underlined. I looked at Schuller.

"Israel and Sarah?"

"From now on, every male Jew has to add 'Israel' to his first name," he said. "It's Sarah for the women. And on passports, the last name is underlined. That means Jew."

I looked at the passport for a long time. The printed name was changing. What I read was "Johannes Israel <u>Bauer</u>."

Schuller said, "I'm very sorry about Guenter."

"Yes, we all are. You worked well with him, didn't you?"

"He's a smart man and a fabulous statistician. I'll miss him very much. Too bad it's a crime now to be a Jew."

"Yes. Isn't it?"

Our eyes met for a moment. He lowered his head. I sensed he wanted to say more, but he didn't. I shut my briefcase and handed the two passports back to him.

"I meant to ask you a question, Dr. Bauer . . . but I don't want to keep you."

"Go ahead."

"Am I supposed to join the party?"

I thought for a second. "Let me answer it this way: within a few weeks we shall have a new Nazi-oriented attorneys' organization which will replace our now-defunct Board of Attorneys. Every lawyer and every prospective lawyer will have to join. It's a closed shop. In that sense, you will be a member of the party."

Schuller stood silent. Again I felt there was more on his mind.

"Anything else?" I asked.

He shook his head.

"Nothing, Dr. Bauer. I'm sorry I kept you."

"That's all right."

"I'll drop by Mrs. Schwartz's home tonight and give her her

passport," Schuller said. "What should I do with the other one?"

"Lock it in your desk," I said.

The rain had stopped. It was dark when I arrived at Grete Fall's apartment. She opened the door herself, wearing a white robe and a red silk scarf loosely draped around her neck. Framed by her light blond hair, her face looked fresh and cool and very young.

We shook hands and she kissed me on the cheek. I had been at her home before. Every room is done in her two favorite colors, white and red. "It's the feminine touch," she explained to me. It is more like a feminine broadside: the effect is jolting.

"Whiskey and water?" she asked.

"Yes, please."

She has a barlike contraption in her living room, a white counter with red leather stools. Every man must feel out of place in her apartment. So do I. I always see myself as a clumsy intruder into a very fragile world.

"Are you hungry?" she asked.

"No, thank you, I'm not."

"I'm having cold cuts for dinner. Enough for two."

She handed me my drink and poured sweet vermouth for herself.

"Thanks very much, but I have a date," I lied.

I had been avoiding getting together with Grete socially. I was aware of the tension between us, and I knew she felt it too. It's the normal reaction of a man and a woman who are attracted to each other. At the beginning of our relationship, I'd come close to getting seriously involved with her, but in handling her contractual and personal legal affairs, I'd soon realized that the private Grete Fall was utterly different from the romantic screen image. Her mind and her emotions were totally absorbed by her career. She'd stay with a man only as long as he was useful to her. As soon as he had fulfilled his serviceability, she'd drop him. I don't think Grete will ever get involved with a man unless she is sure he can further her career. However, she does have one disarming quality—as far as I am concerned: she is scrupulously honest. Prospective victims are forewarned. Unfortunately, however, this caveat presents a challenge to many men who are either mesmerized by her or too vain to face the truth.

Grete walked past me to the couch and sat down. The couch is the only substantial piece of furniture in the room.

"How is Karin?"

"Fine."

She sipped on her drink. The telephone rang. She didn't move. I asked, "Do you want me to take it?"

She shook her head. "Sit next to me, please."

I went to the couch. "You sounded upset when you called me this afternoon," I said.

"I am upset." And after a moment, "I don't know how to start."

She emptied her glass and set it down. Her body moved with her hands. Her head came close to touching the table.

She said, "I'm going to talk to you as my attorney. What I'm going to tell you must be confined to this room."

"That is implicit in the relationship between attorney and client."

"Yes, I know. Get me another vermouth, please."

I took her glass and went to the white counter.

"My mother's husband died twelve years ago," Grete said. "He was Jewish."

I almost lost my grip on the bottle.

"He was not my father," she said.

"What do you mean?"

"My mother had an affair with another man."

"While she was married?"

"Yes. I am that man's daughter."

I went back to the couch and put her glass on the table.

"Of course, this other man was an Aryan."

"Yes."

She looked at me.

"Then both your parents are Aryans."

"Yes."

"Do you know your real father's name?"

"Bernhard von Kling."

"Where is he?"

"He died three years ago in Munich. He and my mother's husband used to be friends."

"I suppose you've already submitted your papers."

"I had to do it while you were away. I did it myself. I don't trust anybody but you."

"You must have needed a statutory declaration from your mother."

"She gave it to me."

"And the authorities accepted it?"

"Of course. They had many similar cases."

"Then where is your problem?" I asked.

"Mother went to confession."

There was a pause. I tried to organize my thoughts. She continued, "She told the priest that she had been lying for my sake. That she had never been unfaithful to her husband. That he had been a wonderful man and that her conscience was torturing her because she had defiled his memory."

"What did the priest say?"

"That she must tell the truth."

I got up and went to the window. The rays of the streetlights were mirrored on the asphalt, still glistening from this morning's downpour. Cars and pedestrians and trucks. The pedestrians moved faster than the cars.

I stood with my back to Greta and asked, "What is the truth?"

"I have my mother's statutory declaration."

"What is the truth?"

She raised her voice and said with her harsh Bavarian inflection, "How the hell should I know? I wasn't in bed with them."

I turned around. She had risen and was looking at me defiantly.

I asked, "What is your mother going to do?"

"I don't know. She told me about her confession on the morning after Victor's party. She wasn't sure then. But last night, we had a fight. I—I almost hit her. I was so furious. I left. I didn't sleep all night. This morning I called you."

"What am I supposed to do?"

"There's a legal aspect to it, isn't there? If she revokes her statutory declaration, she's confessing to perjury."

"Yes."

"Well—"

"There's a human aspect to it, too," I said without much conviction.

She rasped, "Oh, don't give me that bleeding-heart stuff, lover! I'm human and I'm not going to let her destroy my life!"

"You mean your career."

"That *is* my life," she said savagely.

Suddenly she sat down. Her face, distorted in fury and frustration, softened. She said in a half-choked voice, "Please help me, Hans."

"You're acting, Grete."

She looked at me with innocent eyes. "Am I?"

"Yes. You know it and I know it."

Her expression hardened. "Does it matter? Can't you see that I'm scared?"

I sat down next to her. "Let's analyze this logically. With all the cards on the table."

"All right." She shook her head. "It's amazing," she said.

"What is?"

"How well you know me. I can't get away with anything. You cut right through my bag of tricks. That's what I like about you."

She leaned over and kissed me. Her lips were cold.

I said, "Your father died twelve years ago. Twelve years is a long time. Maybe no one ever mentioned that he was Jewish—but you must have known it. The birth certificate which you had to submit would have exposed it. So—you thought of the illegitimate child trick, and in a weak moment, your mother agreed to let you go ahead."

I paused to give her an opportunity to deny it, but she didn't. She kept looking at me, fascinated by her own story.

"You mother signed the statutory declaration. Then she realized, suddenly, what it implied. She had loved your father. By admitting an act of adultery which she had never committed, she had defiled his memory. She was forced to choose between her love for you and her love for the dead man, and couldn't cope with it. She went to confession. Is that substantially correct?"

Without taking her eyes off me, she said, "Of course it is, darling."

"What is your mother going to do?"

"She is going to confess the truth."

"Did you mention the matter of perjury to her?"

Grete shook her head. "I was much too furious. I thought of it only after I got home. I want *you* to talk to her."

I leaned back and closed my eyes. Here we sit, I thought. Under the Nazi laws, two Jews. But we don't accept it. We don't want to be made into Jews. We fight it by cheating and conniving. We are both fighting for our lives. What she has done is immoral—but I have no right to judge her. No one has. Moral standards have been drowned in the flood of savagery and murder. The only thing that counts is survival.

"I won't talk to your mother," I said.

"Why not?"

"Disregard the legal aspect. If your mother committed perjury—so did you. You'll both end up in a concentration camp."

"I know that."

"She must know that too. She might be willing to risk her own life—but not her daughter's, not yours. I don't believe your mother will talk, once she gets calm enough to think it through. But you must help her to get to that decision. She doesn't need an attorney now. She needs a daughter. She needs your compassion, your understanding—your love."

Grete's face softened. Her mouth half opened and she moved her head sideways. The expression in her eyes was loving and humble. She likes the part, I thought.

"Make your mother feel that you're worth the emotional price she is paying," I said. "Then she will—eventually—be at peace with herself."

For a long time, Grete was silent, absorbed in her own loving-daughter image. Then she whispered to herself, "Yes—yes."

She dropped her hands and raised her head. The softness in her face had been wiped off. Her eyes were cold.

"Yes," she said. "I'm so stupid. Yours is the only way."

"I'm sure it is," I said.

It was about seven thirty in the evening when I got home. Hanna had dinner ready for me, but I wasn't hungry. I went to my study and began to write. I tried to keep everything factual without emotional embellishments and I think that I—

May 4th.

I had gotten that far last night when the telephone rang. I had not heard from Karin and I was sure that it was she. I was wrong. A man's voice asked, "Is this Dr. Bauer?"

"Yes, it is."

"This is Inspector Sontag. We've met once before, in Siegmund Schwartz's apartment. That's where I am now. Would it be possible for you to come over right away?"

"What's happened?"

"It's a matter of identification," the inspector said.

In front of the building stood a police car, an ambulance, and an open truck, filled with furniture. Two S.A. men were chatting with the ambulance driver.

The door to the apartment was open. The inspector was in the hall with the same people who had been with him on the morning of Siegmund Schwartz's suicide: the same young policeman; the same thick-set storm trooper, Brause. Apparently, the photographer had already left. Dr. Hirsch was missing. The doctor in attendance was a tall man, probably in his early thirties, blond, with a small mustache and large prominent ears. His name was Tragendorff. The human figure on the stretcher was covered with a white sheet. The hall was bare of furniture.

The inspector motioned to the policeman, who lifted the sheet and folded it back. The impact of the shock was almost unbearable.

The dead man was Manfred Schuller.

"You know this man?"

I nodded. I couldn't speak.

"What is his name?"

I turned away and covered my eyes with my hands. I heard Dr. Tragendorff say, "Give him a moment, Inspector. He's obviously very upset."

"I'm sorry."

It couldn't be true. He had just been in my office. He had been about to stop by and deliver the passport to Mrs. Schwartz. He couldn't be dead.

The door was opened noisily. I turned around. Two brownshirts had entered from the study. Both were young and of average height. One of them had a pale face, devoid of expression, with a small mouth and sharply pointed teeth. He wore rimless glasses. The other bore the insignia of a *Sturmfuehrer*. He was clean-shaven, with deep-set eyes and a face that ended abruptly under his lower lip. He had no chin.

"How long will we have to wait here?" he asked.

"Until I'm finished," the inspector said.

"We have other things to do."

"So have I."

The inspector took out a notebook and pencil and looked at me.

"Would you identify this man for us?"

"His name is Manfred Schuller. He is—was an assistant in our office."

"Your full name again, please."

"Johannes Bauer. Attorney. Von Isenberg, Bauer, and Schwartz."

The inspector jotted it down in his notebook.

"—and Schwartz," he repeated.

"Was this Schuller a Jew?" the pale S.A. man asked.

"No."

"Can you prove that? He acted like a Jew."

"His birth certificate will tell."

"Did you know that Mr. Schuller was here?" Inspector Sontag asked.

"He told me he planned to drop by and deliver Mrs. Schwartz's passport."

The inspector took the passport out of his pocket and handed it to me.

"Is this it?"

I opened it. Helen Sarah <u>Schwartz</u>. "Yes. Where is Mrs. Schwartz?"

"The two Jews are in the bedroom," the chinless *Sturmfuehrer* said.

"What two Jews?"

"The old one and the maid."

I hadn't known the maid was Jewish. In fact, I knew that she wasn't. Dr. Schwartz had mentioned to Klaus that she would have to leave because of the new law. Female servants under forty-five were not allowed to stay in Jewish households. The Schwartzes' maid was much younger.

"Inspector Sontag, what happened here? How did Schuller get killed?"

"The story is that he obstructed the authorities, resisted arrest, and got shot in self-defense."

S.A. man Brause said, "That isn't a story, Inspector, it's the truth."

"You weren't here, were you? We arrived together."

"*Sturmfuehrer* Scharff testified to that. Do you doubt his veracity?"

The chinless brownshirt smiled broadly.

"I want the facts," the inspector said firmly. He turned to the doctor. "Can I speak to Mrs. Schwartz?"

Dr. Tragendorff shook his head. "She's in no condition to be questioned, Inspector. She's irrational and hardly able to form words. She must have gone through a hell of a lot."

"Are you a Jew lover, Doctor?" the pale S.A. man asked. He grinned, baring his teeth.

For a moment the doctor said nothing. He pressed his lips together and stood stiffly, with clenched fists. Then he said, "I consider that question tasteless and insulting. I was called in on this case by Inspector Sontag. Jewish or not—Mrs. Schwartz is my patient."

"That's telling you, Heister," *Sturmfuehrer* Scharff said. He laughed raucously.

"Do you still need me, Inspector?" Dr. Tragendorff asked. "I'd like to leave as soon as possible. I signed the death certificate and I gave the maid a prescription for Mrs. Schwartz."

The inspector shook his head. "I'm sorry, Doctor. I can't let you go. I understand your impatience. I might need your medical opinion during the testimony."

"I'm not an expert on ballistics."

"I know that." Sontag motioned to the policeman. "Get the maid."

The policeman left. Inspector Sontag said to Scharff and Heister, "Please wait in the study until I call you."

"We'll stay right here," *Sturmfuehrer* Scharff said.

The inspector shook his head. "Not during the testimony of the maid. Your presence would influence her."

"She's a Jewess. You'll hear nothing but lies."

The inspector looked at Brause; the storm trooper shrugged. The maid came in with the young policeman. The inspector said calmly, "I won't start until we are alone with the witness."

He turned to me. "I want you to stay, Dr. Bauer."

There was a silence. Finally, the two brownshirts moved to the study. In the door, the chinless one turned and said to the inspector, "You'll be sorry about this."

The inspector did not react. They closed the door behind them. I looked at the maid. Her eyes were swollen and her whole face seemed distorted, as if frozen in a moment of shock.

Her light hair was disheveled: strands of it covered part of her forehead. The fingers of both hands opened and closed incessantly.

"Are there no chairs in the hall?" the inspector asked.

"There aren't any in the whole apartment," said the policeman.

The maid spoke with an effort. "One in my room. One in the kitchen. They—they took all the others."

The policeman left and came back with two straight chairs. He gave one to the girl and she sat down obediently. He gave the other one to the inspector. I leaned against the wall. So did Dr. Tragendorff. Brause stood behind the inspector, and the young cop took a position at the door to the study.

The inspector brought out his notebook and pencil.

"What's your name?" he asked.

"Annemarie Moeller."

"Your age?"

"Twenty-eight."

The S.A. man said, "You're Jewish?"

"Yes."

"Moeller is not a Jewish name?"

"My mother—" the girl said.

Her voice was hardly audible. She saw me and stopped, fright in her eyes. I shook my head slowly. I wasn't sure if she noticed it.

"This line of questioning is irrelevant," the inspector said to Brause.

"If she's an Aryan and employed by Jews, she's breaking the law," the S.A. man said sullenly.

"Who in his right mind would call himself a Jew today if he weren't Jewish?" said the inspector. He sat down. "Tell me in your own words what happened, Miss Moeller."

"Yes."

Her body shook. The inspector looked at Dr. Tragendorff.

"I'm afraid you'll have to be patient with her," the doctor said. "There isn't anything I can do."

"It—it started this morning," the girl said.

"What did?"

"A man—" Pause. "A man in a brown uniform came. With a package. A large package for Mrs. Schwartz."

She described with her hands the size and shape of the package.

"It was wrapped. I didn't know what it was. I put it—put it on the table. There used to be a table here." She stared at the spot where the table had stood. It must have been where the stretcher had been set down.

Dr. Tragendorff said to the inspector, "You can call the ambulance men. Everything is specified on the death certificate and I made some additional notes."

The policeman left the apartment and came back with the two ambulance attendants. The doctor whispered something to one of them, and they carried the stretcher out. I looked after them. That was Manfred Schuller's body under the white sheet.

"Please continue, Miss Moeller," the inspector said. "Take your time."

She swallowed. "Mrs. Schwartz came in. She hasn't been the same since her husband killed himself—"

"Her husband died of a heart attack," Brause cut in sharply.

"Oh, for Christ's sake, let it go!" the inspector said angrily.

"She tried to unwrap the package, but her hands fluttered and I had to do it for her."

She was talking much more fluently now. Much faster. "It was an urn," she said and paused, plainly reliving the terror that had struck her when she first saw it. "An urn like at funerals. There was a piece of paper, red-lined paper, glued on it, and written in ink was the name Siegmund Schwartz. Mrs. Schwartz came closer and I didn't want her to see the urn, so I stood in front of it. She looked and circled the table and stared at it and her mouth fell open and she touched the urn and I said, 'It's nothing, Mrs. Schwartz.' But she walked all around it and saw the name in ink on the red-lined paper and all the time her mouth stayed open. 'Mrs. Schwartz,' I said. 'Please, Mrs. Schwartz,' and she said, 'Siegmund.' She fell on the urn. I had to steady it. She embraced it as if it were alive and I couldn't help myself and cried, and she said, 'Don't cry, Annemarie.' But I couldn't stop. She had been waiting, waiting to bury him, nobody knew where they had taken the body and then it came like this."

She was quiet. So was everybody else. S.A. man Brause had lowered his head. After a while, the girl started again on her own.

"Mrs. Schwartz prayed over the urn in Hebrew, and then she fell on her knees and moved her body back and forth for a long time. I didn't know what to do. At the end, I lifted her up and she said something about God who had taken him, and then she said, 'In Wiesbaden in June'—that sounded long ago—and, 'I'll meet you at the bandstand.' That was all she said. I took her to the bedroom and undressed her and she lay in bed very still with her eyes open and that's the way she is now."

She leaned back in her chair. Exhausted.

"You want to rest for a while?" the inspector asked softly.

She didn't answer. Instead, she went on talking, more and more rapidly, until the words began to overtake one another.

"In the afternoon, the doorbell rang and there was another man in a brown uniform and others with him maybe four or five I don't remember how many and the first one said, 'Heil Hitler, we are coming for the furniture,' and I asked, 'What furniture?' and he said, 'This is the Jew Siegmund Schwartz's apartment,' and I said it was and the man said, 'He won't need them anymore they belong to the German people.' All of them laughed. 'Mrs. Schwartz is still here,' I said, 'she needs her furniture,' and one of them asked, 'What are you doing here in a Jewish house,' 'I am Jewish myself,' I said, and he yelled 'You Jewish sow get out of my way.' He pushed me hard and I fell and they went in all the rooms and started to carry out the furniture. I didn't know what to do, I couldn't speak to Mrs. Schwartz, she was not in her right mind anymore and I was afraid to call the police. They were taking out the piano and one said, 'My wife always wanted a piano,' and the other one looked at me and asked him, 'Did you ever . . .' "

She was groping for a word.

" '. . . did you ever . . . do it with a Jewess? They say they are great in bed.' 'They smell,' said the first one and just as they went out, the nice young man came in with the passport for Mrs. Schwartz. He asked what was going on and I said, 'They're taking our furniture,' and he asked 'Why,' and I said I didn't know and then I told them Mrs. Schwartz was still here but they didn't listen to me. He was very angry and spoke to the S.A. men but they didn't pay any attention to him and he put the passport on the table and said to me, 'I'll call the police.' He went into the living room and when he came out again after a few minutes one of them followed him and asked him, 'What did you do that for you son-of-a-bitch'—that's what he said and another one said, 'Leave him alone, I'll handle the cops.' That was the one the others call *Sturmfuehrer* and then suddenly one of them, the pale one with glasses, saw the urn on the table and asked what it was and said that it would look good in his living room and I said, 'Don't touch it, it's the ashes of Dr. Schwartz.' He said he didn't want the stinking leftovers of an old Jew and tried to lift the lid and I went at him and hit him and the young man who had brought the passport shouted, 'Stop it! Stop it!' He jumped the pale one with the glasses but they were too many. Three of them held the young man and the one they called *Sturmfuehrer* threw me to the floor and they pried the lid off the urn and scattered the ashes on the table. I got up and tried to scrape the ashes together with my hands and then the pale one said, 'Don't dirty your precious Jewish hands. Get me a vacuum cleaner.' The young man broke lose and hit the pale one with his fist. I saw that the *Sturmfuehrer* had his gun out. I screamed but he shot the young man in the back and the young man turned and looked at him and at me amazed-like and he fell. And it was then that the police came."

For a while, none of us was able to move. We did not talk and we did not look at each other. Annemarie Moeller sat in her chair, her head lowered, her hands loosely folded in her lap.

Finally, the inspector rose. He turned to Brause and asked in a hoarse voice, "What do you think of that story?"

I saw in Brause's face that he had been affected too. He hesitated with his answer. Then he said listlessly, "How do I know it's true?"

"Does it sound like a lie?"

Brause paused again before he said, "I couldn't tell."

The inspector raised his voice. "Forget your brown uniform. Tell me, man to man, do you think the girl is lying?"

"No, I don't," Brause said almost inaudibly.

"Thank you," the inspector said. He turned to the policeman. "Bring them in."

The policeman opened the study door and the two S.A. men entered. As soon as Annemarie saw them, she jumped up and cowered behind her chair in a childish attempt to hide.

Dr. Tragendorff leaned forward and watched her closely. *Sturmfuehrer* Scharff asked defiantly, "What kind of trumped-up story did the Jewess tell you?"

He was looking at Brause, but the S.A. man had lowered his eyes.

"I'd like to hear your version first."

"What do you mean by 'version,' Inspector? I'm giving you the facts."

"Go ahead."

"We came to requisition this furniture—"

"On whose authority?"

Scharff stared at him. He touched the holster of his gun. "This is my authority."

The inspector was silent. I had watched him before under similar circumstances. He and I knew that he was going to go down to defeat.

"Is that the gun that killed Manfred Schuller?" he asked.

"Yes. I shot in self-defense. The man—whatever his name—came in and tried to interfere with us. I warned him, but he attacked Storm Trooper Heister. I told him he was under arrest, but he jumped me and I shot him."

"How is it you shot him in the back?"

"I don't know where I hit him."

"Where did the bullet enter the body, Dr. Tragendorff?" asked the inspector.

"The bullet entered the spinal column between the sixth and seventh dorsal vertebrae and pierced the heart. It did not egress."

"I don't understand this medical lingo," Scharff said. He turned to the pale one, Heister. "Do you?"

Heister grinned and shook his head.

"It means Schuller was shot in the back," Inspector Sontag said.

Scharff shrugged. "That's possible."

"When he was jumping you?" the inspector asked.

Sturmfuehrer Scharff was visibly annoyed. "Look, Inspector, what is this grilling? We're not in court here. Storm Trooper Brause, can't you see what this lousy cop is doing?!"

"The girl's story differs from yours, *Sturmfuehrer* Scharff," Brause said.

"What the hell did you expect from a Jewish whore?"

Brause said nothing. Scharff went up to Annemarie Moeller, who was still cowering behind the chair, grabbed her shoulders, and pulled her up. She was whimpering in her terror.

"You're lying, Jew sow!"

The inspector said, "Let her go!"

"I don't take orders from you," said Scharff.

"*Sturmfuehrer* Scharff, don't hurt the girl!" Brause said surprisingly.

Scharff threw the girl across the floor and turned to Brause. "Are you crazy? Do you want me to bring charges against you at headquarters?"

Brause answered listlessly. "No."

"Then, shut up!"

Dr. Tragendorff had rushed to the girl, who lay prostrate on the floor. He knelt beside her. He said, "She should be hospitalized, Inspector. She might be severely injured. X-rays should be taken as soon as possible."

"Can you arrange it?"

The doctor looked at him. "I'll see."

"I'm getting bored with this," Scharff said. "Heister, let's go."

The policeman moved toward them.

"What the hell do *you* want?" Heister said.

The policeman looked at the inspector.

"Storm Trooper Brause, I know I have no jurisdiction over the S.A.," Sontag said. "Can't you do *anything* to bring these troopers of yours to justice?"

Scharff and Heister were watching Brause. He shook his head. "Who knows? The girl might have lied."

The inspector stared at him. "Lied—?"

"Well, she is Jewish, isn't she?" Brause said. He avoided looking at the inspector.

"Heil Hitler," Scharff said. He and Heister left the apartment. There was a pause.

Dr. Tragendorff straightened up. "You mean there's no way of getting those filthy crooks punished?"

"Watch yourself, Doctor," Brause said.

The inspector turned to me. "Dr. Bauer, I wanted you to stay here because you were the only one acquainted with the deceased. Tell me, as an attorney, are there any legal proceedings you could suggest?"

"Legal proceedings don't apply where there is no law," I said. I turned to Brause. "What happened to you? They were both looking at you, and at the critical moment you lost your tongue?"

"I'd rather lose it here than in a concentration camp, Dr. Bauer," said Storm Trooper Brause.

Dr. Tragendorff and I stayed behind after the inspector and the others had left. Dr. Tragendorff helped Annemarie Moeller get up. Her legs were weak, but, together, we managed to walk her, step by step, to her room. The doctor went in with her to examine her more thoroughly.

I waited for him in the hall, seated on one of the two straight chairs. I noticed a small amount of dust on the floor. It looked like dust. I kept staring at it. I couldn't avert my eyes. A foul odor seemed to effuse from it. It grew stronger and stronger until it enveloped me like a poisonous cloud.

"Dr. Bauer, do you feel all right?"

"Yes. How is the girl?"

"It's not as bad as I feared. Nothing seems to be broken, although I would need X-rays to be perfectly sure. She's in shock, but she's coming out of it. She has great energy and courage."

"Yes, she has."

"I wanted to get a nurse for Mrs. Schwartz, but Miss Moeller insists on taking care of her herself. I'll be here in the morning to see how the two of them are making out. Shall we go?"

Outside we walked a few blocks together. Dr. Tragendorff said, "To be honest, I wouldn't know what hospital to take Miss Moeller to. She is Jewish and—"

"I'm sure it's safe to tell you . . ."

"Tell me what?"

"She's not Jewish."

He stopped. "She isn't?"

"No."

"Then why the hell does she pretend—"

"I think you'll find a simple explanation, Dr. Tragendorff. If she were Aryan, she couldn't stay with Mrs. Schwartz. She loves those people."

He shook his head. "That's unbelievable, isn't it?"

We walked in silence. When we reached the corner where we had to separate, we shook hands. He said, "How is it possible for anyone who lives here—now—to retain feelings like loyalty and compassion?" He looked at me. "Do you think there's hope?"

May 5th.

I spent most of the night before last talking to Klaus and trying to get in touch with Manfred Schuller's parents, who live in Osnabrock, North Dakota. It was very hard on them to get this kind of message via long distance phone call. I thought a telegram would have been worse, though.

Late in the evening Karin phoned me and reminded me that we had opera tickets for the first Berlin performance of Richard Strauss's *Arabella.* That is tonight.

May 6th.

It is early in the morning. I could not sleep. That is easy to understand. I have never been so excited. Maybe now everything will take a turn for the better.

But: I must change. Karin is right. I must change. I am much too soft. Too weak. And I am always depressed. That has to stop.

Karin was waiting for me in my apartment when I came home from the office. She wore a silver-colored evening dress. She looked radiant. Her expression changed, however, when she saw my face.

"You're in a bad mood again," she said.

"I'm all right."

She came to me and embraced me. We held each other tightly. Then she moved her head back and looked at me.

"Darling, you're not the same man anymore. Not the man I'm in love with. You're always depressed—"

"I'm sorry, Karin."

"We're going to the opera tonight. Together. A new opera by your favorite composer. What's wrong with that? Can't you enjoy anything anymore?"

She was right. I knew she was right. But how can I enjoy myself when the stink of human flesh is in my nostrils and when my eyes see nothing but tormented faces and scattered ashes? Can I just walk away from that? Round the corner and forget?

Yes, I can. I must. Millions of people all around me know what I know, live through the same experiences. They turn their heads and don't see what they don't want to see. They accept the new way of life. I must learn to live as they live. I am a German. The Germans are a tough race. A strong race. Maybe the weakness in myself stems from that ancient forefather of mine, the great sentimentalist, the Jew.

"I was waiting to hear from you," Karin said. "But you didn't call."

"When was that?"

"On Wednesday. Finally, I went out with Margie and Carl Adriani and—a friend of his."

"Is the friend nice?"

"Yes. I had dinner with him last night."

"I'd better go and change," I said. "It's late."

I passed the door to Hanna's room and she came out and asked me if she could have the evening off. A friend of one of her brothers was in town and she would like to see him.

"What do you hear from Paul?"

"Nothing. But that's my fault," Hanna said. "I never answered his letter."

"You didn't?"

"No."

She did not look at me.

"Have a good time tonight," I said.

Karin and I had a quick drink before we left. As we were waiting for the elevator, I asked, "What's your new friend like? Short, tall, dark—?"

"Blond and tall," Karin said. "His name is Theo Holt. He's a member of the Gestapo."

"Oh, is he really?"

"I know what you're thinking," Karin said. "He isn't that kind of a Nazi, believe me. His best friend used to be a Jew."

"And where is his best friend now?"

"I don't know."

The elevator arrived and we stepped in. In the taxi Karin took my arm and held my hand. By the time we got to the opera, I was in a much better mood. Then, on entering the foyer, Karin said, "Margie and Carl are going to sit next to us."

We had just passed the ticket collector and I stopped.

"Why didn't you tell me?"

"I was afraid you wouldn't go."

We moved on. "You were right."

"But I know how much you like Strauss's music, and it was Carl who got the tickets."

We were walking down the middle aisle. I was thoroughly upset. I did not want to see Carl Adriani again. Not now, not after Klaus had discussed my—problem with him. I could still leave. All I had to do was turn around and—

It was too late. Margie had seen us and was waving at us gaily. Carl Adriani rose.

Our seats were in the sixth row center. We shook hands. Adriani looked splendid in his S.S. gala uniform. Margie's face was flushed. Obviously she was proud to be seen with him.

The orchestra was still tuning. In the strings I could hear some of the Strauss phrases. Karin bent forward and turned her face to me. At least I thought she did. Her eyes went past my face, searching for someone in the audience. When she realized I was watching her, she smiled and leaned back with a sigh. I looked around. Evening dresses. White and black ties. Brown and black uniforms. Two rows behind us, a man nodded and the woman next to him blew me a kiss. Konrad and Barbara Willman.

The tuning of the orchestra petered out. Stopped.

Silence.

Then applause growing stronger as the conductor entered the pit. He stepped up to the stand and bowed to the audience once, briefly. He turned, opened the score, raised his baton. Slowly. Moved his head from left to right, checking the readiness of his musicians. Gave the downbeat.

The curtain rose.

For a while I was engrossed in listening to the transparent fabric of Strauss's orchestration and to the current of gliding and soaring melodies. Then I happened to look at the seat ahead of me.

143 «

A massive neck emerged from a brown uniform coat. The neck passed into the back of the head in a straight line up to the crew cut. Two large ears stuck out like a pair of solid hafts. The flesh of the neck bulged over the collar in a round doubling fold.

I stared at this neck spellbound. It was the most brutish, pachydermatous piece of human anatomy I had ever faced. I felt my body growing rigid and hot with hatred. This neck had tortured, burned, and murdered. My fury seized my hands and clenched them into fists. Raised them. Something touched my arm. Somebody. Karin. I moved my head and saw her eyes on me, eyes full of fright. She took her handkerchief and wiped my forehead gently. My body shook. For a moment, I was unconscious, then I began to hear the music again. The voice of two sisters, free and easy . . . climbing in a surging crescendo to the summit of the melody.

I held Karin's handkerchief in my hand. It was wringing wet. I looked at her. Her eyes were full of fear, but her face was calmer. Her mouth showed the trace of a smile. She leaned back.

Once more I glanced at the neck. It was ugly and fat. I looked at the stage.

At the end of the first act, the applause was strong. I asked Karin if she had liked the music. She nodded, but she averted her eyes. I said that I had suddenly felt sick. She nodded again and rose. Margie and Adriani got up too. As we reached the aisle, Adriani whispered to Margie and she went off with Karin. Adriani turned to me. "Let's talk for a minute, Dr. Bauer."

He pointed to the seat next to him. I sat down, feeling apprehensive. He said, "Opera bores me. I like the theater. The German classics. Shakespeare. Ibsen. I used to lecture on Kleist when I was teaching literature."

I must have looked amazed. He added without a smile, "Don't let the uniform fool you. I used to be an intellectual. A *German* intellectual."

» 144

A fat man in an S.A. uniform squeezed his body through the row ahead of us, aiming for the aisle. I recognized the neck. He stopped in front of Adriani and turned. His face was one big subservient smile.

"Heil Hitler, Carl."

Adriani glanced at him. "Heil Hitler." His tone was cold.

"I hope you're enjoying the performance," the S.A. man said. He was so anxious to please Adriani, he was sweating from the effort.

"I'll have somebody contact your office tomorrow," Adriani said.

"May I respectfully ask—"

"Tomorrow."

He turned back to me. The man bowed twice before he went on. I felt someone looking at me and saw Konrad and Barbara in the aisle, trying to catch my eye. I shook my head. They left.

Adriani asked, "Is Konrad Willman a friend of yours?"

"Yes."

"You know that he's Ludwig Butler's ex-brother-in-law?"

"Yes, of course."

"How close are you to Butler?"

"We've been friends for a long time. Why do you ask?"

"Butler left Germany the morning after the party at Victor Brandt's. Did he tell you that night that he was going to leave?"

"No."

There was a pause. He did not look at me.

"Have you seen Willman recently?"

"I was at his house a few days ago," I said. "Not at *his* house. He and Barbara were staying at her mother's home."

"Then you've met Mrs. Teilhaber."

"Yes."

"A remarkable woman," Adriani said.

I tried not to show how alarmed I was. Was it possible that she *had* denounced her own daughter, Konrad, and—by implication—me? I missed Adriani's next remark and he had to repeat it.

"I said, Karin looks lovely tonight."

"Yes, she does."

He bent down to pick up the program which had dropped to the floor.

"If you don't mind my being personal, I think you are much too lenient with Karin. A man should always remember Nietzsche: 'When you approach a woman, never forget your whip!' "

"That was one of his pseudo-philosophical dictums," I said. "You would hardly apply it to your private life."

It was not meant to be a question, but he answered it.

"It applies to Margie, too. The only difference is that she is an American and the United States is a matriarchal society. The women have the money. And where the money is, there is the power. That's one of the reasons the American democracy is weak and sick. I believe—"

He interrupted himself. "Well, we might discuss that at some other time, at leisure. I suppose you know that your partner, Klaus von Isenberg, spoke to me in your behalf."

"He told me he did."

I tried to appear casual and cool, but Adriani was not fooled for a moment. He knew the stakes as well as I did.

He said, "I've seen your papers and I've also checked your background."

"My family has been—"

He cut in. "That is not what I am talking about, Dr. Bauer. I am referring to your personal record. You were a member of the Democratic Party."

"Yes. That is true."

"Left of center."

I nodded.

"What are your politics today, Dr. Bauer?"

"I am a German, Mr. Adriani. This is my home. My roots are here."

He was silent for a long time. The first bell shrilled, announcing the beginning of the second act.

Finally he said, "To some party members, your answer would be less than satisfactory, Dr. Bauer. I must say that I have always been suspicious of people who converted to National Socialism the minute we came to power. I prefer a sincere attitude. A true evaluation and self-inspired conversion."

The audience began to file back. Adriani glanced at the aisles. "I shall make it short, Dr. Bauer. People whose judgment I value think very highly of you. My personal impression confirms that. I believe that you are honest. I am deviating in your case from the literal interpretation of the law and will inform Dr. von Isenberg of my ruling."

He rose. Margie and Karin were entering our row. I got up too. Adriani shook hands with me.

"Good luck to you."

"Thank you very much, Mr. Adriani."

When we were seated again, Karin looked at me inquiringly. I nodded and she gave me an elated smile.

"I'm happy," she said.

"So am I."

The lights began to dim. I tried to listen to the second act, but I couldn't. I was too excited. Now everything would be all right. My future was secure.

Then I remembered Adriani's question about Butler and Willman. Barbara's mother must have gone to the Gestapo. I wondered if the Willmans knew about it. They were in the audience tonight. Maybe I could speak to them, warn them—no. I couldn't. Not here where Adriani could see us. Thanks to Klaus, I had achieved what I had wanted. It would be stupid of me to take any kind of risk. I must avoid talking to Barbara and Konrad.

Karin squeezed my hand. Her eyes were on the stage. She was listening to the love duet of Arabella and Mandrika. For a moment, I took in the beauty of the melody as it surged to a climax. Karin turned to me and smiled. Suddenly it was not her face anymore. Her nose and mouth shrank and shriveled. The eyes crawled back in their caves. What I saw was the skull. I could not forget the skull.

Karin saw the sudden change in my expression and recoiled. I closed my eyes to blot out the image of the skull. I wanted no part of it. I was fed up with my emotional rampages. I had to stop them. I was not involved. *Obergruppenfuehrer* Carl Adriani, chief of the "Office of the Protection of the Blood," had given me his sanction. I was a German. I was not a Jew. The skull, the ashes of Siegmund Schwartz, the stink of the burning human flesh—all that had to be ousted from my consciousness. I owed that to myself.

At the end of the second act, Karin and I rose. Margie and Adriani remained in their seats. Karin was silent. I took her arm. "I'm sorry, Karin."

She didn't respond.

"I don't feel well tonight. But—"

She raised her head. "Something's wrong with you, Hans. I'm scared."

"Don't be. I can explain it to you—"

Walking slowly in the middle aisle behind the pushing crowd, I saw that Barbara and Konrad had risen too. We went upstairs to the lounge, and after a few minutes, the Willmans caught up with us. The four of us exchanged generalities and talked about *Arabella*. Konrad drew me aside. Immediately I became apprehensive.

"I'd like to ask you a question, Hans," he said.

"Not here."

"Nobody can hear us."

"Call me at home."

"I just saw you talking to Adriani—"

"Not now, Konrad!" I repeated. He was getting very angry.

"What the hell is the matter with you?"

"Nothing."

I turned and saw Margie and Carl Adriani enter the lounge. With them was a young man in S.S. uniform. I asked Konrad, "How do you like the conductor?"

Konrad said nothing. He had seen Adriani too.

"Why don't you join us?" Karin called.

We went back to Barbara and Karin. Konrad looked at me and shook his head.

"Let's go back to our seats," I said.

"Why? We have at least ten more minutes," Karin said.

I noticed she was smiling in the direction of Margie and Adriani. The young S.S. officer was smiling too.

"I'll meet you downstairs," I said.

As I was passing the other group, Adriani called, "Dr. Bauer, I'd like you to meet a friend of mine, *Obersturmfuehrer* Theo Holt."

"Heil Hitler, Dr. Bauer," Theo Holt said.

Adriani was watching me.

"Heil Hitler," I said.

After the opera, we went to Horcher's, the most fashionable restaurant in Berlin, which had become the favorite hangout of the Nazi hierarchy. Adriani had asked Theo Holt to join us, and Karin sat between Holt and myself. As he was talking to her softly, her head turned toward him. Margie said to me from across the table, "I liked *Arabella* very much. Did you?"

149 «

"Yes, I did."

"Why wasn't the government represented, Carl?" she asked. "Strauss is in good standing with the party, isn't he?"

Adriani nodded. "Hugo von Hofmannsthal wrote the book. He was a Jew."

"But he's dead, isn't he?"

Theo Holt looked up. "A dead Jew is better than a live one. But he is still a Jew."

He turned back to Karin, who kept on ignoring me. I saw Adriani and Margie watching us and I began to feel awkward. I asked Karin, "Which act did you like best?"

She moved her head a fraction. "The second one."

The waiter was pouring champagne. Margie said, "I haven't seen you since you came back from St. Moritz, Hans. You used to come around—"

"I've been trying to catch up with my work," I said.

"Karin?"

"Yes, Margie—"

"We must make a date with you and Hans. For drinks or dinner. I've never been to Switzerland. I want to—"

Karin cut in. "Hans has not been feeling well."

There was a pause. Carl Adriani raised his glass. "A toast, Dr. Bauer. To Nietzsche."

We drank. Margie asked, "Why Nietzsche—who is he?"

"He was a profound philosopher," Adriani said. "He knew a lot about women. Don't you agree, Karin?"

"Agree with what?" Karin asked.

After a while, I pleaded a severe headache, apologized to Margie and Carl, and got up. Adriani and Holt rose. I shook hands with everybody. Including Karin.

"Thank you again, Mr. Adriani," I said.

"You are very welcome, Dr. Bauer. Heil Hitler."

"Heil Hitler," I said.

Karin turned around and looked at me with a mocking smile. She did not speak.

A car with the S.A. emblem stood in front of my apartment building, a driver at the wheel, waiting. As I entered, I saw Mr. Heiliger emerge from his ground floor living room, flanked by two brownshirts who were holding on to his arms. His legs dragged. His feet scraped the floor. He yelled, "The boy is lying! He always lies! I just contributed twenty-five marks to the party!"

Another S.A. man came out of the apartment, hauling the large box filled with pictures which I had seen Heiliger carry out of the Gutmans' apartment.

The door was half open and I heard a scream from inside. I walked in. Mrs. Heiliger was holding a big kitchen knife in her hand and had cornered her son, Heinz, who wore his Hitler Youth uniform. The boy was screaming. "Mrs. Heiliger!" I shouted.

She turned and Heinz took the opportunity and ran, colliding with me. I pushed him outside and closed the door. Mrs. Heiliger dropped the knife and stood shaking.

"That swine, that goddamned swine!" she said. "His own father! I'll kill him if he ever shows up again! I'll kill him!"

"What happened, Mrs. Heiliger?"

She stared at me, but I don't think she recognized me.

"That fourteen-year-old bastard—denouncing his father! And Philip loved that scum!" She rushed to the door and stopped.

"I don't know what to do," she said. "What am I going to do?"

Suddenly, her strength seemed to die away. She staggered to a chair and sat down. In a muffled voice, she said, "You're Dr. Bauer, aren't you? You're an attorney."

"Yes, I am."

"Can you please help us? Please help us, Dr. Bauer!"

"Tell me what happened."

"He's a good man, Philip is. A good husband. A good provider. He loves that fat son-of-a-bitch. He was so proud of that bastard."

"What did Heinz do?"

She didn't answer.

"It's almost one o'clock now," I said. "Tomorrow morning—"

"No! Not tomorrow morning! Right now! Tomorrow will be too late. Now, Dr. Bauer, please!"

I pulled up a chair and sat across from her at the table. She took a deep breath.

"You remember the Gutmans, don't you? They were old people. Nice enough. But they were Jews."

"Yes."

"They're in Holland now. In Amsterdam."

"I know. Your husband told me. He was going to send them their family pictures to—"

"Family pictures, oh yes! He was so stupid. He wanted the money!"

"What money?"

"The Gutmans gave Philip a hundred one-thousand mark bills in cash. Ten of them were for us and he was supposed to hide the other ninety in the picture frames and send the whole box to the Gutmans. By last night he had opened the frames, put the money in, and nailed most of them shut. He'd done a good job. He thought it was safe. So did I. He was almost finished: just a couple of pictures left and three more bills. He printed the Gutman address on the box and put everything in his little workroom—just for the night, you know? And then Heinz—Heinz must have sneaked in early in the morning and figured out what Philip was doing. He went to the S.A. and they told the Gestapo."

I remembered Mr. Heiliger's words: "He's growing up in the right spirit. That's why the Fuehrer wants them young."

"Can you help us?" Mrs. Heiliger asked.

"I don't know. There's nothing I can do tonight."

"It's hopeless, isn't it?" she said. "I know it's hopeless."

May 7th.

Today is Sunday, the day of rest. I want to calm down. Hanna is off this weekend, so I'm alone in the apartment. I had a late breakfast and read the Sunday paper, like I used to, in the old days. I know my life has changed and that I must change my thinking accordingly. I am accustomed to analyzing a situation step by step, but I haven't done that recently. I have been afraid something would go wrong, that I would be an outcast in my own country. Now that fear has gone. I am a German in a Germany ruled by Adolf Hitler and his Nazi Party. I must conform to that reality.

I was interrupted by Grete's phone call.

It is late evening.

I am home again.

I know the instinct for self-preservation is the driving force that governs every human being . . . but sometimes it hits obstacles, rooted in the individual makeup of a creature . . . obstacles of an irrational, emotional nature that block its natural tendency to safeguard itself.

I said that I had to make up my mind to stop my "emotional rampages." The trouble is, the events that trigger them don't stop.

As soon as I left Horcher's Friday night, I was confronted with Mr. Heiliger's arrest by the Gestapo: the arrest caused by his own son . . . a fourteen-year-old boy denouncing his own father. Yesterday morning I learned what happened to Mr. and Mrs. Heiliger. After that I met Dr. Tragendorff. Today Grete called and I spent the next ten hours with her. Then Karin came—

How the hell can one cope with so many drastic experiences without getting emotionally upset?

Yesterday, Saturday, I had a morning appointment with Klaus at the office.

As I was leaving the elevator in my building, I found the door to the Heiligers' apartment wide open. I wondered why and knocked on the door . . . rang the bell. No answer. I walked in.

The lights were on in every room. I called Mrs. Heiliger and knocked again before I entered the bedroom. It was empty. So was the adjoining bathroom. All over the apartment were pictures of the Fuehrer, of Goering and Goebbels, and in the boy's room, a large photograph of Baldur von Schirach, the head of the Hitler Youth. Above his bed was the sign LISTEN TO YOUR NEIGHBOR'S TALK and a huge swastika flag.

Mrs. Heiliger must have left in great haste. She had always impressed me as a very meticulous person. It was not like her to leave the door open and all the lights turned on.

Klaus was at the office when I arrived. We were alone. Saturday is not a working day. I told him first of my talk with Adriani. He already knew about that: Adriani had called him at home. Klaus told me how happy he was that this unpleasant problem had been solved. We didn't talk about it at great length. For some reason, we both felt embarrassed when the subject came up. However, we were now ready to reorganize the office staff and to discuss the question of a potential third partner. Magda and Hedi had made out lists of prospective candidates for office clerk and secretary. Hedi had added a note confirming that all persons on the lists held the necessary papers testifying to their Aryan descent.

Klaus had some names of attorneys jotted down who might be interested in joining our law firm. Only a few of them were acceptable. Some had been admitted to the bar within the last few weeks, qualified only by the length of their membership in the Nazi Party. Most had taken over established practices of Jewish lawyers who had either left the country or been disposed of. I knew only one of the listed lawyers personally: August Hammer, a man with an excellent reputation and a good personality.

We had some sandwiches sent up. While we were eating, I told Klaus about Mr. Heiliger. He asked, "Have you done anything about it?"

"No. What could I have done?"

"Well—you could have tried to inquire, carefully, of course, just to be able to tell Mrs. Heiliger what had happened to her husband. They'd never tell her anything."

I shook my head. "I don't want to get involved."

Klaus chewed for a while before he said, "A question concerning a man's whereabouts doesn't get you involved, Hans.

You have a perfectly legitimate reason for it. He's your apartment house manager and he's disappeared."

"I wouldn't know whom to call."

He looked at me. "Let me try. That woman must be going out of her mind."

I said nothing. There was an unexpressed reproach in his attitude which I resented. He got up. "I'll make a quick phone call," he said and left for his office.

When he came in again he nodded and said, "I've set it in motion. I hope they'll get back to me." He crumpled the wrappings of his sandwich and threw it in the wastebasket. Then he hesitated for a moment. "I hate to bring this up, Hans . . . but Adriani mentioned the money he expects from us."

"How much?"

"One hundred thousand marks."

"For Christ's sake—"

"A voluntary contribution to the welfare fund for the National Socialist Party."

"He's crazy."

"He told me confidentially that your friend Victor Brandt paid two hundred and fifty thousand."

"Two hundred and fifty—" I started to laugh. "Margie told Karin that she refused to go to bed with him until Adriani agreed to attend Victor's party."

Klaus started to laugh too. "He's hardly the type to let himself get blackmailed by a woman, is he?"

For a moment, it was like the old days, the two of us happy, relaxed. Then we remembered the subject at hand.

"About the money—" I said.

"Yes, the money."

I thought for a moment.

"This is my personal affair. The firm has nothing to do with it."

"I wouldn't say that, Hans. The fact that you're able to continue here is of great value to the office."

"Thank you. But Klaus—this money is my personal responsibility anyway. I insist on that."

"All right, I'll make you a proposition," Klaus said. "Take whatever money you can spare out of your personal account, and then cover the rest with a bank loan—for which the firm will offer the collateral. Don't answer me now. Think it over. Now, let's go to work. What's on next week's calendar?"

We discussed one case, which we both thought could and should be settled out of court. Then I read aloud: "Samuel Rosenthal versus Eberhardt Schmidt."

I looked at Klaus. He said, "Forget it."

"I don't know that case."

"You were doing acrobatics in St. Moritz," Klaus said. "Siegmund Schwartz prepared the case. In February. Eberhardt Schmidt was the junior partner of Samuel Rosenthal, Inc., Interstate Transfer and Storage Company. Rosenthal is a Jew. Schmidt is a party member. On February sixth, Schmidt announced he was taking over the company and that Rosenthal was out. Rosenthal's suit involves a demand for accounting and an injunction against Schmidt. Rosenthal was our client—but you can't represent a client who's disappeared."

"Why did we ever take the case?"

"Remember, it happened in early February, Hans. It was supposed to be a test case. At that time, nobody knew that gangsterism would be legalized."

"Gangsterism—if anybody ever heard us—"

Klaus looked at me. "You and I are not 'anybody.' "

"I know. But we must be more careful."

"Careful between the two of us? You must be joking."

I said nothing. I didn't know what was right or wrong anymore. Shortly afterward, he went to his office and started to work on a brief, and Dr. Tragendorff called and asked me to meet him late in the afternoon. He sounded very upset.

An hour later, Klaus came back in and sat down. "I've just heard from Franz, my contact with the party. The one I asked to investigate the status of your Mr. Heiliger. He said he was sorry, but he was too late. The man is dead."

I had not liked Heiliger, but that came as a shock.

"Franz said it would have been impossible to interfere. Heiliger tried to smuggle out ninety thousand marks to a Jew who'd gone abroad. He'd accepted ten thousand marks as a bribe. That rates as a 'crime against the state.' "

"How did he die, Klaus?"

"He was taken before the so-called people's court in the cellar of an empty building. The 'trial' lasted all of five minutes. He was shot right then and there."

After a moment I said, "At least they didn't torture him."

Klaus did not move. He looked at me. "There's more. It seems that Mrs. Heiliger found his body in the cellar where it had been left. She had been searching for her husband all night." He paused and took a deep breath. "There were rats in the cellar. When the woman saw the condition the body was in, she went berserk. She found an old, corroded sickle and ran out into the street. She killed one brownshirt and wounded three others before she got killed herself. The *Sturmfuehrer* who reported the . . . incident quoted her last words: 'That goddamned fat bastard.' "

"She meant her fourteen-year-old son. He denounced his father."

For a long time we were both silent.

"He's an orphan now," Klaus said. "And he'll get a promotion in the Hitler Youth."

I met Dr. Tragendorff at Mampe on the Kurfuerstendamm. I was a few minutes late and I looked for him outdoors first, and then inside, among the booths. He was in the back. On the table stood a half-empty beer mug and a bowl of pretzels. He nodded at me when I sat down. He did not smile.

"I've been sitting here for more than an hour," he said. "This is my fourth beer. I'm well on my way to getting drunk."

I ordered a whiskey and soda.

"I'm sorry to incon—inconvenience you, Dr. Bauer. I thought I should give you some facts of life. I presume that you understand the meaning of the word 'facts.' "

"Of course."

"According to the dictionary, a fact is a thing done or performed, something that has really occurred or is the case, a datum of experience as distinguished from conclusions."

My whiskey came and he raised his mug. "Heil Hitler."

"Heil Hitler," I said.

He drank deeply and set his mug down. "Recently, Dr. Bauer, the facts have assumed a character that contradicts the very definition of the word. They have overstepped the borderline of reality and established themselves as a new type of fact, 'experiences' in some land of incubus."

He raised his head to get the waiter's attention. With a sweeping gesture of his right hand, he stuck his forefinger into the empty mug.

"You want me to tell you about some of the neoteric facts?"

"Please do."

Four brownshirts came in and sat down in the booth next to us.

"Undoubtedly you do remember Mrs. Helen Schwartz, the widow of the Jewish attorney, Siegmund Schwartz, who shot himself and suffered a heart attack after his death."

"Don't speak so loud," I said.

"Thank you," Tragendorff said to the waiter who had brought him another beer. One of the brownshirts turned around and looked at us. Tragendorff raised his mug and toasted him. "Heil Hitler."

The four men answered in unison, "Heil Hitler."

"Give the devil his due," Tragendorff said.

I put my hand on his arm. I whispered, "Please be careful. You'll get us into trouble."

He nodded. "Speaking about trouble. I visited Mrs. Schwartz several times. She has no other doctor and I don't give a damn whether she's Jewish or not. She's sick and needs a physician."

The S.A. man turned again and stared at Tragendorff.

"Heil Hitler," Tragendorff said.

This time there was no answer. I whispered, "If you don't lower your voice, I'm going to leave."

Dr. Tragendorff changed to a stage whisper, which didn't improve the situation.

"The last time I saw her, her pulse was slow. Much too slow. Her speech almost inaudible and utterly inco—incoherent. Annemarie Moeller was there, you remember her, don't you, the girl who said she was Jewish because—"

He noticed the brownshirt watching him closely and thrust his head in the S.A. man's face.

"What is it, sir?"

"I'm listening," the S.A. man said. He was a sturdy type, with a red face and a pug nose.

"May I inform you, sir, that this is a private conversation between two German citizens?"

"You don't talk like a German," the brownshirt said.

"How would you know?" Tragendorff said. "You don't *look* like a German to me."

The whole room went quiet. I rose. "Let's go."

"Just a moment," the S.A. man said. He turned back to Tragendorff. "What do I look like to you?" he asked.

"The man's drunk," I said to the brownshirt. "Let me take him home."

"He's not too drunk to answer my question. What do I look like to you?"

"Like a Jew," Tragendorff said and burst out laughing.

The four brownshirts shot up and stood bolt upright. The first one crossed to our table. I pulled Tragendorff's arm and he came to his feet, but the brownshirt smashed his fist into the doctor's face. Tragendorff stumbled and fell. There was blood on his mouth.

"Don't hit him, he's drunk," I pleaded. "He doesn't know what he's saying. He's been a member of the party for ten years."

"Heil Hitler," Tragendorff said.

I motioned to the waiter, who had been standing close by, watching. He handed me the check and I paid. The S.A. man had not returned to his booth. One of the other brownshirts took him by his shoulders.

"What the hell, Mallinger!" he said. "The guy's smashed."

"He called me a Jew."

"Anybody who looks at you knows he had to be joking," I said. "I'll take him home and put him in a cold shower."

"Let him go," the other brownshirt said. "Forget it. You hit him, now forget it."

He propelled his friend back to the booth next to us. I dragged Dr. Tragendorff from his seat and walked him out.

In the taxi Tragendorff said, "I'm sorry." He was holding a handkerchief to the right corner of his mouth. His face looked haggard and pale. "I'm almost sober now. It hurts like hell."

"You could have gotten us both killed," I said.

"I should have hit him back," Tragendorff said. "I was the best amateur middleweight in the Medical Association. I could have laid him flat. That fat fag had no punch."

I looked at his face. "It'll do till the next time."

"Where are we going?"

"To my place," I said.

"Don't, stop the car. I've got two more house calls to make."

161 «

"You couldn't possibly do it in your condition," I said. "You can call your office from my house."

He refused to take a shower, so we went into my study and I made a pot of strong coffee for him. Tragendorff was sobering up fast. After he'd called his office and told his nurse where he could be reached, he hung up and stood for a moment without moving. Finally he said, "I must apologize to you. There's no excuse for my irrational behavior. I guess it's been too much for me. I phoned you because I wanted to talk to you. I had to talk to somebody I trusted."

"Go ahead."

He went behind the desk and sat down. I had drawn the curtains and it was dark in the room. Only the desk lamp was lit and the circle of light hit Tragendorff's long-fingered hands, which played nervously with the paraphernalia on the desk until he folded his hands tightly in an effort to calm himself.

"When I saw Mrs. Schwartz's condition," he began, "I consulted a colleague of mine, a neurologist, and his urgent advice was to hospitalize Mrs. Schwartz immediately. He diagnosed her case—I am going to use simple terms, Dr. Bauer—as traumatic neurosis, caused by a severe emotional shock. This is curable, but it could take a long time. Annemarie Moeller became hysterical. Mrs. Schwartz had just received her affidavit from her sister in Chile. She had applied for a visa. If she had to go to a hospital now, she would never get the visa. I told Annemarie that in her present condition Mrs. Schwartz was ineligible for any visa to any foreign country anyway, but the girl wouldn't listen to me. She threw herself across Mrs. Schwartz's bed and refused to move. My colleague had left; I didn't know what to do. I went to another room and phoned some of the hospitals. None of the ones I'm connected with take Jewish patients. There's only one Jewish hospital left in Berlin equipped to deal with neurological cases, and that one is overcrowded and understaffed. I argued with them, used my Aryan authority, and finally got Mrs. Schwartz admitted. Then I asked the hospital to send an ambulance and went back to Mrs. Schwartz's bedroom."

He paused and leaned forward. His face, with the small mustache and the shock of blond hair, emerged from the darkness and entered the circle of light. Dr. Tragendorff is a young man, but his face was heavily lined. It didn't look young anymore.

I poured a fresh cup of coffee and set it next to him on the desk. He smiled. "I'm all right."

"Yes, I know."

He waited until I was back on the couch where he could not see me. That seemed to make him feel better. He continued, "Annemarie stood in the door to the bedroom, silent, her eyes pleading. I shook my head and went to the bed. Mrs. Schwartz lay there, still. She had no idea who I was. 'It is good to die,' she said. 'After the music is over, I'd like to die.' I said, 'Don't talk about dying.' She frowned in an effort to listen to me. It was as if she were trying to capture the sound of words. Maybe it was the sound of music from far away. Annemarie came up to me and bent over the bed. She wore a loose little dress. I could see her breasts. They were lovely and I wanted to touch them and I hated myself for thinking that at that moment . . . but I couldn't help getting excited when I saw her breasts. 'I ordered an ambulance,' I said. Annemarie began to cry. Mrs. Schwartz turned her head and said something in Hebrew which I didn't understand. I asked Annemarie, but she didn't understand it either. She was still crying. I put my arm around her shoulders and said it was best for the woman to be in a hospital. Annemarie shook her head violently and said, 'They're going to kill her. I know it.' I felt her body and got more and more aroused, but I was ashamed of my feelings and moved away from the girl. Suddenly, Mrs. Schwartz rose in her bed and screamed, 'Come back! Come back!' Annemarie brought her face close to hers and said, 'He'll come back, Mrs. Schwartz. He'll come back.' The doorbell rang. The girl straightened up, trembling in fear. I left the bedroom and walked through the empty hall to open the door. But it was not the ambulance—in fact, Dr. Bauer, the ambulance never came—it was *Sturmfuehrer* Scharff, the one without a chin, you remember him, don't you? He had come with his aide, I forget his name. They demanded to see Annemarie Moeller, and then one of the scum recognized me and asked me what I was doing there. Was the Jewess still there? And wasn't I an Aryan doctor? I was afraid for the women and I was afraid for myself. I said, 'Mrs. Schwartz is in danger of dying and I cannot let her die.' And *Sturmfuehrer* Scharff asked, 'Why not?' At that moment, Annemarie came in the hall. She stopped as she saw the uniforms and turned to leave. 'That's her!' the brownshirt said. The *Sturmfuehrer* went after the girl and took her arm and hauled her back into the room. 'You lied to us,' he said. 'I've checked your papers. You're not Jewish.' She said, 'But I am,' and the *Sturmfuehrer* started to laugh and said, 'You're a sexy slut, but you're an Aryan in a Jewish home and you are under arrest.' The girl freed herself and spit at him and he laughed louder and the other S.A. man came from behind and grabbed her buttocks and Annemarie screamed and hit him. I stood there not doing anything, Dr. Bauer. There were two of them and they had guns and I was scared. Too scared to move. I was shaking, but I knew that if I protested, it would be the end of me. Annemarie looked at me. Once. Then they knocked her down and carried her out. I thought I would go insane. I must have moved toward them without knowing it because one of the brutes pointed his gun at me. And I stood still. They went."

His voice had come out of the darkness, speaking very fast in an unbroken stream of words. When he stopped, I could hear the heavy sound of his breathing.

"Anything you did would have meant suicide," I said.

"I know that," he answered. "That doesn't keep me from being ashamed of myself."

I wanted to speak, but he continued: "I went back to Mrs. Schwartz. She was lying in the same position as before. I looked at her face closely. Her skin was flaccid and gray. Her lower lip was loose, the mouth half open. Her pupils were enlarged. I don't think she could see me, but she seemed to feel somebody's proximity. She said, 'The boat will leave soon.' I took her right hand and felt her pulse. It was slow, irregular, and very weak. I wondered if she had eaten. I found the kitchen and saw a cup of broth, a dish of cereal, and a glass of milk. I took the cup of broth into the bedroom, raised Mrs. Schwartz's shoulders, and tried to make her drink. She pressed her lips together. I talked to her, but it was obvious she didn't understand me. I took the broth back into the kitchen. When I returned to the bedroom, I found Mrs. Schwartz sitting up in bed. I tried to make her lie down, but she resisted. She seemed determined to get up. I stepped back and watched her. She rose slowly, moved her legs out and down, and slid easily into her soft slippers, then propped her hands against the bed and straightened up. She stood. Then she began to walk, bent forward, with an eager expression on her face. Her body seemed to ask for more speed than her legs could supply. The door was open. She walked through the corridor and I followed her. She went to the hall and from there to her husband's study, where she opened the door and stopped. Her body was swaying. I was afraid she would fall, so I stood behind her without touching. She looked around the empty room and seemed to realize that the furniture was gone. She walked to the place where the desk must have been and turned her head, bewildered. Then suddenly she fell to the floor—except that as I rushed to her, I realized that she hadn't fallen. Obviously, she was where she wanted to be. She wouldn't move from the spot. The telephone was in one corner. I picked it up and called the Jewish hospital again. They were very sorry, they said, no ambulance was available. Maybe they'd have one in a couple of hours. I phoned my office and was told about two urgent calls, one an emergency. I had to leave. Mrs. Schwartz lay cowering on the floor, staring at something on the wall. I had no idea what she was staring at. The wall was empty. I knelt next to her and tried to get her attention. I said that I had to leave and that I would tell the manager to watch for the ambulance and let the attendants in. I knew she didn't understand what I was saying, but there was nothing else I could do. I said I would come by later and make sure she'd been picked up. Her face was lifeless. As I left, I could feel the silence of the room and the woman's loneliness. . . . Late in the evening, I went to the house again. The manager said there had been no ambulance for the Jewish woman. He came upstairs with me. He rang the bell. Nobody answered. He got his master key and started unlocking the entrance door . . . but the door was open. We looked in every room, but we couldn't find Mrs. Schwartz. She was not at the hospital. She had disappeared."

Long after Dr. Tragendorff had left, I sat in my study unable to decide what to do with myself. Something was closing in on me, I didn't know what.

I thought of Tragendorff, of his shame, his feeling of guilt. For some reason not clear to me, I felt guilty myself. I remembered Konrad Willman: "Guilt itself is a sin—a most deceptive one. It will corrupt your soul and your mind. It perpetuates your sin and makes you its slave."

I thought of Annemarie Moeller, of her courage, of her defeat. Of her great devotion that had been repaid with rape and murder. Everything decent was going down to defeat.

» 166

Where was I heading? Or was it too late to ask? Suddenly, I smelled again the odor of burning human flesh. I saw before me the skull and the naked eyes. I heard the girl's tortured voice.

Then I remembered that her name was Berta.

May 9th.

That was Saturday. That's as far as I got in my so-called diary. The last part of the entry leads back to another emotional rampage, which I had promised myself to renounce. I won't mention it again. I'd only repeat myself. I want to write about Sunday. Sunday, the seventh of May. It began with Grete's call. Her voice sounded weak and fumbling, as if she were drunk or drugged.

She said, "Please come as soon as you can. I need you desperately."

Her eyes were swollen. She wore no makeup, no lipstick. Her mouth trembled when she saw me and she embraced me silently, tightly, her head on my shoulder. She wore a white robe.

"She's dead," Grete said.

I tried to loosen her embrace, but she held on.

"Your mother?"

"Yes."

"I'm so very sorry."

Her body tensed. She dropped her arms and walked away from me. "I came home last night after an early dinner with Becker—he's directing my next picture. I worked on the script

167 «

and then I called Mother. It was before nine o'clock. There was no answer. She'd told me she'd be home, but I thought she might have changed her mind. I called again at ten."

She sat on the couch, speaking very softly.

"Again no answer. I began to get nervous. She never goes to bed after ten."

I sat down next to her.

"I called again at ten thirty, at eleven. By that time I was scared. I took a cab to her apartment—I have a key—the corridor was lit and I turned on the light in the living room. Everything was in perfect order. A glass of tea was on the table, half full, next to her favorite chair. Then I saw a strip of light under the bedroom door."

Grete paused and swallowed, then she looked at me and began to cry. The tears streamed down her face, but she continued to talk.

"Hans—she was lying on her bed, I thought she was asleep. No. That isn't true. I was trying to . . . but . . . I *knew* she was dead." Her voice broke.

"Don't," I said. "Don't talk."

"I want to."

"Not now, Grete."

"I'll be all right in a moment."

I sat without moving. I could think of nothing to say or do. She lowered her head, her light hair swinging over her face, and remained like that for a few minutes. Then she began to speak again, very fast.

"An empty medicine bottle on her night table. And a note. A note to me. 'I took some pills to sleep better. I love you, my darling.' I cried, I touched her face, I kissed it . . . it was cold. I didn't know how long she had been dead and her cold face frightened me. I knew I had to do something, and then I remembered her doctor's name. I looked for Mother's purse—it was on her dressing table—the black alligator purse I had given her on her last birthday. I opened it. Mother was dead, but her purse was still alive, filled with her things, lipstick and pencil and—"

Grete's voice was racing. In an effort to slow her down, I touched her hand. She seized my hand and held it in a tight grip.

"I got her notebook, found the doctor's number. He was out on an emergency. I phoned you, Hans, I didn't know what else to do. You weren't home. You couldn't be reached. I bent over my mother's face and watched her mouth. Maybe she was still breathing. Maybe she wasn't dead. The phone rang—it was the doctor. He arrived ten minutes later . . . and covered my mother's face. He was very gentle. He said he had to call the police: it was obviously suicide. While we were waiting, he asked if I knew of anything that could have driven her to it. I said I didn't. I lied. I knew why she had done it. So do you. Don't you, Hans? You know why she did it! Don't you? Answer me!"

She was shouting. I got up. "Yes. I can imagine why she did it," I said. "The tension was too much for her."

She screamed, "What the hell are you talking about?! What fucking tension? Can't you ever say anything straight? I killed her!"

I went behind the white counter of the bar and took a glass.

"That's an idea," she said more calmly. "Give me a drink."

"What do you want?"

"Nothing sweet. Something very strong. What do you have?"

"Whiskey."

"I want that too."

She came to the bar and sat on one of the red stools. I poured.

"More," she said.

I poured more.

"No water."

"Grete, you're not used to—"

She tore the glass out of my hand and some of the whiskey spilled. She drank and put the glass down.

"You want to hear the rest?"

"That's up to you."

She emptied her glass and set it down in front of me. I poured, but less than before, and she took the bottle and filled her glass to the rim. "Your drink's too weak, too," she said, and poured more whiskey into my glass. I reached for the bottle, but she held on to it. It would have been foolish to fight for the bottle. Maybe that's what she needed—getting drunk and passing out. She touched my glass with hers.

"Drink with me."

We drank. She shuddered. "It tastes terrible, but it's great. Isn't it great, Hans?"

"Yes, it is," I said.

"I've never been drunk. Do you believe that?"

"No."

"It's true. How many times have you been drunk?"

"I've never counted."

"Make it once more. Get drunk with me now."

"No."

"For my sake, please, darling. Don't let me get drunk alone. I don't want to be alone."

"I'm here," I said.

"Not close enough."

She leaned over the counter and, gripping my head with both hands, opened her mouth and kissed me. Her mouth was hot. I could feel her tongue. I pulled my head back.

"Goddamned coward," she said.

My drink was much too strong, it began to affect me. My drink and her mouth.

"Come here," she said.

I emptied my glass.

"Another one for you," Grete said.

"All right."

She hadn't finished hers. Her eyes were hazy now, her face flushed. I went to her and she pressed her body against me. Her breasts. Her thighs.

"Now, let's drink."

We did. She set her glass down and put her mouth on mine.

"Fuck me, please," she said.

I tried to shake my head. She stepped back and let her robe fall off. She wore nothing underneath.

"I want you to fuck me. Please, Hans—"

We fell asleep on the floor. I woke up before she did and looked at her there, her mouth half open, snoring lightly. Her face looked drained and very pale.

I got up and went into her study, a small corner adjoining the bedroom, furnished in red and white, of course. I looked at the pictures on the wall. Photograhs and posters: Grete Fall at the opening of her film *The Girl Who Couldn't Lie;* next to her, Paul Becker, her director. Stills taken on the set, some with her leading man, Werner Thiel, who had been her lover while the film was shooting and after that returned to his wife and three children. A poster from the first motion picture that had made her a star four years ago, *The Fourteen Karat Love,* "presenting the new young German star, Grete Fall." I glanced at the film magazines. In one of them was a full-page photograph of "Dr. Joseph Goebbels, *Reichminister* of Public Enlightenment and Propaganda, with Mrs. Goebbels and the young motion picture star Grete Fall." Mrs. Goebbels had a frozen smile on her face. Grete was very beautiful in a white ermine coat.

I turned the pages without seeing them, feeling depressed and shaken, then leaned back and closed my eyes. It was shortly before noon.

I seemed barely to have closed them when Grete's voice woke me. She had changed into a red robe and draped a white scarf around her neck, but still wore no makeup or lipstick.

I asked, "What time is it?"

"Three o'clock. Do you have to leave?"

"Do you want me to?"

"No. Stay with me, please. If you can."

"I've made no plans for today," I said.

She knelt down before me. "I'm sorry," she said.

"Don't be."

"I didn't want it to be like that for the first time."

I took her hand. She said, "I wanted it badly and I was drunk."

"Yes."

"It could have been anybody. You know that, don't you?"

"Yes."

"That's what makes me so sad."

"I understand."

"I'm glad it was you," she said.

"So am I."

"Really?"

"Yes."

She withdrew her hand gently and rose. "I don't know what I'm going to do," she said. "My picture's supposed to start shooting two weeks from tomorrow."

"Work will help you. Do you have a cigarette? I forgot my case."

She took a small silver box from her desk. "Give me one too."

I lit both cigarettes.

"I can't go on," she said.

"Go on with what?"

"Working in pictures. I can't see myself on the set, playing silly scenes, making love to some stranger and always thinking of her. What I did to her."

"I'm going to say something cruel, Grete: it won't make any difference to her anymore."

She turned her back to me. "That's a terrible thing to say."

"It's true."

There was a pause.

"What about me?" she asked. "My feelings? My life?"

"Your life is acting. You know that yourself."

She shook her head violently. "That's changed, Hans. Mother's . . . death changed everything. It was my acting, my goddamned ambition, that killed her. How can I ever forget that?"

I got up. "Maybe you'll never forget it," I said. "But you'll learn to live with it. Giving up acting would only make it worse. And you'd never do it, darling. You can't do it."

She was silent. After a while she started to cry and left the room. I went into the kitchen to see if I could find some coffee. There was a pot on the stove, more than half full, and I turned on the gas to heat it up. As I stood watching it, my mind was blank. What a blessing it is that sometimes one's mind goes blank.

"I'll have my coffee black," Grete said.

She took out cups and saucers.

"The same for me."

She poured and we took our coffee into the living room. The counter of the bar was clean: she had removed the glasses. We sat on the couch. We caught each other looking at the empty floor space between the counter and the table. She half-smiled and I tried to think of something else.

"This is excellent coffee," I said.

"Yes, it is. I'm a pretty good cook."

"Really?"

"Well, I used to be. Now I don't have the time. Anna does everything."

"She's not here today, is she?"

"She's off on Sundays," Grete said.

The telephone rang, rang twice more, and then stopped. Grete got up and waited. When it rang again, she picked up the receiver.

"Yes, Willie."

She listened. "The funeral is private," she said. "Completely private. That's the understanding. Don't tell the press where it's going to be." She listened again. "Well, if they should find out, I want to be protected. I'm not going to speak to any of them."

Pause.

"No, Willie, please, don't. I want to be left alone, that's all." She hung up and stood for a moment, frowning.

"Your mother was Catholic," I said.

"Yes."

"She committed suicide. The Catholic Church forbids burial in consecrated ground."

"It's going to be all right," she said.

"You must have powerful connections."

She avoided my gaze.

"Yes."

I stayed with her until six o'clock that evening. There were more phone calls from her publicity man, Willie. The studio seemed to be taking care of everything: the reporters, the undertaker, the cemetery.

"When's it going to be?" I asked.

"Tomorrow afternoon. I don't want you to be there. I don't want anybody to be there. I want to be alone with Mother."

"I'll do whatever you want me to do."

"Send her a bunch of snowdrops. They were her favorite flowers."

The newspaper arrived. On the third page, it carried the item that Mrs. Franciska Fall, mother of the famous young motion picture star, had died of an accidental overdose of sleeping pills. Her daughter was in a state of shock. She could not be reached for comment.

For most of the afternoon, we sat on the couch together in silence. Once in a while, her head would fall back and she dozed off—then she'd wake with a start and look around as if she weren't sure where she was. Her face would shadow then, and she'd cry.

When it was close to six o'clock, she said, "I'm going to try to sleep. I'm very tired."

She got up and stumbled, and I reached out to steady her.

"Maybe I'm still drunk," she said. "Would you do me a favor?"

"Yes."

"Wait here until I'm in bed. I'll call you."

She left. I was alone in the twilight of the room. I went to the window: it looked gray and hazy outside. The streetlights were on, and the cars were turning their lights on too. I wondered what kind of day it had been.

Grete's voice called me.

She was in bed, her pale face on a white pillow, her body covered up to the neck with a white blanket. She took my hands and pulled me close. We kissed each other gently.

"I hope you sleep well," I said.

"I will. I'm half asleep now. But I'm afraid of waking up."

"Do you want me to stay?"

She shook her head. I went to the door.

"Darling—"

"Yes."

"I'll never act again."

The door to the Heiligers' apartment stood open, and I saw light inside. I stopped and looked. Heinz Heiliger was there, in his shirt sleeves, his back to me. On the floor was a suitcase which he was just closing. It seemed too heavy for him, for he had to bend down and push it outside through the open door. Then he straightened up and saw me. He froze.

I pressed the button for the elevator.

"I'm moving out," Heinz said defiantly.

"I thought you would."

"My parents are dead."

"Yes. I heard about it."

He kept staring at me. He was wondering if I knew why and how his parents had died.

"My most heartfelt condolences," I said.

He gave me another defiant look, went inside, and slammed the door. I stepped into the elevator.

I went to the liquor cabinet in my study, took out a bottle of whiskey and a glass, and opened the bottle. Then I got a whiff of the whiskey and put them both back.

I turned on the radio, and listened to the news. Hitler had made a peace-loving speech. Von Ribbentrop had returned to London. By government decree, the two leading Berlin newspapers had ceased to exist. One of the publishers and several of the editors had been arrested. The Association of German National Jews had declared their unfailing loyalty to Germany and to the Hitler government. The stopping of a truck by members of an S.A. storm troop had revealed a printing press inside; apparently Jewish-inspired pamphlets against the regime were being printed while the truck drove through Berlin. Five men and two women were arrested and brought before the people's court. The penalty for "crimes against the state" was death.

Konrad's cadaverous driver, Satan, came to my mind. I remembered Konrad saying something about a pamphlet in his living room. Should I call them? No, it was too dangerous. Their telephone was tapped.

I grew more and more restless. My thoughts began to overlap. I couldn't stop them. Konrad and Barbara . . . Grete Fall . . . Karin and Jimmy Charters . . . Karin and Theo Holt. . . . They were in bed together. I saw them. He was kissing her breasts. Adriani stood by the bed, watching them, wearing a cardinal's scarlet robe and a cardinal's hat. He smiled at the lovers and blessed them, not with the sign of the cross . . . with the sign of the swastika. It hung, diamond-studded, on Grete Fall's nude body. The chain was long and the swastika oscillated before her genitals. . . . Konrad stood in a room that was the people's court. The floor was swarming with rats, hundreds of them; they were climbing on his body and Gustaf Angermann sat in the judge's chair and laughed. . . . I was not asleep. I knew I was dreaming. I had dreamed all that before. . . . Grete Fall kissed me. . . . Mr. Heiliger bit off the tip of his cigar and spat at me. "You're nothing but a dirty Jewish swine." But I knew he was dead. . . . A door opened. Someone came in. I didn't know where I was. The room had no walls. It stretched endlessly into darkness. I couldn't see the door . . . but someone had come in . . . a woman. I smelled her perfume. It had the odor of decay and rot. I saw the yellow skull and the bloody incision where her mouth had been. It came closer . . . the stench was choking me . . . it touched me and I screamed—

Two hands clasped my shoulders and shook me.

"Hans, what is it?"

Karin's voice. I opened my eyes. I hadn't realized they'd been closed. I was lying on the couch. Karin stood next to me.

"Please say something. Answer me."

"Yes."

"What was it? A nightmare?"

"I don't know," I said.

She went and turned on all the lights. It hurt my eyes.

"What happened to you?"

"I must have fallen asleep."

"You screamed," she said. "You screamed when I touched you."

"I didn't know it was you. Please turn off some of the lights."

Part of the room fell dark. It was twilight again. I liked the twilight. It was better than the glaring truth of the day. I sat up. I could see Karin. She was wearing something tight-fitting and low cut in orange and black. I had never seen that dress.

"You must go to a doctor," Karin said.

"I'm not sick."

"Maybe you just don't know it. I tell you, Hans, something is wrong with you."

"That's true," I said. "Something is wrong with me."

"In the opera, you stared at me as if you'd never seen me before. You stared at me in horror."

"It wasn't you," I said. "It was another woman."

"Are you in love with her?"

"You can't be in love with a skull."

She came very close to me. "A skull?"

"Yes. It had once been a face. But I've never seen the face. I've only seen the skull."

She kept looking at me. "I called you early this morning. I was worried about you. I kept calling and then, finally, I decided to come over."

"I was at Grete Fall's. Her mother died."

"Yes, I read about that. Why did she kill herself?"

"She didn't. She had a heart attack."

"The newspaper said—"

"The paper is lying."

"—she took too many sleeping pills."

"A heart attack. People don't kill themselves. They die of heart attacks."

She bent down to me. "Hans—"

» 178

"I can see your breasts, Karin. You have lovely breasts. I'd like to kiss them again."

She stood up straight. "What's happened to you?"

"I'm an Aryan now," I said. "I have my diploma. A certified Aryan! Didn't Adriani tell you?"

"Yes, he did."

"We could get married now, couldn't we? But it's too late."

"Yes."

"You wouldn't have married a Jew."

"I would have married you, Hans. I wanted to marry you. You turned me down. I'd have gone anywhere with you—money or not. But you never believed I would. You never demanded anything from me. And demanding is part of love."

I got up and put my arms around her. "You're so wise tonight."

She kissed me. "Wise and sad."

"Until the next love comes along."

She broke away from me. "We were together for almost four years, Hans . . . but you still know nothing about me."

"I know about Jimmy and I know about Theo Holt."

"And that's it to you?"

"Isn't that enough?"

"No. No, it isn't. And there is nothing to know about Theo Holt."

"Not yet, maybe."

"Yes, Not yet," she said harshly. "And as to Jimmy—you know he meant nothing to me. I only used him."

We stood there facing each other . . . then suddenly this whole confrontation seemed unreal. Karin was unreal. I was unreal. If I'd made a genuine effort at that moment, maybe I wouldn't have lost her—but I couldn't. We'd been lovers. Now we would be lovers no longer. It was sad, but it was unimportant. There was no room for love anymore in my life. Love belonged to the radiance of an abundant past. To yesterday.

Karin had gone to the door.

"Are you leaving?"

"Yes."

"Do you have a date?"

"I had a date with you. You forgot."

"I'm sorry."

"Yes."

I moved to open the door for her.

"No, don't. Don't take me out. I'll find my way," she said. She opened the door and turned once more.

"Friday night at Horcher's you said, 'Heil Hitler.' That was the first time I heard you say it." She looked at me with a mocking smile. "You'll never be a Nazi," she said. "Don't try."

She left. She must have paused in the hall for a while because some time went by before I heard the entrance door close. When I went into the hall, I saw a key on the table. I felt a sudden stab of pain. Karin had put it there. I didn't touch it.

I saw the light in the kitchen and went in. Hanna was sitting at the table and with her was an agreeable-looking blond man in his shirt sleeves. He was just finishing a plate of ham and eggs and a stein of beer. Both got up when they saw me, and Hanna introduced him to me as her brother's friend from her hometown.

He took his coat from the chair next to him and put it on. It was the brown coat of an S.A. uniform. He was six feet tall and must have been about Hanna's age. We exchanged some polite questions and answers. I went to my bedroom.

I had not looked at Hanna. I had been thinking of the nice boy in Stockholm who had hoped she would join him as soon as he was settled.

It is now Wednesday, the 10th of May.

I am falling behind, but I cannot help it. We had some very hot days. It is hot tonight. The windows in my study are wide open, but it hasn't cooled it off at all. I can't stand heat too well, the kind of city heat that is stale and wet and makes your shirt stick to the body. Mountain heat is different. There, the air is crisp under a brilliant sky. The full sun hits the snow and warms and bronzes the face.

As boys, we used to ski a lot. There was no ski lift then; we carried our skis on our shoulders, carefully balanced, our shirts off. We climbed in the deep snow, using each other's footprints, across the glacier with its blue-green crevasses, up to the summit. We lit a fire in the hut, opened our rucksacks and threw our raw potatoes in the ashes, then let them glow until their skin was black and crusty, their flesh soft. We drank hot chocolate and ate the potatoes. The black skin was the best part.

Then we fastened our bindings and started down in the powdery snow. We used stem turns and christianias to stay clear of trees and snow-covered brooks. Sometimes we had to jump over half-buried fences and trunks. All that came easy to us.

After many years, I skied again in St. Moritz. I didn't like the ski lifts. Climbing up had been half the fun. The hut was now a high-priced restaurant with large sun patios and multicolored deck chairs, where chic ladies and sporty gentlemen in ultra-stylish outfits ordered the latest fashionable drinks in many languages.

But the sun, the clear air, and the powdery snow were still there. Still the same.

* * *

My desk lamp is lit. The only light in the room. It grants me safety and quiet isolation. My yearning for solitude has grown stronger, and with it an aversion to bright light. It almost amounts to fear. During the past few days, I have been getting up before dawn and arriving at my office before the morning twilight changes into day. When the sun comes up, I draw my curtains.

"You're sitting in the dark, Dr. Bauer," Magda said on Monday.

"That's the way I want it," I said.

Klaus finds it depressing. He doesn't understand this new habit. Several times I caught him watching me closely, as if he were looking at a stranger whose behavior puzzled and troubled him. I don't blame him. My state of mind changes constantly. It's nothing I purposely try to bring about; I simply can't control it. An element of confusion obscures my memory and disarranges my experiences.

On Monday afternoon, I sat in my office, catching up on one of the many cases we had taken on during my four months' absence. The case was not likely to reach the courts before the early part of September.

The buzzer on my desk went off. Magda's voice said, "Dr. Bauer, *Obergruppenfuehrer* Adriani would like to talk to you."

I picked up the receiver. A woman said, "I'll put the *Obergruppenfuehrer* on, Dr. Bauer."

After a moment, I heard Carl Adriani's voice.

"Heil Hitler, Dr. Bauer."

"Heil Hitler," I said. Karin's last remark came to my mind. I almost stumbled over the words.

"I'd like to ask a favor of you," Adriani said. "I had a phone call this morning from the Ministry of Justice. It seems you are in negotiations with a Dr. Koenig regarding a partnership in your law firm. Is that correct?"

Surprise silenced me.

"Dr. Bauer—"

"Yes."

"Is my information correct?"

"Yes and no," I said with an effort.

"What does that mean?"

"Dr. Koenig would like to join our office," I said, "but we decided against it."

"That is most unfortunate," Adriani said.

There was a pause.

"You saw Dr. Koenig at Victor Brandt's party," I said. "I don't think you were favorably impressed by him."

"I don't remember meeting him."

"He's not a very reputable lawyer," I said.

"The minister of justice disagrees with you. He is personally interested in Dr. Koenig's career."

"I see."

"I hope you won't be difficult about this, Dr. Bauer. I promised the minister to intervene in Dr. Koenig's behalf."

"I can assure you I shall be most cooperative whenever—"

He did not wait for me to finish. He said, "I would appreciate it if you could arrive very soon at a mutually satisfactory deal with Dr. Koenig."

I was getting angry. "Mr. Adriani, I am not alone in the firm. Klaus von Isenberg is my partner. Neither of us considers Dr. Koenig up to the standards our office has maintained and shall continue to maintain. Dr. Koenig is a cheap shyster."

His return came back. Cold and hard. "You don't have to lose your temper, Dr. Bauer. I fully expect you to reevaluate Dr. Koenig's qualifications and come to terms with him." He added, "I trust I am making myself clear."

"I'm afraid you are, Mr. Adriani."

He broke the connection. I sat motionless. After a while I realized I was still holding the receiver to my ear and I put it down.

So that was to be the arrangement. One hundred thousand marks in cash. Plus promissory notes. This was the first one. He had not lost much time in presenting it. "I trust I am making myself clear."

That son-of-a-bitch! What the hell was I going to do? I couldn't suddenly switch positions and tell Klaus I'd made a mistake. "I'm sorry, Klaus, I was thinking of the wrong Dr. Koenig. *Albert* Koenig. *Alfred* is an honorable man." I couldn't do that. I had to be honest with Klaus.

I was not very articulate when repeating Adriani's talk to him. I was furious. Too . . . embarrassed. He listened to me calmly, sitting at his desk. When I finished, he got up and started to pace. I felt tired and sat down.

He said, "I hate to do it."

"Do what?"

"Take Koenig into the office."

"That's out of the question, Klaus!"

We were both thinking. I asked, "Could you talk to Adriani?"

"Of course, but it wouldn't make any sense. No matter who speaks to him, *you're* his game."

"The professional quarry—the Jew."

He looked at me. "Hans, don't."

"Can't you see? Here I am, dangling between Heil Hitler and Ahasuerus. Another Nietzsche image—'the tightrope dancer.' "

The light in the room was too bright. I shaded my eyes with my hand. I heard Klaus say, "You must see a doctor, Hans."

"Somebody told me that yesterday. I'm not sick."

"There's been too much pressure on you."

"Karin said I should see a doctor."

"She's right."

"Yes. She's always right. She also told me I shouldn't try to be a Nazi."

"You're not a Nazi."

I got up. "Then what am I, Klaus? I'll tell you what I am. An Aryan by the grace of Adriani, and by his ill will a Jew."

Klaus had resumed his pacing. Now he stopped. "I'm going to call Dr. Koenig and ask him to come and see us."

"Don't do that, Klaus. Not on account of me."

"On account of us, Hans. We're in the same boat. And we want to keep our team intact. Between the two of us, we should be able to keep a shyster like Koenig under control."

When I came home on Monday, a man I did not know opened the entrance door to the apartment house.

"Heil Hitler. You're Dr. Bauer, aren't you?"

"Yes."

"Allow me to introduce myself," the man said. "I'm the new manager. My name is Adolf Wirt."

His short mustache covered precisely the space between the wings of his nose and his upper lip. The black hair was combed onto the forehead. His small eyes looked as if they were permanently squeezed together. He wore a swastika armlet and a swastika button in his lapel.

"Nice to meet you, Mr. Wirt," I said.

"Thank you, Dr. Bauer. My wife's name is Elsa. We have two lovely little daughters, Hilde and Kaete, four and seven years old. Kaete's already in the Hitler Youth. We're very proud of her."

"I hope you and your family will be happy in your new home." I pressed the button to bring the elevator down.

185 «

"Thank you very much," Mr. Wirt said. "Please be assured that my wife and I will be at your service day and night."

"Thank you."

"Thank *you*, Dr. Bauer."

The elevator arrived and I got in. Mr. Wirt leaned forward and said in a low, confidential tone, "I understand that my predecessor met with a fatal accident—"

"He did."

The elevator door was closing.

"Do you know how it happened?"

"No, I don't. You might ask his son, Heinz Heiliger. He's in the Hitler Youth too." I began to move up.

"Thank you, Dr. Bauer. It was a privilege to meet you."

We have made the deal with Alfred Koenig. He came to the office for the first time today.

This is a new entry. It is almost a week later.

Tuesday, the 16th of May, 1933.

Koenig has taken over Siegmund Schwartz's office. He brought his own secretary, a girl by the name of Renate. She is tall and blond, wears her hair in plaits, and dresses in blouses with stand-up collars and tight-fitting skirts. She never forgets to say Heil Hitler. Magda and Hedi don't like her at all. They're afraid of Renate.

Koenig wants a new desk chair and a new carpet. Both chair and carpet have retained the odious smell peculiar to the Jews. Klaus said perhaps Dr. Koenig's Aryan nose was indisposed.

Desk chair and carpet were new. After that setback, Koenig mentioned that his secretary had been with him for ten years. She was a jewel. She wasn't used to sitting in one room with other secretaries. She needed her own private office. Klaus and I said she would have to be satisfied with the existing accommodations.

Dr. Koenig was not in a good mood. He said that he expected full cooperation from us. He knew it had taken outside pressure to get him his partnership in spite of his eminent qualifications. He asked for access to our files, so he could get acquainted with the activities of our office. I told him we would provide his secretary with a key to the filing cabinet. Would that be satisfactory? Quite.

A few days after the funeral, I talked to Grete Fall. She was in a rush: the wardrobe for her next film had to be selected and tested. The shooting date had been moved up. The picture was to start in ten days. She hoped to see me soon, for lunch or for a quick drink.

"I'll never act again," she'd said.

It would be unfair to remind her of that.

Thursday, the 18th of May.

I had to break off the other day because the doorbell rang. It gave me a shock, I don't know why, perhaps because I wasn't expecting anybody. I heard Hanna cross the hall and open the entrance door, and I listened . . . but I couldn't hear anything. I became more and more tense.

Then came the knock on the door. Hanna said, "A letter for

you, Dr. Bauer. The boy won't give it to me. He says he has to hand it to you personally."

I went out and saw a boy of sixteen or seventeen standing in the door. "Dr. Bauer?"

"Yes."

He gave me a small envelope. "For you."

I reached in my pocket for a tip, but when I looked up, the boy had gone. I heard him run downstairs. I opened the envelope and read the note.

> Dear Hans, Please meet me tomorrow evening between six and six thirty near the K.D.W. department store. In case you can't make it, try on one of the following days. Same time. I won't wait longer than six thirty. This is urgent. Please try. Keep it a secret and destroy this note. Barbara.

Barbara. Barbara and Konrad again. They seem to be determined to get me into trouble. Now I'm supposed to meet her secretly at the K.D.W., the best-known department store in Berlin, located in the Tauentzienstrasse, where everybody runs into everybody else.

I can't take the chance. I'm not involved in their activities. Ludwig Butler isn't *my* ex-brother-in-law. I have to think of myself, of Klaus, the firm—

"Yes, Hanna."

"Will you be home for dinner?"

"I don't know."

"Well, I just—"

"If you want to take the evening off, go ahead."

"Oh, thank you, Dr. Bauer."

I wish I could talk to someone, but there isn't anybody. Klaus, of course, but he's done enough for me. He's got too much on his own mind anyway. Karin—yes, maybe a year ago. But now she's gone.

No one could help me with this anyway. This must be my decision. And I've made it. Under no circumstances will I go and meet Barbara.

The telephone rang. I was still in the hall. It rang again. I went to my study and picked it up.

"This is Carl Adriani."

Mechanically I said, "Heil Hitler."

"Could I see you, Dr. Bauer?"

"When?"

"This evening."

"What time is it now?"

"Seven o'clock."

"Where would you want to meet me?"

"I'm at Margie's now. If you could come here—I won't keep you long. Quite informal, Dr. Bauer. We'll have a drink and talk."

I don't remember how I got there. Margie's place isn't far from where I live. I either walked or took a cab. It was cool, I recall. The Kurfuerstendamm was crowded with people going to the movie houses and to the theaters . . . I must have walked.

I hadn't been to Margie's for a long time. She opened the door for me. She wore a velvet house gown, I noticed, but it wasn't really a gown: underneath it, she wore pants. Her face looked different; maybe she'd been crying. She took my arm and, for a moment, leaned her head against me.

Adriani was using the telephone in the living room. He wore a dark-blue robe and a scarf around his neck—it was the first time I'd seen him out of uniform.

He turned and nodded at me, continuing his talk; he seemed

189 «

to be speaking harshly to somebody. I couldn't hear the words. The room was familiar to me: not very large, but exquisitely furnished with carefully selected antiques. Some of them belonged to Karin. Where was Karin? I hoped I wouldn't meet her.

Margie asked, "Would you like a drink?"

"Yes, please."

"Carl likes aquavit."

"I prefer whiskey, if you have it."

"Of course. I'm an American, remember? Ice?"

"Yes, please, and a little soda."

She fixed the drink and gave it to me. My hand shook. Margie noticed it, but made no comment.

"I had a letter from my father today," she said. "He's ordering me home."

"Ordering?"

"Yes. Some friend of his at the American embassy wrote him about Carl."

"And he doesn't approve?"

"Father despises the Nazis. The thought that his own daughter is linked to one is intolerable to him."

"What are you going to do?"

"I don't know."

Adriani had finished his telephone conversation and hung up. "I'm glad you came, Dr. Bauer." He shook hands. "I hope you'll excuse my informal attire. The robe is a present from Margie."

He took a small glass from a bed of shaved ice and filled it with aquavit. "Have you had dinner?"

"No. I'm not hungry."

Adriani motioned with his head to Margie.

"Linda has everything prepared," she said.

"I'd like to talk to Dr. Bauer for a few minutes."

"All right. I'll take my drink along," Margie said. She took her glass and left the room. At the door, she turned and looked at me. I'd no idea what the look implied. Maybe it was meant to be encouraging.

Adriani pointed at a chair. "Sit down."

I did. He remained standing. "You broke with Karin, didn't you?"

"Our relationship was over. It died a natural death."

"Too bad for her."

"Why do you say that?"

"Because I know her. She's not self-reliant. She needs you more than you need her."

He sat down very close to me. Without his uniform, some of his rigidity seemed to have left him. Lacking the support of the stiff collar, his face looked softer, his wide, sensual mouth and long eyelashes were more pronounced. He said, "I'm glad you followed up on my suggestion concerning Dr. Koenig."

"That wasn't a suggestion, was it?"

"You might call it blackmail," he said without a smile. "I took advantage of your vulnerable position."

He was talking very gently, in a subdued voice. It served the same purpose as the casual robe. It was intended to make me feel relaxed.

"You're toying with my life," I said.

He shook his head. "Not unless you force me to."

"That means, I'm safe as long as I comply with your—your —"

"Extortion," Adriani said. "Don't be afraid of insulting me. You can't. I prefer to call a spade a spade. It prevents mis-understandings."

He emptied his glass and rose to pour himself another drink. "May I freshen your whiskey?" he asked.

He sipped the aquavit and smacked his lips. "I love this stuff. It has a pure, clear taste. Why don't you try it?"

"I prefer whiskey," I said.

He sat down again and crossed his legs. "How are the Will-mans?"

The question had the hoped-for effect: it jolted me. I'd not yet destroyed Barbara's note. It was in my right coat pocket.

"I haven't seen them recently."

"Not since you talked to them at the opera?"

"No."

"Have you heard from them?"

"No."

"Isn't that rather strange, Dr. Bauer?"

"Not at all. Sometimes we don't see each other for months, especially when he's working. He's rehearsing the new Gerhart Hauptmann play now."

"No, he isn't," Adriani said. He looked at me sharply. His tone of voice had changed, too. It was the prosecutor's voice. "I did presume you knew that, Dr. Bauer."

"I didn't."

Adriani paused. He uncrossed his legs and leaned back in his chair.

"Konrad Willman has not been to the theater since Monday last week. I know. I tried to reach him."

"Did you call him at home?"

"Their house has been vacated."

"Vacated?"

"Yes."

"And you don't know where they are?"

"No. Do you?"

"I told you, I haven't heard from them." I got up.

"Another whiskey?" Adriani asked.

"No, thank you." I set my empty glass on the table.

"A few days ago there was an incident," Adriani said. He'd lowered his voice again and began to talk in a bored, monotonous manner, as if he were tired of telling the story.

"Somewhere in Lichterfelde, a truck was stopped by one of our S.A. patrols. Inside the truck was a printing outfit with all the necessary equipment. Six men and two women were busy printing pamphlets against the government. It solved a problem. We'd twice succeeded in breaking up these criminal activities, but the pamphlets had continued to appear. We'd not been able to discover the new hiding place. Five men and the women were taken into custody. The sixth man escaped."

"I heard about the truck," I said.

"You did?"

"Yes."

I was pacing now and managed to get behind Adriani's chair, out of his sight. I didn't want him to look at me, lest he see my apprehensiveness. He didn't turn. He said, "We'd never been able to find who wrote those treasonable leaflets—until now. One of the captives supplied the name under a certain amount of duress."

He paused and added, "The writer is another friend of yours, Dr. Bauer. Ludwig Butler."

"Butler?"

"Yes. You sound surprised. You didn't know that? No, of course not. It took us several days to get the information."

"Is the man still alive?" I asked.

"The man was a woman. That amazed me. Women are more capable of withstanding pain than men. In answer to your question: no. Due to a technical mistake, she is not alive anymore."

I stood still. Adriani rose and faced me.

"You're not sick, Dr. Bauer, are you?" he asked softly.

"I've not been very well recently," I said.

"That's what Karin told us. You should see a doctor."

"Yes."

He went to the aquavit bottle. "I need another one," he said.

"I've had a rough day. Don't worry, though." He looked at me. "I never get drunk."

"May I ask why you wanted to see me, Mr. Adriani?"

He was pouring his drink, his back to me. "That's pretty obvious, isn't it? We haven't been able to find Mr. and Mrs. Willman. I thought you might know where they were."

My tension exploded into anger. "How many times must I repeat it—I haven't seen the Willmans and I haven't heard from them!"

"I'm sorry you're annoyed with me," Adriani said calmly. "I can understand it. It's an awkward situation for you to be in."

"I have nothing to do with this whole affair," I said firmly.

"I didn't imply you had." He raised his voice. "The fact is, Dr. Bauer, that we sent an . . . investigator to Mr. Willman's house and found Mr. and Mrs. Willman gone, the house deserted. Why, Dr. Bauer? It could have been just a coincidence. They might suddenly have decided to move. But it could also have been that somebody tipped off Konrad Willman—our sixth man, for instance—and that your friend decided he didn't care to be exposed to questioning by the Gestapo."

"Why should he be afraid, Mr. Adriani? I'm sure Konrad has nothing to hide."

"Then why does he hide himself, Dr. Bauer?"

"I can't answer that."

"There, you see."

He dropped into his chair and went back to his former, casually monotonous approach. "Why don't you sit down and have another drink?" he asked.

I went to the table and poured a whiskey. I succeeded in holding my hands steady.

"To make this short," Adriani said, "—Margie doesn't like to dine too late—if you should hear from your friends, I would expect you to contact me."

I was silent as the infamy of his demand sank in. He continued, "It's really quite harmless, Dr. Bauer. The Gestapo is interested in having some questions answered, that's all. No threats, no coercion. If Konrad Willman is not involved in this matter—and I agree with you, I'm quite sure he isn't—nothing will happen to him. On the other hand, Dr. Bauer, if he should have participated in a treasonable act, you wouldn't hesitate to cooperate with us in the interest of your country which you love so much—would you?"

"No, I wouldn't."

There was nothing else I could possibly have answered at that moment. Later, when I was by myself, I could—

Adriani rose. "I'm glad you didn't disappoint me and that I judged you correctly," he said. He touched glasses with me. "Heil Hitler."

"Heil Hitler," I said.

He took the aquavit bottle and set it down. "I've had enough."

He put his arm around my shoulder. It felt like lead. I shuddered at his touch. "You're sick. You might even be running a temperature," Adriani said, concern in his voice. "You must go to a doctor. I'll talk to Margie about it."

Suddenly I heard myself shout, "Don't! Stop it!"

I shook myself free. He stood and looked at me. With an effort, I said more calmly, "I'm sorry. It's only—everybody's been telling me I'm sick, I should see a doctor—it's been too much. Too much."

"Yes, I can understand that," Adriani said. He ignored the subterfuge and went to the heart of the matter. "You're a very sensitive person—so am I. But we're also both sophisticated men. You realize that you can't always be rigid about basic conceptions and ideas. If you want to survive, you must be flexible . . . you must adjust your thinking to the demands of the times."

195 »

The demands of the times. The demands of Hitler and his Nazi gang:

Denounce your father and your mother.
Listen to your neighbor's talk.
Torture and kill whoever is against you and too weak to resist.
Betray your friends.
"Fair is foul, and foul is fair: Hover through the fog and filthy air."

Maybe the Fuehrer had taken his philosophy from Shakespeare's witches. He might have read *Macbeth*. And if he hadn't, Goebbels had, I'm sure of that. He used to be a pupil of Gundolf, the eminent professor of literature; Gundolf had published a new German translation of Shakespeare's works, even though it turned out to be inferior to the classic translation by Schlegel and Tieck. Goebbels must have read *Macbeth*. Maybe he was the one who had decided to build the Third Reich on the witches' chant.

Margie forced me to stay for dinner. There was a lot of small talk, mostly Adriani's: his soliloquy. Margie and I were silent. At one point she said to me, "You're not eating anything, Hans."

"I'm sorry . . . I'm not hungry."

Without looking up from his plate, Adriani said, "Which boat are you planning to take, Margie?"

"Boat—?"

"Yes—back to the States. Take a German one, the *Bremen*. To please your father. She leaves next Sunday."

Margie burst into tears, got up from the table and left. I said nothing. I'd no idea what had happened between them. Maybe she thought he wanted to get rid of her. Maybe she was right.

Adriani's table manners were atrocious. He was wolfing down his dinner, his face almost touching his plate, shoveling the food into his mouth, sometimes using his hands. It made me sick to watch him. At the same time, it gave me a measure of satisfaction to see his civilized and worldly behavior collapse.

He did not look up as Margie came back into the room. She sat down. Our eyes met. Her mouth showed the trace of a contemptuous smile.

"You eat like a pig," she said.

For a moment he stopped chewing, but he said nothing, nor did he change his position.

"I don't know how I ever managed to suffer through meal after meal, watching your disgusting exhibition."

His plate was empty. He shoved it aside. "On Sunday, your suffering will be over," he said.

Silence.

"I'm glad," Margie said in a hard voice. "I must have been blind."

He straightened up. "You weren't blind, my love," he said. "Not in bed. You had your eyes wide open."

I went home as soon as I could. Down at the servants' entrance, I saw two shadowy figures melted into one. When I approached the front door, the shadows separated. In the dim light I recognized Hanna and her S.A. man. I turned my head.

In my bedroom, I took out Barbara's note and read it once more, then I tore it up into tiny pieces. Wouldn't that be a celebration for Adriani if he could catch me at a clandestine meeting with Barbara or Konrad! He could march the Jew to a concentration camp and have some good, clean fun with him.

This is a new entry.

I won't mention any more specific days or dates. I cannot write every day—we are very busy at the office. The new laws and decrees make it necessary for us to reexamine and revise many of our pending cases. The pre-Hitler legal structure is being disassembled piece by piece, while the Nazi judiciary prepares the new German civil code.

A week has elapsed since I received Barbara's note. I see in the newspapers that another director has taken over the rehearsals of the Gerhart Hauptmann play. No reason has been given for the change.

I find I get irritable and tense every afternoon between five and five thirty. I see Barbara in the crowd on Tauentzienstrasse making her way slowly from one corner to the other, looking for me. Waiting for me. The note said it was urgent. Obviously, they are counting on me for help. But I cannot help them. If I ever got together with her or Konrad, I would have to inform Adriani.

I was in Klaus's office when Dr. Koenig came in. For the first time since he had joined us, he wore his S.S. uniform.

"Am I disturbing you, gentlemen?"

He gave us a crooked smile and sat down opposite Klaus, who was at his desk. I sat on the couch.

"What is your rank in the S.S.?" Klaus asked.

"*Untersturmfuehrer*," Koenig said. "I'd like to tell you—"

"I am a major in the German army," Klaus said. "I am not in the habit of wearing my uniform in our law office."

"Any objection to the S.S. uniform?" Koenig asked icily.

Klaus answered in the same tone. "Only to a member of our firm displaying it during office hours."

"I am acknowledging your reproach and stand corrected," Koenig said stiffly.

His answer irritated me. "Look, Dr. Koenig, let's not be so pompous about everything. Why did you come in? What can we do for you?"

I detest the man. I know the feeling is mutual. Dr. Koenig swallowed. "I read through most of your files and I must say I'm very favorably impressed. You've met with much success."

"Thank you, Dr. Koenig," Klaus said. He gave the line a soulfully benign connotation.

"I haven't seen all your files, though, have I?" Koenig asked.

"We don't know what you've seen," I said.

"Some of your records seem to be missing."

"What makes you say that?" Klaus asked.

"Well, I remember one specific litigation some time back. One of the names involved was Bitterfeld, wasn't it?"

Klaus and I exchanged looks. It didn't escape Dr. Koenig. A thin smile appeared on his face.

"How *is* Gustaf Angermann these days?" I asked. "I hope he's gainfully employed."

The question took Dr. Koenig by surprise. He paused, pretending to search his memory. "Angermann—oh, yes. I've run into him once or twice. He used to work for you, didn't he?"

"Yes. Until he was fired," Klaus said. "You're undoubtedly referring to Axner versus Bitterfeld."

He unlocked one of his desk drawers. "Here's the file, Dr. Koenig. Study it at your leisure and turn it over to the Gestapo."

Dr. Koenig rose, indignant. "How can you accuse me of such nefarious intentions, Dr. von Isenberg?"

"I'm not accusing you. I'm just anticipating your next move."

"Nothing could be farther from my mind," Koenig said firmly.

"I'm glad to hear that. Now, what is it you wanted to know?"

"I understand that case was highly controversial," Koenig said.

"Not any more controversial than your qualifications as an attorney," Klaus said calmly.

I looked at him, surprised. Koenig said, "I object to these insinuations! I shall complain to the Ministry of Justice—"

Klaus cut in, "Do that. Do that right away."

He took a sheet of paper from the same drawer. He said, "I must apologize to you, Hans, but I did expect some dirty business from Dr. Koenig . . . and I did some research on my own to protect us."

He turned to Koenig. "You're not a doctor of law, Mr. Koenig. You've never had any legal training. In the opinion of a well-accredited handwriting expert whom I consulted, the signature of the dean of the University of Freiburg is forged. You never attended that university. The law school certificate is, undoubtedly, your own product, a self-fabricated document— as such, not badly done. You used these two fictitious instruments to be accepted on the legal staff of the Nazi Party and that, in turn, got you admitted to the Board of Attorneys under heavy pressure from your Nazi colleagues. I think this information would be most interesting to certain members of your party and to the minister of justice himself."

Koenig had paled. "None of this is true," he said. "Your expert's sold you a pack of lies and you've fallen for it."

"Yes, I have, Mr. Koenig."

Koenig was trying desperately to regain his dignity, but Klaus gave him no chance. He said to me, "What we know gives us sufficient reason to void our contract with him."

"Yes, of course."

"I can't see it that way," Koenig said. "Even if I did make a mistake and my memory slipped—which I don't concede at all —our contract is valid."

Klaus shook his head. "Again, you give us proof that you don't know anything about law. We accepted you as a partner in the firm because you gave us to understand you were a qualified attorney. But you aren't. Misinterpretation with fraudulent intent constitutes 'false pretense.' And 'false pretense,' designed to obtain money or material values, is a crime."

Koenig gave up. He looked at Klaus, then at me. "What do you want me to do? I relinquished my own practice—"

"You didn't relinquish very much," Klaus said. "Your income last year was sixty-five hundred marks, after taxes."

Koenig's mouth began to tremble. "Please, Dr. von Isenberg, Dr. Bauer—consider that my reputation is at—"

Klaus cut in sharply, "What reputation—?"

Koenig sat down and lowered his head. Klaus said, "If my partner agrees, we might allow you to stay with us—what do you think, Hans?"

I shrugged. "In certain situations, he could be of value to us."

Koenig broke in, "Yes, I'm sure of that. I'll do my utmost—"

"As an errand boy," Klaus said. "A go-between, whenever we need a favor from the party. As a flunky—"

"Please, Dr. von Isenberg," Koenig said. His voice was hardly audible.

I loathe the man, but I thought he had had enough. "Let's go back to work," I said. I looked at Klaus. He had not heard me. He was breathing heavily, his face flushed, his mouth distorted.

"I don't give a damn about your feelings, Mr. Koenig," he said savagely. "I like your whining even less than your impudence. You are a miserable creature. A blackmailer. A fraud. Repeat that with Dr. Bauer as a witness, and we will tolerate you in our office."

There was a pause. Koenig raised his head. "I can't."

Klaus rose from his desk chair and went up to Koenig. "There's a lot of money in this deal, Koenig. You have a family.

You might even have a mother. If we throw you out and inform your friend, the minister, and the Board of Attorneys, it won't be easy—"

Koenig shouted, "I am a blackmailer and a fraud!"

He buried his head in his hands.

"You forgot the miserable creature."

Tonelessly, "—a miserable creature—"

Klaus went back behind his desk and sat down. I saw the storm of fury slowly ebb in him. There was no satisfaction in his face, just a tense agitation, akin to fear.

Koenig got up. He stood motionless and looked at Klaus, but Klaus did not see him. Koenig turned. Our eyes met and held. He despised himself, but he had taken the insults and the humiliation because he wanted to stay at all costs.

"I'm sorry," he said softly.

When he had left, Klaus said, "I regret nothing."

"You enjoyed it, didn't you?"

"Yes. I could have trampled him underfoot, literally. I'm learning, Hans. I'm learning the method and the execution. I'll make a great Nazi."

I shook my head. "Don't say that." But I'd had the same thought watching him. For a moment he was silent and his body seemed to relax. But the fear was still in his face.

"What price living in the Third Reich," he said.

Later, at the end of the day, I was signing letters, Magda was waiting.

"Any more calls?" I asked.

"Just one—you were in conference and the call didn't seem important. He said he'd call you later at home."

"Who was it?"

"He didn't give his name."

"Didn't you ask?"

"Oh, sure. But he hung up."

I finished signing and handed Magda the folder. She went out.

Who could it have been? Barbara or Konrad? Konrad. She said it was a man. Under the circumstances, he wouldn't have left his name. I looked at my desk clock. Five thirty. Suddenly, I felt very tired. I leaned back in my chair and closed my eyes.

Now we have a flunky in our office. A genuine Nazi flunky— but a dangerous one. He'll be at our beck and call, but he'll never forget his humiliation. He'll wait for his opportunity. I know Klaus; he'll never get it. Any time he tries to rebel, he'll be faced with exposure.

Just like—

It's a hateful comparison, I don't want to think of it. But it fits. The similarity is obvious. What Klaus is to Koenig, Adriani is to me. I am at the same time blackmailer and victim. And there we have the exact analogy: blackmailer versus victim equals Nazi versus Jew.

In the evening, the mysterious phone call came to my house. A man's voice said, "Dr. Bauer?"

I knew that voice. Where had I heard it before?

"You might remember the case I treated at your request— recently?"

Dr. Hirsch.

"Yes, I do."

"The patient's out of danger, but she's still quite ill."

"Is she at the hospital?"

"No. They were short on beds. At the moment, she's staying at my home."

"Doesn't she have parents or other relatives?"

There was a pause. Dr. Hirsch said, "I've tried to get in

touch with . . . the other interested party, but I can't reach them. I must consult with somebody. Would you know where I could find them?"

"No, I'm sorry."

"The point is, she can't stay here for very long," the doctor said. "I'm cramped for space."

Why did he have to call me? I have nothing to do with this. I was at the Willmans', accidentally, when she arrived. I helped them get a doctor. That's all.

"Dr. Bauer—"

"Yes."

"I didn't know if we were still connected."

"Let me give it some thought," I said. "Where can I reach you?"

"I'm in the phone book," Dr. Hirsch said.

I am writing this *much later*.

Some of the details I remember only vaguely, but I know I made my decision on the evening Dr. Hirsch called me. I was at home. One lamp was lit. I'd left my study, so it couldn't have been my desk lamp. I must have sat in the living room. There was music. Music of great beauty. Yes, I was listening to "Libera Me," the last movement of Verdi's *Requiem*: "Deliver me, O Lord, from eternal death on that dreadful day when the Heaven and the Earth shall be moved, and Thou shalt come to judge the world by fire."

I remember it now clearly. I saw before me the dreaded image, the yellowed skull with the naked eyes and the bloody incision that had once been a mouth. And then the image changed. The eyes began to live. The mouth opened. I was frightened, and the power of the choir and the orchestra heightened my fear.

I can't account for every one of my movements. I know I could still hear the music when I left. I must have forgotten to shut off the radio. The next thing I remember is a door opening. Dr. Hirsch stood in the light that spilled from his apartment out onto the staircase. He was so thin. His body drowned in his suit.

"My quarters are small," he said.

He had one room, furnished with heavy armchairs, two large couches, and a clutter of old-fashioned art objects and books. There was little space to move.

"All the expensive junk," he said, "from the apartment I used to live in." He raised both arms in a gesture of frustration and regret.

In the back hung a curtain, which he pulled aside. It enclosed a small kitchenette and a clothes closet. A bed had been squeezed in and filled the room in its entirety. It was impossible to reach the stove or the closet without first removing the bed.

The girl had her back turned to us. She seemed asleep. Pointing at the lack of space, the doctor said, "You see?"

I nodded. "How is she?"

"Better. What she needed was a plastic surgeon to rebuild her face. There was one at the hospital and he started on her, but the next day his affidavit for Brazil came through and he had to leave."

"And there is no other plastic surgeon in Berlin?"

"Not a Jewish one."

"What about your affidavit, doctor?" I asked. "To Mexico, wasn't it?"

"Yes. I have it."

"When are you going to leave?"

"Soon," he said.

I saw from his expression that he didn't want to talk about it. The girl moved.

"Is there somebody with you?" she whispered.

"Yes. A friend of the Willman family. You won't remember him," Dr. Hirsch said.

She turned slowly. I saw her face.

It was rigidly bandaged from the chin up. Behind the bandage, I could see that her hair had been shaved off. Her cheeks had filled out—her head was not a skull anymore. The eyes, still without brows, were part of her face again: they looked enormous. Her nose was in a cast. When she opened her mouth, I saw that some of the teeth she had lost had been replaced. The color of her skin was gray, her forehead heavily lined. She asked. "Who are you?"

Her restored voice sounded very strong, but it came out of an old woman's mouth.

"I am Hans Bauer . . . a friend of Barbara's and Konrad's. I was at Mrs. Teilhaber's house when you came in."

"You saw me then?"

"Yes."

"How dreadful," she said.

"Dr. Hirsch called me."

"I promised him," Dr. Hirsch said. "He wanted to know how you were getting along."

The girl turned to me. "Isn't he a saint?"

Dr. Hirsch shuddered. "God forbid."

"A Jewish saint," the girl said.

The telephone shrilled.

"There are no saints in the Jewish religion," Dr. Hirsch said as he went to take the call. For a moment, he couldn't find the telephone. When it rang again, he discovered it on the floor between one of the couches and his desk.

The girl asked, "Have you seen Barbara and Konrad? How are they?"

"They're fine," I lied.

"They've been very good to me and they aren't even Jewish."

"Some Aryans are very decent."

"What are you?"

"I am not a Jew."

She looked at me. Her eyes were very beautiful, I thought.

"Why did you come here?" she asked.

"I wanted to see you."

"Why?"

"Because—because—you are all alone, aren't you?"

I saw her eyes getting moist and I said, "I don't want to upset you."

She shook her head. "You don't."

"Maybe you shouldn't talk so much."

"I love to talk. For a long time, I couldn't—but I've recovered very fast. Don't you agree?"

"Yes. Very fast."

"Dr. Hirsch isn't at home very much. I don't have anybody to talk to."

The doctor came back from the telephone. He was putting his overcoat on.

"I have to leave," he said. "It won't take long. It's in the neighborhood." He reached for his satchel. "Can you stay until I get back, Dr. Bauer?"

"Yes."

"Good. Don't answer the doorbell and don't answer the telephone," he said. He opened the door and added, "Washroom and toilet are two flights down." Then he left.

When we were alone, the girl looked at me again. "Will anybody ever fall in love with me again?" she asked.

"Why, of course."

"But my face looks terrible still and it won't look much better
—ever."

"It isn't bad now, Berta," I said. "I'm sure it'll be lovely again
once everything is healed."

"You know my name."

"Just Berta."

"Berta Gruen . . . you know, my face was the first part of
my body they hit," she said, "when the interrogation began.
After every question, one of the S.A. men slapped me. 'Answer,
you Jewish sow!' I'll never forget that man. His face was wide
and flat, his nose half-squashed; its wings stretched almost to his
cheeks. His breath stank of onions and stale beer. He had long
arms like an ape and huge hands. He broke every bone in my
head. I told him nothing. I don't think I could have talked, even
if I'd wanted to. There was so much blood in my mouth. And
my teeth—I had to spit them out and I spit them right in his
face. After that he used his fists."

She had turned her face to the wall with the kitchenette. She
spoke more to herself than to me.

"I don't remember how long that lasted. I thought it went on
forever. Finally, I fainted. They poured water on me until I
came to again. I was drenched, and so tired that another S.A.
man had to hold me. He stood behind me and clasped his arms
around my body. His hands squeezed my breasts, and while the
questioning went on, and the first S.A. man hit me, I felt—"

She paused for a moment.

"I felt the man holding me getting excited—sexually excited.
I was so full of terror that I screamed . . . I thought I did . . .
and then I must have fainted again. I woke up in a different
room. They had taken off my dress. I was alone with two
brownshirts. They stripped me. I couldn't resist: I was much
too weak. One of them grabbed my legs and held them apart.
The other one opened his pants and got inside me . . . and
after him, the one who stank raped me, I don't know how many

times. I didn't faint. I prayed to God to let me die . . . but I didn't die. Another man came in. He wore a black uniform. I couldn't see his face—there was too much blood in my eyes. I remember, though, that the two S.A. men let go of me. I was nude and dirty and I knew my breath was as foul as theirs."

Her voice was fading. She seemed exhausted and stopped.

"Don't talk about that anymore," I said very softly. I was barely able to bring out the words. "You mustn't do that to yourself. You must try to forget."

She turned to me and shook her head.

"No . . . no . . . I've never told anybody. I have to— empty myself of it—I must talk. Can't you understand that?"

"Yes."

"The two S.A. men picked me up and carried me to a chair. Then they left. There was a table, on it some oddly shaped things. I didn't know what they were. The man in the black uniform sat across from me. I only saw his hands, I never got to see his face. I remember he had a soothing voice. He said he wanted to give me one more opportunity to talk. If I didn't, he would be forced to hurt me very badly and he would hate to do that. He said it was against his nature to torture people. And then he asked me, 'Where is Walter Stengler?' "

She interrupted herself.

"Walter Stengler had been my lover—he wasn't anymore; we'd parted only a month ago—but we were still friends. Walter is a Communist organizer. He'd escaped and they wanted to know where he was hiding. They thought I had to know, that's why they arrested me: a Jewess with a Communist lover. I did know where he was, but I couldn't betray him."

He wasn't her lover anymore. Only a friend. But she couldn't betray her friend.

She continued.

"I told the S.S. man that I hadn't heard from Walter and that I didn't know where he was. Maybe he'd gone abroad. He said,

'We're sure he's still in Berlin.' I was so frightened, I couldn't speak. I just shook my head. He said, 'I'm very, very sorry'— I'll never forget the tone of his voice, it sounded as if he really meant it. But then he leaned across the table and reached for something on both sides of my chair. It was a wide belt, and he strapped me into the chair very tightly. He was careful not to touch my naked body, but there must have been some sharp metal underneath the belt. It cut my skin and hurt. He took one of my hands and stretched my arm across the table. He rigged something I couldn't see . . . then after a moment, I felt the most excruciating pain I had ever suffered. It felt as if my whole body were being torn apart. I went out, cold. When I came to, I don't know how and when, he asked me again where Walter was hiding. I pressed my lips together. Blood shot out of my mouth and then the terrible pain came again. I fainted ten times. Ten times he brought me back and started all over again . . . questions . . . torture. The last time I came to, I was lying on a cot. I thought my hands were on fire, they hurt so much. I tried to raise them, but I didn't have the strength. I moved my head and saw that both my hands were heavily bandaged. I could feel and hear the throbbing of the wounds. Blood was all around me . . . on the cot . . . on the floor. Then I realized that the S.S. man who had talked so softly had pulled out my fingernails, one by one."

She stopped and I got up. She had gone through unspeakable pains of torture and I could not take the mere telling of it. I wanted to walk away from the bed, away from the horrible image which I would never be able to lose again. But there wasn't anywhere to walk. I stood squeezed in between the heavy pieces of furniture, took out my handkerchief and wiped my eyes.

Once more her voice:

"Worse than the pains was the doubt. Part of the time I had not been conscious and, even between my fainting spells, strapped in the chair, I'd been in a continuous state of terror. I'd no way of knowing if I had talked. I couldn't walk. Two brownshirts I hadn't seen before carried me on the cot through a long, dark tunnel and set the cot down in front of a door. They opened the door and I saw a very small cell—a hole about my size. They put me in, upright, and locked the door. I stood there nude. The weight of the bandages pulled me down, but I could do nothing but stand. There was no room for sitting or falling. The four walls were so close, they touched my body. I don't know how long I stood there, it must have been several days and nights. After a while, I became hungry . . . no one came. It got so I could think of nothing but food. Then the blood in my mouth began to dry—I'd swallowed a lot of it; now I was thirsty—I craved a drop of water. Finally, the door opened. The first S.A. man came in, the one who stank. He held a pitcher of water and a plate of meat and cheese, but he didn't give them to me. He asked me the same questions again, and when I shook my head, he went off with the water and the food. I don't know what I did after that. I wasn't in my right mind anymore. I still don't know if I betrayed Walter in the final hours."

I moved one of the chairs closer to the bed. "I'm sure you didn't."

She looked at me. "You're crying."

I touched my face. "I wasn't aware of it."

She pulled her arms out from under the blanket, her hands still bandaged, and reaching for my hand, put it between her two. We sat in silence. I felt my tears running down my cheeks. She kept looking at me. Her lips formed something akin to a smile. It was as if she were trying to console me in my sorrow. After a while, she withdrew her hands.

"How did you get away?" I asked.

"I was unconscious when they took me out of the cell," she said. "When I came to, I was back in the first room where the interrogation had started. The S.A. man who had questioned me was there, and many others. I was lying on the floor . . . somebody must have dressed me. One of the men said, 'You can leave.' He pointed at the door. 'The door is open.' I asked, 'Did I talk?' 'Talk about what?' the man said and the others began to laugh. 'Did I talk? Please tell me!' I don't know if I screamed, I don't think I had the strength for it, but I remember that I was screaming in my mind. 'Get out, you Jewish tart, before we kill you,' the man said. I tried to get up, but it was impossible. I could hold on to nothing with my bandaged hands. Finally, I started to crawl to the door and all the S.A. men burst out laughing. I had to get away from the jeering and the shouting and I reached the open door. I was outside and I could see the lights of the gate at the end of the compound . . . it was so far away . . . I knew I would never get there. I crawled. Every few minutes, I had to stop and rest—then about midway to the gate, I saw the boots of two S.A. men. I didn't dare look up, I was too scared. One of them reached for me and I asked him not to beat me. He picked me up and held me in his arms. It was dark and the other S.A. man turned on his flashlight to look at my face. It hurt my eyes. I heard one of them say, 'What the hell did they do to her?' And the other one cursed, but then the first one said, 'You'd better shut up.' One of them asked me where I wanted to go . . . I thought and thought and I remembered that Barbara and Konrad had moved to her mother's house and that the house was close to the camp . . . but I couldn't remember her mother's name. They took me to the gate and one of them said, 'We can't let her out without her release papers.' They searched my clothes and couldn't find them. The guards came out. The men put me on the ground and they all stood there and looked at me . . . they were very quiet . . . one of the guards went to the phone and when he returned, he moved us on. The two S.A. men carried me out and asked me again where I wanted to go. I still couldn't remember the name, but I thought I could recognize the house, I'd been there before. I couldn't talk, only whisper, but they understood. They took a motorcycle and put me on the back seat. I couldn't sit up, so they placed me horizontally across the seat, my head and legs hanging down, and strapped me on. One of the men got on and drove off with me. I must have lost consciousness, because the next thing I remember is being close to the house and the S.A. man stopping and getting off. He raised my head and talked to me, then he walked his motorcycle slowly along the street until I motioned to him that I recognized the house. He removed the straps and set me on the ground. I didn't even thank him, I was still numb . . . but later I prayed for both men. For a while, I lay quietly, too weak to move, then I crawled to the driveway. After many attempts I managed to pull myself up, I don't remember how, and knocked on the door."

I don't know how long the silence between us lasted. I could think of nothing to say. All words have been inadequate. And that is how I feel now: inadequate. I made my deal with Adriani because I didn't want to be a Jew. I am not a Jew. I want to stay in my country. But now I keep asking myself: where is my country? Where is the Germany I love?

Someday I will say "Heil Hitler" to a man in a black uniform and he might be the same man who pulled out Berta's fingernails, one by one. He and I will have a drink together and I will try to be pleasant to him, because I have to. I have joined them. I am playing their game. And by joining them, I am condoning their reign of terror and fire and rape. I am an accessory to their crimes. I am as guilty as they are.

I heard Berta's voice. "Dr. Bauer—"

"Yes."

"You look sick."

"Yes, I am sick."

"Why don't you ask Dr. Hirsch—" She stopped and said, "Oh, no, I forgot. He isn't allowed to treat you."

213 «

"A doctor can't help me," I said. "It's not that kind of an illness."

She looked at me, her eyes asking a question. But she did not speak and I did not answer.

"Where are you going to go from here?" I asked. "Where are your parents?"

"They emigrated to the United States as soon as Hitler came to power. They were smart. I refused to join them because I wanted to stay with Walter."

"Can't they send you an affidavit?"

She shook her head. "They're too poor. Maybe later, when my father earns more money. Dr. Hirsch said he might be able to get me a visa to Mexico."

"To Mexico? You need an affidavit there too."

"He has one, and he hopes he can get another one for me."

"He's a remarkable man," I said.

There was a pause.

"May I ask you something, Dr. Bauer?"

"Of course."

"You don't hate Jews, do you?"

"I wouldn't be here if I did."

"That's what I thought," Berta said. She hesitated before she continued. "You've seen me only once—what was left of me. You couldn't—I mean—it's impossible that you were worried about me. Why did you really come here?"

"To exorcise a ghost."

"Am I the ghost?"

"I couldn't forget your face," I said.

She stared at me. "I didn't have a face then."

"Thinking of it used to frighten me," I said. "I tried hard to forget it—but now I know that it saved me."

A key turned in the lock and Dr. Hirsch returned. "How's the patient?" He threw his overcoat on one of the couches.

"It was good to talk to Dr. Bauer," Berta said.

"You shouldn't talk too much and you know it," Dr. Hirsch said. "I'm sorry about the delay, Dr. Bauer. You've been here much too long. It wouldn't be good for either of us if you were seen here. I'll make this very short. I don't think Miss Gruen is safe here—or anywhere in Germany. She should leave the country as soon as she can. For that, she needs her papers. Miss Gruen gave them to Mrs. Willman because she feared she would be arrested—which happened two days later. I haven't been able to get in touch with the Willmans and I would much rather stay out of this. It's dangerous for a Jew to make himself noticeable. I thought you might be able to get Miss Gruen's papers from Mrs. Willman. Have you seen them lately?"

"No." I couldn't suppress a smile. It seemed that, step by step, decisions were being made for me. Maybe that would make everything much easier.

Dr. Hirsch misunderstood my smile. "Of course, you as an Aryan can't comprehend the predicament of the Jews. Frankly, I hate to ask a favor from you, but I'm not asking it for myself."

The girl had listened silently. "Dr. Bauer is our friend."

Dr. Hirsch shook his head. "No Aryan is our friend."

"I don't blame you for your opinion, Dr. Hirsch," I said. "Let me just say . . . I'll see what I can do."

"I appreciate that," he said stiffly. "I don't want to be rude, but I must urge you to leave now."

I went to the bed. Berta raised her head and looked at me. "Thank you, Dr. Bauer."

Dr. Hirsch was impatient. He ushered me out as fast as he could. When we were in the corridor, I asked, "What about the Mexican affidavit? Can you really get another one for her?"

"She had no business talking to you about that," the doctor said. He didn't answer my question. "Please try to contact Mrs. Willman as soon as possible."

"Do you think they'll try to arrest her again? She couldn't go through this a second time."

"No, she couldn't," Dr. Hirsch said. "In case that should happen—God forbid—she has a cyanide pill."

He turned and went back into his room. As he closed the door, he said, "Good night, Dr. Bauer."

The next day.

Good night, Dr. Bauer.

Good morning, Dr. Bauer.

Did you have a good rest last night? Did you have nightmares or did you sleep peacefully? The sleep of the just.

Konrad Willman says that guilt is an ignoble emotion. I hope you didn't suffer from it, Dr. Bauer. I hope the tortured body of Berta Gruen did not appear in your slumber. Or did you dream that you yourself strapped her body in the chair, pulled out her fingernails, one by one? You wore a black uniform, Dr. Bauer. You were sweating. You looked at Berta Gruen's naked body. She was dead. You had killed her. That's why you screamed in your dream. And you were still screaming when you woke up.

Good morning, Dr. Bauer.

Heil Hitler!

I spent the day in the office. I'd felt fatigued when I got out of bed, but gripped by an excitement that made me restless and impatient.

"You look as if you hadn't had any sleep," Klaus said.

"I didn't get much last night."

He shook his head and said nothing.

"I know what you're driving at," I said. "You want me to go to a doctor. You think I'm sick."

"You *are* sick," Klaus said. "Take a week off. Try to relax."

"I just took off four months."

"That was different."

We were waiting for a client and were alone in Klaus's office. He asked, "Did you hear from Adriani again?"

"Yes."

He looked at me. I knew he expected me to talk, but I couldn't. He said, "I've been wondering all along."

"What about?"

"If you would be able to take it." He was sitting at his desk, and I at the far end of the couch. We were separated by the entire length of the room. "You know what I mean, don't you?"

"Yes, I know what you mean," I said.

He opened the file on his desk and glanced at it cursorily. "I heard yesterday that the quota for the United States wasn't full yet."

"Why are you telling me this, Klaus?"

He continued turning the pages. "I have friends in New York and in Boston," he said. "I might be able to get you an affidavit."

I laughed. "Do you want to get rid of me?"

He looked up from his file. "Exactly."

The intercom buzzed. Hedi announced our client. We had no other opportunity to talk to each other. During the rest of the day we were never alone.

I spoke to Alfred Koenig for a few minutes. He came to my office to "clarify his position," as he phrased it. He was very apologetic, but the irritating fact was that his "humble" attitude was much harder to take than his former arrogance. After he had concluded his brief statement, there was no dignity left in him. It was an embarrassing performance. I was glad when he left.

I had made up my mind to meet Barbara. I had to get Berta's papers from her and, at the same time, I could listen to what she had to tell me. That's as far as I had thought it out. I didn't know what I would do after I had seen her. I didn't want to think about it. I wasn't committed to anything. I had no intention of letting my emotions wreck my life. Maybe there was a way to satisfy Adriani without betraying my friends.

I took a cab to the Kaiser Wilhelm Memorial Church and walked from there to the Tauentzienstrasse. I was at the K.D.W. department store at five minutes past six. It was the evening rush hour, the street was crowded. Twilight was setting in. I passed the store, went up to the end of the next block, and turned back.

Barbara was standing in front of one of the show windows. She must have been watching me in the reflection of the glass. When I came close, she turned and said, "Hans, how nice to meet you!"

She sounded so genuinely surprised that I was reminded of the many times in the past when I had admired her on the stage. "Are you in a hurry? Can you walk with me for a few minutes? I haven't seen you for a long time."

"Yes, it has been a long time," I said.

Her next sentence came out just as cheerfully. "I'd almost given up on you."

"It wasn't easy for me to come," I said.

"I know. We're both grateful to you. We left our place. We were warned that the Gestapo would arrest Konrad."

"Why?"

"Our friend who is now in Paris. The writing he did at our house—"

"Where do you live now?"

"We change quarters every night. Konrad doesn't go out anymore. I do—very rarely—only if it's urgent."

We walked leisurely. She had put her arm in mine and was smiling at me. We might have looked like two people in love.

"Who warned you, Barbara?"

"Remember our driver? We used to call him 'Satan.' He was inside one of the trucks the Nazis caught. You might have read about it."

"Yes. Was he the sixth man who escaped?"

Barbara frowned. "He came to see us in an S.S. uniform—he scared us to death. He'd learned that one of the printers had broken under torture and told the Nazis that our friend had written the pamplets. Unfortunately, that printer had been at our house to pick up the pamphlets."

"But you and Konrad didn't know anything about this—?"

"Who would believe that, Hans?" She added rapidly, "I want to make this short. I don't want to take any risks."

"Are you being followed?"

"No. I've been very careful, Hans. I've never taken the same route twice coming here. If I weren't sure nobody had trailed me, I'd have left before you got here." She squeezed my hand. "Something else. You know how much Mother hates Konrad and you remember the evening that girl—"

"I saw Berta last night."

"You did—?!" She seemed startled. "How is she?"

"Better. She needs her papers. That's one of the reasons I'm here."

"Konrad has them. We'll mail them to you tonight. Mother went to the Gestapo and—"

I gasped. "She couldn't have done that, Barbara!"

"She did—and I must say, I expected it. I know my mother. She denounced Konrad for harboring a Jewish escapee from the reeducation center and for associating with Jews and Communists. Add this to the story about our friend in Paris and you know we have to get out of Germany."

"Can you?"

"We have the opportunity now. Konrad's been invited to direct a play in London. We asked for an affidavit and visa. Our agent in London knows the situation. The officials there will deal directly with the British embassy here. The German authorities aren't involved. We've asked that the papers be sent to you. You're the only person Konrad and I trust. That's why I was so anxious to meet you, Hans. They should arrive any day now."

"But what about exit permits?"

"We're buying them."

"Buying—?"

"Yes. Don't you know how corrupt some of those Nazi officials are? It'll cost us another fifty thousand marks. That's not too much for two lives."

"Where shall I send the papers, Barbara?"

"To the post office at the Potsdamer station, box 205. I'm so grateful you're doing this for us."

We walked in silence. It was getting dark. The streetlights came on. Barbara said, "When we talked about the truck, you mentioned the sixth man who escaped. How did you know about that, Hans? It didn't get into the papers."

"I must have read it somewhere," I said.

We separated the way we had met. Cheerful and affectionate. We kissed.

I didn't want to be alone that evening. I called Victor Brandt, but he and Eva had gone out for dinner. I was tempted to call Karin, but thought better of it. It wouldn't have made any sense. Then I phoned Grete Fall. She was alone. She was working on her new script, but she'd love to see me if I promised not to keep her up too late.

I hadn't talked to her since the night after her mother's death, and I felt odd when she opened the door, dressed in a white, fluffy lounging robe. We kissed medium casually, then she held on to me and looked at me for a long time.

"I'm as embarrassed as you are," she said with a smile.

The manuscript was on the couch. I picked it up, careful not to lose her place, put it on the table, and sat down. She came and sat next to me.

"It's a terrible part," she said.

"What are you playing?"

"A girl who is forced to join the Hitler Youth. First she hates it, then she becomes a fanatical Nazi. It ends with an apotheosis, glorifying the Fuehrer and the Third Reich."

"That sounds like fun," I said.

She sighed. "Every picture is going to be like that."

"Of course."

"You don't look well, Hans," she said.

"People have been telling me that."

"What's wrong?"

I didn't answer her. Instead, I got up and went to the bar. "Do you mind?"

"Help yourself."

"What about you?"

"Not tonight. I have to work."

I poured some whiskey into a shot glass and drank it down.

"How ambitious are you?" I asked.

She raised her head. "Very ambitious. Very, very ambitious."

"Acting is everything to you?"

"Yes, everything," she said in a harsh voice. "It's my life."

"And you regret nothing."

I didn't say it as a question. After a moment, she said, "I regret that my mother died."

I saw the tears in her eyes and said, "I'm sorry, Grete."

"Why do you ask these questions?"

"I envy you," I said. "You have one goal and one goal only. You don't give a damn how you get there, because reaching it is more important to you than anything else in the world. You lie for it, you cheat for it, you—"

I broke off. She continued, "I kill for it. Is that what you wanted to say?"

"I didn't want to say it."

I set my glass on the counter and went back to the couch. Grete took my hand. "You know how guilty I felt," she said softly. "It—it tore me to pieces."

"Yes."

"But it's as you told me then. I've learned to live with it."

"It didn't take you long."

"I know." She brought her face close to mine. "Why did you come up here tonight?"

"I didn't want to be alone," I said.

She turned her head. I rose again. "I'm very restless. I don't know what to do with myself."

"What is it that bothers you, Hans? Tell me."

I leaned with my back against the counter, bracing my elbows on its top. I said, "Suppose the Nazis found out about you."

She was startled. "How could they?"

"I said, 'Suppose.' "

"That's impossible, Hans. Why try to figure out something that is—"

I cut in. "Bear with me, please."

"All right. They find out about me."

"And they use their knowledge to blackmail you."

"How?"

"First, a minor case: you are in rehearsal with a play. The Nazis force you to accept a leading man who is a very bad actor, but an old-time party member. If you don't comply, they'll expose you. What would you do?"

"That's a silly question," Grete said. "I'd take the guy they want."

"Without any compunctions?"

"I'd be furious, but I wouldn't have any choice, would I?"

"No, you wouldn't."

She shrugged. I asked, "Now, suppose someone denounces me as a Communist."

Grete was getting very angry. "What kind of a game is this, Hans? What's the purpose?"

"I'm curious, that's all."

She shook her head. "There's more to it."

"No, there isn't."

"All right. Have it your way," Grete said. "The Gestapo think that you are a Communist."

"You're the only one who knows where I'm hiding. They ask you—again threatening to expose you. Would you tell them where I am?"

"No, Hans, really! This is going too far."

"Would you?"

"I can't answer that."

"Why not?"

"Tell me what this is all about."

"Would you betray me?"

She rose and stood very close to me. "Yes!"

"That's what I thought. You're honest."

"I wouldn't like to do it," she said.

The telephone rang. Grete went to take the call. "Hello—"

She listened. Her expression changed. *"Now?"* she asked.

She glanced at me and listened again. "No, it's not convenient at all."

She turned her back to me and listened again. She said, "Yes, I see," and hung up. She turned back to me. "I'm sorry, Hans, but you must leave. I'm expecting a visitor." Her voice was low, but it sounded stubborn, almost defiant.

"It must be an important man," I said.

"He is. He should be here in a few minutes."

She went to the bar and put my glass under the counter.

"He travels fast," I said.

"He does. I don't want you to see him, Hans."

I was already on my way out. "Thanks for the drink, Grete."

She came after me, her face flushed. She embraced me and whispered, "I told you I'd do anything for my career."

I didn't move and she dropped her arms.

"Yes, you did tell me that," I said.

When I reached the street, I saw a black Mercedes limousine drive up to the entrance of the building. The chauffeur and the man next to him jumped from the car to open the door for their passenger.

I went on. I didn't want to know who Grete's visitor was.

The day of decision.

I know this title sounds dramatic—it certainly doesn't fit a diary—but I've long ago given up trying to record events from day to day. I wrote this headline after the whole narrative was finished.

Grete answered my questions the way I expected her to. My talk with her clarified my own position. With Klaus's help, I had complied with Adriani's first demand. Now I was faced with his second blackmail proposal. This one had nothing to do with our firm. It involved nobody but myself. It gave me a choice: betray my friends or put myself in jeopardy.

The instinct for survival dictated self-protection at any cost, regardless of loyalty or friendship. But that also brought up the very real, rational question: would I be able to live with my decision afterward? Would I be capable of facing the brutal fact that I was a murderer? In other words: did I qualify as a Nazi?

Klaus didn't think I would. Proof of it was his offer to get me an affidavit—but once I had committed myself to protecting my friends, an affidavit wouldn't help me anymore. It'd be too late for that. I had no illusions about the consequences.

Barbara had said I was the only person she and Konrad trusted. That was flattering, but I must say I felt embarrassed about it. The last time I had talked to Konrad at the opera, I had not behaved like a friend. I'd been interested only in pleasing Adriani then. It was amazing they still had that much faith in me.

In spite of Barbara's assurances, I never believed that my meeting with her had remained secret. I suppose I have too much respect for the proverbial German efficiency, especially today. It was inconceivable to me that Barbara had not been followed and that, in turn, I had not been identified by one of the Gestapo agents.

The next day, Hanna brought my breakfast and my mail to the study. Among the letters was a bulky one addressed to Konrad Willman, Esq., c/o Dr. Hans Bauer. I took a large envelope, addressed it to Konrad Willman, post office Potsdamer station, Box 205, and stamped it. I looked once more at the address. Box 205. Wouldn't it have been more logical to have had the papers dispatched to that address directly instead of sending them first to me? Maybe the Willmans had been afraid the Gestapo would discover who had rented the box. No, that was impossible. If they'd been afraid of exposure, they wouldn't have asked me to forward the papers. I should have asked Barbara about that, but I hadn't had a chance. She'd been scared, in a great rush—it hadn't occurred to me to ask for an explanation.

While eating my breakfast, the excitement of the day before took hold of me again. I tried to wade through the newspaper, but I couldn't concentrate on reading. I put the paper aside. I was so tense I couldn't even use my letter opener to check the rest of the mail.

Next to the lamp on my desk stood the telephone. I waited for it to ring. It loomed black and large. I stared at it. It seemed to grow until I could see nothing else in the room. I folded my hands to keep them quiet and stretched my arms across the desk to be closer to the phone. Waiting. My fingers began to hurt. I kept my hands tightly clasped. My knuckles were white.

Then the phone rang. The sound shook my whole body. I picked up the receiver and heard the dial tone. Puzzling. I put the receiver back on the hook and waited.

The door to my study stood half open. I heard Hanna's steps crossing the hall. The telephone had not rung. It had been the bell to the entrance door.

I listened. The noise of the door opening. A man's voice, "Heil Hitler." Then, "We'd like to see Dr. Bauer." I went out into the hall. Two men in S.S. uniform stood there, talking to Hanna. She turned when she heard me. "Dr. Bauer, these two gentlemen—"

One of them cut in, "Heil Hitler, Dr. Bauer."

Hanna watched me, her eyes full of fear. I said, "Heil Hitler."

"*Hauptsturmfuehrer* Lentz," the first one said. Pointing at his companion: "*Untersturmfuehrer* Krippe."

"Heil Hitler," Krippe said.

Lentz said, "Orders from *Obergruppenfuehrer* Adriani. He wants to see you in his office."

"Now—?"

"Yes, Dr. Bauer. We hope we aren't causing you any inconvenience."

"I was about to leave for my office."

"Sorry."

Hanna gasped. I looked at her and smiled. She nodded, close to tears, and went out.

"If you'll excuse me, I have to call my secretary," I said. "I have many—"

Lentz cut in. "I am instructed to tell you, Dr. Bauer, that you are not to make any phone calls from your home. You might be able to notify your office later."

I thought of the letter I was supposed to mail, but didn't think they would let me go back into the study.

"I have some letters on my desk," I said. "I have to check them before I leave. Some of them might be urgent."

Lentz thought for a moment and motioned to Krippe, who followed me into my study. I stood at the desk. Krippe watched me closely. In a sudden move, I seized the telephone receiver. Krippe rushed forward. "Stop that, Dr. Bauer!"

He slammed his hand on the cradle. I used the moment of distraction to slip the bulky letter into my pocket. I said, "I'm sorry, I forgot."

"No more of that," Krippe said. "We have to go."

I left the study, trailed by him.

"I'm ready," I said to Lentz. "Just let me tell Hanna I'm leaving."

He made no objection. I opened the door to the corridor and called, "Hanna!"

She came immediately. I took a few steps inside and threw the letter in her direction. I looked at her. She picked it up and nodded.

"I should be back in a couple of hours," I said.

She pressed her lips together.

"Good-by," I said.

The three of us left.

The floor of the large hall was black marble. Pillars divided it in the center, and to the left and right heavy doors, widely spaced, led into offices guarded by men in S.A. uniforms. Adriani's office was at the far end of the hall. Lentz and Krippe said, "Heil Hitler," to the S.S. man at the door; he responded and let us in.

Four secretaries were working in the anteroom, all young and attractive, none of them in uniform. The girl next to the door marked HSPF (Higher SS and Police Fuehrer) got up from her desk.

"This is Dr. Bauer," Lentz said.

The girl smiled and went to the intercom to announce me to Adriani. As I watched her, Lentz and Krippe left without my noticing it. I had to wait a few minutes. Once in a while, one of the four secretaries looked up from her typewriter and gave me a smile. It was a very friendly office.

Adriani's door opened and an S.S. officer came out, young and tall and, from the way he walked, obviously imbued with his own importance. The girls chimed in unison, "Heil Hitler, *Standartenfuehrer* Liegman."

He said, "Heil Hitler, ladies," and walked through and out.

The first secretary motioned to me and opened the door to Adriani's office. As I went in, she said, "This is Dr. Bauer, sir."

Adriani rose.

The room was spacious. Adriani's desk stood at the far end of it, quite a distance from the door. I knew the design. I had seen photographs of Mussolini's office.

Adriani remained standing and shook hands with me across the desk. There was no "Heil Hitler."

I asked, "What does this mean, Mr. Adriani? You send two S.S. officers to pick me up. I'm not allowed to use my telephone—"

"All just routine, Dr. Bauer. Don't be upset," Adriani said.

"I am not a criminal," I snapped.

He pointed at a chair and sat down himself, leaned back and closed his eyes. Then he sat up straight. "Have you seen Karin lately?"

"No, I haven't."

"Margie's leaving Sunday on the *Bremen*," he said. "Karin's going with her."

"To America?"

"Yes. For a short time only. She'll be back."

I didn't comment.

"Margie's very unhappy," he said. "She had an accident. Cut her face."

I watched Adriani. The satisfaction on his face was plain. He seemed about to add something, but then didn't. I crossed my legs and folded my hands.

"There's no reason for you to be nervous, Dr. Bauer."

"Offices like this always make me nervous," I said.

In spite of its luxurious marble floor and a large Persian carpet, the office gave a spartan impression, with its sparse furnishings and incandescent lighting. The dark green heavy curtains were drawn. On the walls were an oversized photograph of Hitler and a smaller one of Heinrich Himmler, head of the S.S.

"You remember our last conversation in Margie's apartment?" Adriani said.

"Oh, yes."

"We spoke about your friends, Barbara and Konrad Willman." He looked at me. "We still haven't been able to get in touch with them."

"You haven't?"

"No."

He reached for a cigarette and offered one to me. I declined. I kept my hands clasped.

"A great number of Gestapo agents are tied up on this project," Adriani said. "I'd hate to waste their time. However—"

He lit his cigarette, drew on it, took it out of his mouth, and examined the burning end of it.

"—they have been able to catch sight of Mrs. Willman on several occasions. It would have been very easy to have picked her up. But they didn't—at my suggestion. I hope she'll lead us to her husband, eventually. Trying to get his whereabouts from her through interrogation would be rather messy, I'm afraid."

He put the cigarette back in his mouth.

"I'm going to be frank with you, Dr. Bauer. I hope you'll reciprocate. So far, your friend Mrs. Willman has outsmarted the Gestapo. Agents have trailed her to numerous apartment buildings, only to lose her inside. Her husband was not at any of those locations."

In a sudden move, he leaned forward and said, "Now give me the information you have."

It was an old courtroom trick and I was too experienced to be impressed by it. I was certain I had been seen with Barbara.

"I ran into Mrs. Willman accidentally," I said.

He raised his eyebrows. "Oh—when was that?"

"Yesterday afternoon on Tauentzienstrasse, near the K.D.W."

"I see."

He crushed the cigarette in his ashtray and leaned back in his chair.

"I must say I'm disappointed in you, Dr. Bauer," he said in a mournful voice.

"Why, Mr. Adriani?"

"I thought we had an agreement. Or am I wrong? Weren't you supposed to call me if and when you had some information on the Willmans?"

"It happened only yesterday afternoon," I said.

"At ten minutes past six. You walked together for about fifteen minutes. You were home at five minutes to seven. Between seven o'clock last night and a quarter to ten this morning, when I finally sent for you, you had, in my modest opinion, plenty of time to contact me."

"Maybe I made a mistake," I said. "Maybe I underrated the

importance of my meeting with Mrs. Willman. The fact is, Mr. Adriani, I don't have any new information."

"Don't you know how to reach them?"

"No, I don't."

"Couldn't you find out?"

"I asked Mrs. Willman, but she wouldn't tell me."

"Why not?"

"She thought it was better if I didn't know."

Adriani closed his eyes for a moment and opened them again. "That means she doesn't trust you," he said. "Remarkable. You're such an honest man."

I was silent. He opened the middle drawer of his desk, took out a small piece of paper, and put it on the desk for me to see. It was a snapshot of Barbara and myself. We were walking arm in arm, smiling at each other and talking.

"Take it, Dr. Bauer. Look at it," Adriani said.

I had to unfold my hands and reach for the photograph. My hands were shaking badly. I knew Adriani observed it.

"A very good likeness," I said.

"Yes, it is. Evidently, you were talking to each other. May I ask what the conversation was about? It seems improbable to me that you were just exchanging gossip."

I thought fast. "Mrs. Willman is very unhappy about her mother," I said.

"Mrs. Teilhaber?"

"Yes. It seems she informed the Gestapo that her son-in-law had harbored a young Jewess, an inmate from the nearby concentration camp."

"We call it a reeducation center," Adriani said.

"I happened to be at Mrs. Teilhaber's house when that girl came in. She was not an escapee, Mr. Adriani. She was let go by the people in charge."

Adriani nodded. "There, you are right. I had the case investigated. She was interrogated—"

"—and tortured."

"Under the circumstances," he said, "the application of physical force is part of the interrogation."

"She was more dead than alive when I saw her."

"That is regrettable." His tone was sharpening. "It is doubly regrettable because it was unnecessary in her case. At the time of her interrogation, her boyfriend, Walter Stengler, had already been taken into protective custody. The center was notified too late."

I felt the impact of his words bodily. Berta Gruen had suffered for nothing. Her body had been wrecked because somebody had been late in making a phone call. Suddenly, my hatred of the man behind the desk became overwhelming.

"What happened to him?"

I realized that my voice was hoarse. Adriani's reaction came fast and hard.

"What business is that of yours, Dr. Bauer? How do you explain your surprising interest in state criminals and their Jewish whores?"

It took all my willpower to restrain myself and to remain in my chair. I said nothing, but Adriani was watching me closely. He knew how I felt.

"To satisfy your warmhearted compassion for Communists and Jews—Spengler was executed. Hanged."

Adriani's face had undergone a change. Its hard and handsome structure was distorted, almost unrecognizable. His mouth was half open. I saw the saliva in the corners of his mouth. He got up from his chair and walked around his desk until he stood close to me. His legs touched my knees. Raising his voice, he said, "It seems to me your compassion for Jews is not an accident, Dr. Bauer. It is inside you, part of you. It stems from your subhuman ancestry."

I jumped up and he stopped and retreated a few steps. I was beside myself.

"I don't know what a Jew is like, I've never felt as a Jew, but —by God!—if I have to choose between being like you and your gang and being a Jew—I'd infinitely prefer being a Jew!"

Adriani looked at me. His mouth closed. His face lit up. It gave me a shock when I realized that he was smiling. He moved backwards, step by step, watching me, until he reached his desk chair. All the time, he was smiling. He sat down and took out some papers from his middle drawer. His voice was calm. The smile was gone. Occasionally consulting his papers, he said, "Your meeting with Mrs. Willman was not accidental. She had been observed at the same location, Tauentzienstrasse, for eight consecutive evenings, always at the same time. From six to six thirty. She was obviously waiting for someone. She was waiting for you. It is improbable, if not impossible, that in your fifteen-minute-long conversation, nothing was said about their where-abouts, their present plight, their plans for the future. All this is vital information which would lead to the arrest of an enemy of the state. I am asking you now, Dr. Bauer, to give us all the information you have on Mr. and Mrs. Willman."

"I have no information," I said.

He looked at me and said softly, "If you maintain this untenable position, Dr. Bauer, I shall have to turn you over to the Gestapo for interrogation."

I was silent. At that moment, I felt no fear. Adriani lowered his head. He waited. As nothing came from me, he continued, "I further advise you that due to a clerical error by one of my subordinates, your personal papers have been incorrectly evaluated. In checking your records myself, it has come to my attention that you are of Jewish ancestry. You have made a deliberate effort to hide this from the responsible officials and tried to pass yourself off as an Aryan. You are a Jew. I am notifying you herewith that the laws and decrees concerning the Jews which have been issued under the collective title 'Laws and Decrees for the Protection of the Blood' apply to you in full."

He stopped and glanced again at the papers. "That is all, Dr. Bauer."

He put the papers back in the folder and leaned forward. "I might add that I personally regret this turn of affairs. It was not my choice. It was yours. I had hoped that our relationship would develop in a . . . different direction. But I must say that I had my doubts about you from the very beginning. When I called you an honest man, I meant it. Too bad."

"Do what you have to do," I said. "I'm tired of your voice."

Adriani's face reddened. He pressed a button on his desk harder than necessary.

Hauptsturmfuehrer Lentz entered and stood at attention at the door. Adriani motioned to him. Lentz walked the distance to the desk. Adriani handed him the folder.

"The Jew, Hans Bauer, is in protective custody and ready for interrogation," he said.

He did not look at me again. He remained seated as Lentz handcuffed me and led me out.

Hours later, I found myself in a Mercedes limousine. I wasn't scared. I felt nothing. Maybe I was convinced that none of this was real. I could not be sitting here, handcuffed to *Hauptsturm-fuehrer* Lentz. It didn't make sense.

I had been waiting for hours in different offices. Handcuffs off. Handcuffs on. I didn't know why I had been kept waiting. I talked to nobody. No one spoke to me.

Now it was evening. Twilight had changed to darkness. The car was going very fast. I'd asked Lentz where he was taking me, but he hadn't answered. We came to a crossing, and the Mercedes slowed down to turn into a side road which was unpaved and full of holes.

Suddenly, I knew—and as the eerie experience of my first ride toward the camp repeated itself and I remembered my terror, the same fear struck me again. I saw the glaring lights and, closer, the outlines of the massive structure, the towers at the corners, and the searchlights slowly turning in a full circle. Three hundred and sixty degrees.

Now the searchlight hit the Mercedes and stayed on it. The main gate raced toward us, flooded in white, flanked by brown-shirts armed with rifles.

The driver rolled down his window. I heard the "Blue Danube" waltz blaring from the loudspeakers. What selection would they play for me?

For a few seconds, the car stopped at the gate. There was an exchange of "Heil Hitler." Then we drove on.

We entered a brightly lit room. It was crowded with people. I saw S.S. uniforms and brownshirts, secretaries behind type-writers and a few men and women handcuffed as I was. Lentz went with me to a group of S.S. officers who stood in one corner of the room. One of them laughed very loudly. He turned as we approached. Lentz stood at attention.

"Heil Hitler, *Sturmbannfuehrer* Linsing."

Lentz did not go with me into the next room. It looked familiar to me. It fitted Berta Gruen's description of the room where she had been raped and tortured. I saw the table, the riggings, and the chair with its straps.

Linsing led me in. One S.S. man and two brownshirts were waiting for us. It gave me a jolt when I recognized Gustaf An-germann. He grinned at me. I'm sure this was the happiest moment in his life.

"Special assignment," Angermann said. "I gave up a delightful rendezvous tonight when I saw your name on the list."

Linsing turned sharply. "What's that?"

Angermann shrank. He stood at attention. "I know this Jew, *Sturmbannfuehrer* Linsing."

"Take off his handcuffs," Linsing snapped.

Angermann stepped up to me and took off my handcuffs. He took a long time doing it and it hurt.

"You scum!" I said.

He slapped my face hard. I gathered all my strength and hit him in the crotch with my foot. He doubled and fell. In the next instant, I was on the floor myself.

"I wouldn't repeat that, Jew!" Linsing said.

The other S.A. man picked me up and Linsing floored me again. I lay still. I heard Gustaf Angermann groan. After a while, my head cleared and I rose by myself.

The other S.S. man had stood motionless. He was very young. He looked as if he were about to get sick.

Linsing said to the other S.A. man, "Take care of Angermann." He straddled a chair. "What's your name, Jew?"

"Hans Bauer," I said.

Linsing motioned to the young S.S. man, who handed him a folder. Linsing glanced at it. The next question came as a surprise to me. "You're a friend of Ludwig Butler's?"

"Yes."

"You know that Butler is a traitor?"

I kept silent. Linsing reached for a horsewhip behind his chair and lashed my face.

"Answer, you Jewish swine!"

"I didn't know he was a traitor," I said.

The whip lashed out again. This time, it hit my neck.

"Do you know it now, Jew?"

I shook my head. The whip hit my groin and the pain was excruciating. I dropped to the floor.

"You want more of that, Jew?"

"No."

It cost me an effort to get out that one word. Linsing said, "Up, Jew!"

I turned on my stomach. It hurt like hell. From a crawling position, I managed to rise. It took a long time.

"Is Ludwig Butler a traitor?"

Oh, for Christ's sake, I thought. Why not? He's gone anyway. I said, "Yes."

"So you have a traitor for a friend, Jew."

I said nothing. He took the hard stem of the horsewhip and hit my face. I felt the blood running down my cheeks. I said, "Yes."

I didn't care if it made sense or not. Linsing opened the folder and glanced at it again.

"Did you know he was going to leave the country?"

What is this? I thought. I'm here because of the Willmans. Why does that son-of-a-bitch jump at—

The stem of the whip came down squarely on the top of my head. The pain was unbearable. I couldn't take another one like this.

"Yes, I knew it."

"And you lied about it, you lousy Jew!" Linsing shouted. He raised the whip. Suddenly, his face paled and his body slackened. He seemed near collapse. The other S.S. man had remained next to him and he helped Linsing get off his chair. Linsing dropped the whip. He rose slowly and turned to the brownshirts. Angermann was up, too, his face purple.

"I leave this Jewish swine to you," Linsing said. "Have fun."

His back stooped, he went out, followed by the other S.S. man. I could see relief in the younger man's face. I was only semiconscious. Angermann came up to me close, too close. His breath stank of garlic and stale beer.

"Strip, Jew!" he shouted. His saliva hit my face. I wanted to vomit. "Take your clothes off! Strip!"

I didn't move. He picked up the horsewhip and lashed out at me. Again. Again. Again.

237 «

With my dim eyes, I saw the dance of the howling dervish, the orgasm of the ecstatic flagellant. The lashes fell so fast, they came as one. One great fire of pain ravaged my body, nullified me, and finally, in a transport of bliss, lowered my ashes into clouds of peace.

I was enclosed in an urn. I could not move. It was black inside. I could not see. There was no noise. The storm was over. Ashes to ashes.

Somebody must have lifted the lid. I saw the ocean, the wide horizon. The waves rose high and broke. Some of the foam spilled into my urn. It felt like ice. The waves came closer, turned over the urn, crashed inside it. I was drenched.

I tried to open my eyes. I saw white and red: a young girl's favorite color. I knew the girl. The red was blood. I was stretched out on a white cot . . . and the pains came back, in a crescendo. There was a sound like a scream. I didn't know where it had come from. A voice said, "The Jew is awake."

I saw a brown shape. It held something over my head. It looked like a bucket. The shape could speak. "I'll give him some more," it said.

The bucket turned upside down and the water splashed on my head and on my body. It must have gone right through my clothes.

"Up on your feet, Jew!"

I recognized Angermann's voice. I turned my head. I could see him. He sat on a chair. He was holding the horsewhip in both hands. The other S.A. man set the bucket down. He went behind me and lifted me from the cot. I saw that I was naked and felt ashamed. Angermann rose from his chair and dropped the whip. My legs gave out, but the brownshirt held me.

"Look at the almighty Dr. Hans Bauer," Angermann said. "Just a dirty, naked Jew."

"How come he isn't circumcised?" the other S.A. man asked.

"Yeah, why aren't you circumcised?" Angermann asked. His hand touched my genitals. I recoiled.

"Nice and big," Angermann said.

"All Jews have big ones," the other S.A. man said.

"Stand up straight!" Angermann shouted.

"He can't, Angermann."

"Let go of him, Billig. I'll hold him."

He grabbed my penis and pulled. It hurt badly. I'd thought nothing could hurt me anymore. Billig stepped back, laughing uproariously at Angermann's attempts to keep me balanced.

Suddenly, Angermann dropped his hand. I fell and hit my head. "That Jewish swine is pissing all over me!" he shouted.

Billig was doubled over, laughing so hard the tears ran down his cheeks. I did not pass out. I felt nothing but shame. This was the ultimate measure of degradation.

I saw Angermann go through a door and heard the water run. Billig stood over me, still laughing. "Only a goddamned Jew could think of that," he said.

I closed my eyes. After a while, I heard Angermann come back. Smelled the stink of his breath. "You're going to pay for that, Dr. Jew!" he said.

Billig's voice asked, "What do you want to do with him?"

"We'll give him the rest cure."

I opened my eyes and saw him grab my legs.

"That's against orders," Billig said.

"To hell with that! I give the orders!" Angermann shouted.

"All right."

Billig took hold of my head. They put me on the cot, then they picked up the cot and carried me through a long, dark tunnel. I knew where the tunnel ended. Berta Gruen had gone the same way. They set me down at a door. Angermann opened the door. Billig lifted the cot up to a vertical position.

"It's against orders," Billig said again.

"Forget it," Angermann said.

He slammed the door shut behind me. My knees buckled. I tried to let myself down straight, but I skinned my knees and the movement hurt so much that I gave up. I clawed the walls with my hands, trying to hold on to them.

Berta. Berta had survived. I shall survive. They did not pull out my fingernails, one by one. Maybe they forgot. Berta's face did not frighten me anymore. It was not a skull. It was a lovely face. I wanted to see it again. Hanna mailed the letter. Barbara and Konrad. Box—box what? They didn't ask me any questions about Konrad. Only about Butler. He was in Paris. Safe.

I must have dozed off. My whole body was burning. My hand. I couldn't feel my hand anymore. I was hungry. Berta had been hungry too. I shivered. I was naked and it was cold. My fingers hurt and I pressed the palms of my hands against the wall. Berta Gruen had survived. She had suffered much more than I had. It had been for nothing. Her boyfriend had already been dead. I would never tell her that, and I hope she never learned about it. The man in the black uniform. His arms stretched across the table. Jewish sow.

I felt that I was about to pass out. I was afraid of it and hoping for it. Maybe I could die. They'd find a Jewish corpse in the cell. Berta did not die.

Blank.

Resonance.

I saw a face I knew. It was close to me. It had a smiling mouth.

"Hans," said the face.

"My name is Berta Gruen," I said. "I am a Jew."

The face pulled back. I couldn't see it anymore. I heard its voice.

"He's coming to."

There was another face. Thin and haggard. I knew that face too.

"Dr. Bauer."

"I am a Jew."

"We are all Jews here," the face said.

Something touched my arm. The face dissolved.

I woke up. I opened my eyes. I felt great pain, but I could see. I was lying in bed. I tried to raise my head. It hurt. My head was bandaged. Something was hammering inside it. I saw many beds, beds after beds, crowded against each other. And faces in all of them.

I saw a man in a white coat bent over one of the beds. He was thinner than ever, his face furrowed and very pale, a ghost of a man. He walked toward me.

"Dr. Hirsch," I said. "How long have I been here?"

"Two weeks. How are the pains?"

"Bad."

"See if you can stand it, just for a little while. We're short on sedatives."

I nodded.

"Dr. von Isenberg was here when you first came to," Dr. Hirsch said. "I promised to call him."

I listened to him talk. I had forgotten the sound of a human voice.

"How is Berta Gruen?" I asked.

"She is still at my place. She got up for the first time a week ago," Dr. Hirsch said. "Now she's walking quite well. Her papers came. She's going to go to Mexico."

"On your affidavit," I said.

"It was easy to have it changed."

"What about you?"

"Berta Gruen has been asking about you," he said.

"She saved my life," I said.

Dr. Hirsch looked at me. "You mustn't talk too much. You may not have realized it yet, but your whole body is bandaged tightly. The less you move, the better."

"Yes."

I felt I was getting short of breath. I asked, "How did I get here?"

"Dr. von Isenberg called our hospital," he said. "He'll tell you about it."

"Yes."

"I'll give you a sedative in about an hour. The government cut our ration in half."

The pains were getting worse. I passed out before Dr. Hirsch came back. I was still unconscious when he gave me the sedative. I must have slept for a long time.

When I woke up, I saw Berta Gruen. She sat in a chair, close to my bed. She wore a dark suit. Most of the bandages had been removed from her head. Her face, though still distorted, looked fuller. Her eyebrows had begun to grow.

She smiled at me. It was a poor smile; her face muscles were still very weak. I liked her smile. It made her look younger again.

"Well, here I am," she said.

"Yes. I'm glad. Now I can tell you—"

I raised my head. It hurt. But I could see her better.

"Tell me what?"

"I wouldn't have survived without you," I said. "I thought of you and what they'd done to you. And how courageous you'd been."

She shook her head. "You just imagine that."

"It was very real to me," I said. "You know that I'm a Jew."

"Yes."

"I didn't want to be a Jew. I don't know anything about Jews."

"It starts with pain," she said. "That much you know."

"Are you religious?"

"Yes."

"I don't know anything about the Jewish religion."

"You can learn, can't you?"

"Jesus Christ was a Jew. I learned that a long time ago."

"The Jews don't recognize him as the Messiah. They're still waiting for the Messiah to arrive."

"Make him come fast," I said. "We need him."

Dr. Hirsch came to my bed. He said to Berta, "You must go back. I gave you five minutes."

He helped her get up. Looking at me, she said, "I can walk by myself."

She stood.

"Dr. Hirsch got me an affidavit for Mexico."

"I'm very happy for you," I said.

She smiled. "I'll leave as soon as I'm fit again. It'll be another month, but I have my passport and my exit permit."

"I wish you luck in Mexico," I said.

She nodded. "We'll talk to each other before I leave."

The next evening, Klaus came to see me. He put his briefcase on the chair and sat on my bed.

"How are you coming along?"

"Dr. Hirsch promised he'd stitch me together again," I said. "It seems most of my ribs are broken. I've some bad wounds on my genitals and the bones in my head need repair. Other than that . . ."

He didn't smile. He looked worried and tense.

"Tell me what happened, Klaus."

"You want a report. Are you sure you're up to it?"

"I'm just going to listen to it," I said.

"Well, all right."

He put his briefcase on the bed and sat on the chair. "On the day you were picked up, Magda called your home. You were an hour late for an appointment."

"I wasn't allowed to phone."

"Yes, I know. She spoke to Hanna, who told her what had happened. I called Adriani and he asked me to come to his office. I got the whole story directly from him."

He stopped. I asked, "How about Barbara and Konrad? Did they get to London?"

He looked at me.

"Are you sure you want to hear that part of the story?"

I raised myself up.

"The Gestapo didn't catch them?" I asked. "Please tell me."

He still hesitated. Then he took a deep breath. "Your friends, the Willmans, are in perfect health. They couldn't be better. Konrad is directing the Hauptmann play and Barbara—"

"They didn't leave?"

"They never had any intention of leaving, Hans. Your friends Barbara and Konrad sold you out to save their own skin. They framed you."

I stared at Klaus.

"They saw you at the opera with Adriani. Something must have happened there between Konrad and you. In any event, they thought you'd become a Nazi. When they realized the Gestapo was looking for Konrad, he went to Adriani, told him about you and Butler, about Butler's message, the one you gave to Konrad—about, well, everything that made you look like a double-crossing son-of-a-bitch. To prove your disloyalty to the Nazis, they offered to frame you. Barbara met you 'secretly' to tell you about their predicament and their so-called plans. They knew you wouldn't betray them to Adriani. They counted on your friendship and your integrity for that."

We were both silent. I said, "They were my friends."

Klaus nodded.

"I'm so stupid, Klaus. You can be glad you're rid of me. In the back of my mind, I knew something was wrong, but . . . I trusted those two."

Klaus said, "As long as the Nazis stay in power, you can't trust anybody. The whole regime is built on betrayal and lies. It affects everybody who stays in this country which used to be Germany."

My head sank back on the pillow. I was very tired.

"Like Berta Gruen," I said. "All the pains for . . . nothing. And you know, Klaus, I felt so—noble inside. I'm glad I didn't know."

I saw that Klaus was moved, but he went on talking. "In fairness to Adriani—although he's as vicious as the rest of them —he ordered a 'token' interrogation. At least, that's what he told me. He didn't know you'd be up against the worst sadist in the Gestapo and—of course—he couldn't have known that Angermann would use the opportunity to take his personal revenge."

I said, "As soon as I feel stronger, I must decide what I'm going to do with myself."

"You're going to the United States," Klaus said.

"How?"

Klaus smiled. "I wrote to a friend of mine in New York for an affidavit for you after you came back from your first meeting with Adriani. I was sure you could never change into a Nazi."

He picked up the briefcase from my bed and took out some papers.

"I'm different," he said. "Some Teutonic element in myself makes me fight them with their own weapons. I'll manage, at least for a while."

He handed me an envelope.

"These are your affidavit and your exit permit."

I looked at him. "Klaus—" My voice gave out and I had to start again. "How can I ever—"

"You're not supposed to talk that much," Klaus said. "Here's your passport."

I took it and opened it. I saw

Hans Israel <u>Bauer</u>.

I looked at it for a long time.

"My graduation papers," I said.

A prominent German playwright and vocal anti-Nazi, Felix Jackson barely managed to escape Germany with his life in 1933. For four years, he lived in Budapest and Vienna, then in 1937 producer Joe Pasternak and director Henry Koster brought him to the United States, and Jackson began to write for Universal Pictures. His screenplays quickly earned him two Academy Award nominations—for *Destry Rides Again* and *Bachelor Mother*—and Jackson turned to producing pictures, as well. In the late forties, he left motion pictures for television (still in its early days) and wrote and produced for, among other shows, *Silver Theater, Studio One, Playhouse of Stars, Four Star Playhouse, The Don Ameche Show* and *The Paul Whiteman Show*. From 1959 to 1965, he served as Vice President of West Coast Programming for NBC, before retiring to become a free-lance writer. He is the author of two earlier novels, *Maestro* and *So Help Me God*. He lives in Sherman Oaks, California.